TRACKED

STALKER'S MOON, BOOK 2

ELLIE FERGUSON

Hunter's Moon Press

Print ISBN: 978-1-949901-05-4

E-Book ISBN: 978-1-949901-06-1

Cover design by Sarah A. Hoyt

For more information about this book and other books by the author, check out her website.

Thank you for your support.

To my wonderful son for supporting his crazy mother's wish to be a writer, even when it meant having to listen to her plot at him when he should have been doing his homework. I love you, son.

The way home is fraught with danger.

CHAPTER ONE

"Lady, I said to hold still!"

The cop, who looked all of thirteen, held me against the hood of his squad car and finished cuffing my hands behind my back. As he did, lightning flashed overhead. I turned my head and stared down the alley, praying my imagination was playing tricks on me, that I hadn't seen movement in the dark shadows. Damn my bad luck and the cop's even worse timing. If only he'd been a few minutes later, I'd have finished the job and been well away from here.

Don't get me wrong. Under different circumstances, and most definitely with a different partner, I wouldn't object to being cuffed. I might even enjoy it. After all, there's nothing wrong with a bit of role-playing between two consenting adults, especially if it led to spectacular sex. But neither of us were playing and I most certainly wasn't consenting – at least not in *that* way.

Hell, all I wanted to do was survive the next few minutes. Unfortunately, the possibility of that happening grew smaller with each passing moment.

God, I hate my job sometimes.

With the cop's forearm still holding me against the hood of his car, I blinked through the rain and sniffed. Nothing. Not that I really expected anything different. Once again, the wind shifted, this time blowing toward the alley opening. That, along with the cop's fear and the smells of the car engine, made it almost impossible to scent my prey. Not good, not good at all.

Still, there was one small blessing, if you could call it that. The cop was human. That meant the stench of death clinging to me didn't call out to him. He couldn't smell its foul odor any more than he could read my mind. Fortunately, science hasn't progressed that far. The last thing I needed was some gung-ho cop mucking about in my head, especially considering my activities of the last half hour.

The dark of night combined with the rain also helped. It kept him from seeing any blood that might have splashed on me during the kill, just as it kept him from seeing the bruises I knew marked my face. Nor could he see the way my jeans were torn at the left thigh where the feral managed to get in one good bite before I'd slit its throat and taken its head. Both the bruises and the bite would heal soon enough. What worried me was what forensics might reveal should the cops decide to check my clothes or look too closely at the alley.

Well, I'd worry about that later – assuming there was a later.

"Look, officer." I tugged ineffectually at the cuffs and then tried to straighten, only to be slammed back against the hood. The sharp, bitter taste of blood filled my mouth and I spat, sorry the rain would wash the results from the hood. Damn it, this was getting old fast.

A clap of thunder sounded overhead, rattling the windows in nearby buildings and drowning out anything he might have said. Unfortunately, it also drowned out any sounds that might have come from the alley. The alley I could barely see as the rain beat down even harder. By the time I saw anyone, or anything, emerge from the shadows, it would be too late.

I've always known death would come for me one day, but I'd planned to meet it head-on, fighting. I wasn't one to "go gently into the night." Now it looked like I'd meet it head-on, but there'd be little I could do about it.

Lightning streaked across the sky, followed almost instantly by another clap of thunder. The storm was right on top of us and didn't seem to be moving anywhere fast. I sensed more than felt the cop fumbling with his radio. Taking advantage of his inattention, I twisted slightly, sliding out from under his restraining arm. Before he could react, and probably shoot me for trying to escape, I turned and straightened. But I didn't move away from the squad car. Instead, I planted my butt against the fender and stood there, looking to my left, never taking my attention from the alley.

Another flash of lightning – damn, Mother Nature was pissed about something tonight – and the shadows near the mouth of the alley shifted. My breath caught, and I fought the urge to react. The instincts born of a hunter tried to force me toward the alley, toward my prey. Common sense and a strong desire to survive stopped me. Even so, my wrists strained against the cuffs. My heart pounded. Fear, stronger than any I'd felt in a very long time, filled me. Cuffed like this, I was helpless, and I didn't appreciate it one little bit.

Wasn't it enough I'd been forced to kill that night? Did I have to die as well?

"Damn it, lady, I told you not to move!"

The cop's voice cracked as he dropped his radio and fumbled at his hip for his gun. If the situation wasn't so serious, it might actually be funny. Maybe it would be in a decade or two. But for now, it was deadly serious and even more dangerous.

Praying I wasn't making a fatal mistake, I tore my attention from the shadows shrouding the alley and focused on the cop. Maybe he really was as young and inexperienced as he looked. The way the hand holding his gun shook seemed proof of it. So did the fact he hadn't secured me in the squad car while he checked the alley. He might not have told me what he thought he'd seen me do, but I could make a pretty good guess.

At least if he'd followed standard procedure, I'd be out of the rain. Instead, he had me standing there in the rain, cuffed like a common criminal.

Believe me, I might be many things but common I'm not and that's something he'd soon discover if he didn't get us out of there.

I waited, expecting Volk to appear from the shadows at any moment. He'd already surprised me once tonight. That came close to costing me my life. He might still succeed, thanks to the cop. At least I'd had the satisfaction of knowing I'd dealt with one of Volk's ferals before everything went to hell. But damn it, Volk had already cost us so much. How many more would die before we managed to kill him and contain the rest of his followers?

I closed my eyes and fought for control. The hunter inside me wanted out. She knew the danger we faced and railed against it. She knew how to deal with this foolish human and she knew how to deal with Volk. All I had to do was release control and let her loose.

Part of me wanted to do just that. God, how I wanted to. But cuffed as I was, it would be beyond foolish. I couldn't shift with my arms secured behind me. At the very least, my shoulders, not to mention my elbows and wrists, would be dislocated in the shift. More likely, they'd be broken. Neither result would heal quickly. Besides, Hollywood had a number of things wrong about our kind, not the least of which was the process of shifting between human and animal. It wasn't quick, nor was it painless. I had no doubts that before the shift was over, the cop would put a bullet in my brain and that would seriously suck.

The sound of leather scraping against the pavement seemed to fill the air even though the cop gave no indication he'd heard it. My eyes snapped open and I once more focused on the shadows down the alley. I tensed, ready for flight. I'd risk a bullet in the back to facing Volk with my hands cuffed behind me.

Death was close. I could feel it. How long would it toy with me before finally striking?

A moment – or an eternity – later, I slowly exhaled. Whether I shivered from the cold or from relief, I didn't know, and it really didn't matter. But my money was on relief. After all, no monsters –

human or otherwise –emerged from the shadows. Better yet, I was still alive. Maybe my luck was finally improving.

I doubted it, but a girl can always hope.

Not that I was about to relax. I knew Volk. I'd been tracking him for more than a month now. I'd seen what he could do and knew he wouldn't hesitate to send one of the ferals in to distract the cop so he could personally deal with me. Fear once again licked at the edges of my self-control and I fought it down. I needed to stay calm and I needed to figure out some way to convince Officer Do-Good to get us the hell out of there.

Most nights, the last place I wanted to be was a jail cell. Right now, however, the thought of being safely locked behind solid walls and strong bars sounded very, very good.

"Look, officer," I began again as the sounds of a distant siren reached me. It wouldn't be long before others joined us. Whether that was good or not, I didn't know. It might be enough to convince Volk to withdraw. It might also force him to strike now, before reinforcements arrived. "I don't know what you think I did or who you think I might be, but I swear I was just out for a walk. You'll find my ID and motel key in my back pocket if you'd just look." I let a hint of frustration creep into my voice. He'd expect it and God knows I certainly felt it.

"Lady, I read you your rights. I suggest you exercise the right to remain silent, because there is no way you were out for just a walk. I *saw* what you did!"

Great, just great. Once again, my luck ran true to form. I'd been stopped by Billy the Boy Scout, always true to duty. I'd lay odds he was one of those who always believed what he saw, no matter what the truth might be. Hell, with my luck, he also believed everything printed in the paper or reported on TV because the media would never lie or show bias.

Well, if he wasn't careful, I'd shatter all his illusions. It was bad enough he'd cuffed me and hadn't followed procedure by placing me in the squad car before securing the scene, something that might keep us both alive a bit longer. The fact Volk still lingered in the area only made matters worse. When the wind shifted a moment earlier, I'd caught his scent: that foul, carrion-like scent I'd learned to associate with him long ago. I'd felt his amusement in that moment. I'd become the mouse to his cat, most definitely not a position I enjoyed. If Officer Do-Good didn't do something soon, I would because I refused to die in this back alley.

No more than five minutes could have passed from the time the cop had cuffed me and his back-up arrived, but it had been five of the longest minutes of my life. In that time, I'd gone from anger and frustration at being interrupted before I could finish dealing with Volk to bone-chilling fear and I'd had just about enough. The only thing keeping me from doing something that might be exceedingly foolish was the thought of how it would only cause more trouble, trouble no one would thank me for.

I dipped my head and tried to wipe the rain from my eyes with my shoulder – Have I said I hate being cuffed? It's damned inconvenient – Then I turned my attention to the car now parked behind the squad car. Interesting, it wasn't a marked unit. Instead, it was a black SUV. To the untrained eye, it looked like any number of other SUVs on the market these days. But I didn't have an untrained eye. I saw the reinforced bumpers and other special after-market add-ons that told me it had to belong to one of Coyote Springs' detectives.

The driver's door opened, and a man stepped out, a very tall man. A man who, in the quick flash of lightning, looked like he was as much at home in a gym as he was patrolling the streets. He wore black slacks, black shirt and a CSPD windbreaker. His shield hung from a chain around his neck. He paused long enough to frown up at the rain before closing the distance between him and the uniformed officer in long, quick strides.

Then the wind shifted again, and every instinct came alive. The scent of the newcomer was headier than the most expensive cologne. My other self, the white tiger that had been fighting for release, pressed once more against my control as she recognized one of our own. This newcomer, this mountain of a man, smelled of the grasslands. Whether that was good or not had yet to be seen. Like the normals, shape-shifters have their bad seeds.

God, I really hoped he was one of the good guys.

At least he looked like he knew what he was doing as he looked around. His eyes slid over me before he focused on the deeper shadows of the alley. Nothing about his expression or the way he held himself betrayed his thoughts. Surely, he realized what I was. There was a remote possibility he hadn't. If that was the case, I didn't want to call attention to my true nature. So, I reasserted control over my tiger and prayed the newcomer got us far away from the alley and soon.

Instead, he turned his attention to the uniformed officer and motioned for the younger man to join him. After a quick warning for me not to move, the young cop complied. I leaned against the fender of the squad car, wondering what was going to happen next and not liking how they kept me standing there, wet and cold, while they talked. I strained to hear what they said but couldn't quite make it out. There was something about "patrol", "flash", and "blood" and that was all. Nothing I hadn't expected.

"Did you find anything when you searched her?" the newcomer asked, turning to look at me with the jaundiced eye of a cop who'd been on the streets long enough to know just how fatal it can be to take anything for granted. "You did search her, didn't you?"

"No, sir." In the light form the head lamps, I saw the uniform swallow nervously. "I secured her and figured it best to wait for back-up before doing anything else."

Oh my God, he was worried I'd yell sexual harassment? Give me strength.

"Please tell me you at least secured the scene."

"N-no, Chief Kincade. I didn't think I should leave her unattended."

For a moment, Kincade said nothing. I'm not sure he could. Frustration and disbelief radiated from him. In the light from the two cars,

I saw his right hand fist at his side. I might be the one cuffed, but Officer Do-Good was the one in real trouble. Not that I had much sympathy for him just then.

Kincade took another step forward until he stood almost nose to nose with the uniform. "Let me get this straight, Officer Snyder. You arrested this woman you say you saw kill someone. You cuffed her, and I assume you read her her rights." Officer Snyder gave a jerky nod. "But you didn't search her, and you didn't secure the scene, even though it's raining and any evidence there might be is being washed away. Worse, you didn't check to see if there might be someone in need of medical attention further down the alley. Nor did you check to see if she might have an accomplice hiding in the shadows, waiting for the right moment to shoot you and free her."

"I-I—"

"Stay here."

With that, Kincade moved to stand before me. His left hand closed around my left arm and he gave a slight tug, just enough to let me know he wanted me to come with him. Since he was moving toward his SUV and not the shadows of the alley, I was more than happy to oblige. Not only would the SUV keep the rain off me, it would offer some protection against Volk should he still be nearby and decide to strike.

"Lean back," Kincade said after helping me into the back seat.

I did as he said and watched as he secured the seat belt across my waist. He cinched it tight and then gave it a tug to make sure it wouldn't loosen. Then he bent. Before I could react, much less ask what he was doing, he shackled my ankles, the short chain running through a metal loop in the floor.

He straightened and quickly glanced over his shoulder to where Snyder stood looking miserable as the rain continued to beat down on him. "I don't know who you are, lady, but I know *what* you are. I also smell the blood on you. As soon as I check the alley and make sure you haven't left me a mess I can't explain away, we are going to have a chat. What you tell me will determine whether you go to jail and get to call your lawyer or if you go straight to my clan leader to explain why you're hunting in his territory without permission."

Mouth suddenly dry, all I could do was nod. He gave me a long look before slamming the door, locking me inside the SUV. I might be out of the rain, but I had a feeling I was also in more trouble than I'd been in before. Hunting in another clan's territory without permission from the local Alpha could a capital offense. My own Alpha assured me he'd see to it my way was cleared wherever my hunt took me. But if he hadn't, facing Volk might actually be the lesser of two evils.

It wasn't long before Kincade emerged from the shadows. Relief filled me — well, relief and a touch of worry — and I watched as he once more approached Snyder. It was easy to see that Kincade hadn't found anything to substantiate what Snyder had reported, not that that helped me. Kincade had smelled the blood on me. As a shapeshifter, he'd know it was the blood of one of our kind. Hopefully, he'd remember to tell his Alpha that. Killing one of our own kind was a serious offense but not the automatic death sentence hunting a normal would bring down on me. Still, I was relieved he hadn't come across Volk. Hopefully, he'd be able to convince Snyder he made a mistake and I'd done nothing wrong. Then, if my luck continued to hold, he'd call his Alpha and find out I was authorized to be in their territory and they weren't to interfere with my hunt. If that happened, and I knew it was a very big if, I'd soon return to the hunt.

For the moment at least, I didn't have to worry about becoming Volk's next victim.

Kincade said something to Snyder that had the uniform hunching his shoulders and staring at his feet like a kid getting a very effective dressing down. Then Kincade nodded to the squad car, the implication clear. He stood there, watching as Snyder moved slowly away from him, feet dragging through the water. Part of me felt sorry for the kid. He'd had the misfortune of stumbling upon something he wasn't prepared to believe in, much less understand. Then he'd been dressed down by his boss. My night might have sucked, but it had been even worse for Officer Snyder.

"We both got lucky," Kincade said as he slid in behind the steering wheel. "The rain washed away the most obvious evidence of what you were doing in that alley and whoever else was with you or your target got the body away before anyone else could see it." He slid the key in the ignition and a moment later we drove off with a squeal of tires. "And now you're my problem. Name and clan?" The last was snapped out and I knew better than to keep quiet.

"Maggie Thrasher, Northern California clan, Eureka pride."

He nodded but said nothing else. Instead, he radioed Dispatch that he was transporting the suspect to County. My heart beat a bit faster. Surely, he wasn't really going to do that. County jail meant more than fingerprinting me and taking my photo. Thanks to a recent Supreme Court ruling, it meant the cops could — and, with my luck, would — take a DNA sample from me. That was one of our kinds' biggest fears. Modern science had finally advanced to the point where it was quite possible some overly-ambitious lab tech would spot the difference in our DNA from normal human DNA. Once that happened, our secret would be out and none of us wanted to risk the panic that was sure to follow.

Shapeshifters might be stronger than normals and much more difficult to kill, but we also were in the vast minority. That's why we have always done our best not to let our existence be known. We've seen what fear can do to people. We've seen it in our own kind when a new shifter form suddenly appears. If our existence became public knowledge without the right groundwork being laid, there would be bloodshed and too many on both sides would die.

"Where are we going?"

Did he hear the worry in my voice?

"To see my Alpha. He'll either tell me you are cleared to be here or he won't. For your sake, you'd better hope you've told me the truth and he knows why you're here and has approved it. We had trouble with trackers coming here without permission last year and trying to take his mate against her will. He won't take kindly to another tracker trespassing in our territory."

I swallowed once, mouth tight, as memory of my own clan leader telling us about his visit to the Texas clan and the reasons for it. I'd known then that Declan hadn't told us everything. There were gaps in the story about how the clan leader for the Northern California clan had hunted for a female shapeshifter for years, ever since she'd spurned his advances as a fifteen-year old after her parents' deaths. He'd somehow discovered she was living in the Dallas-Fort Worth area and had sent trackers after her, without notifying the Texas clan leader of their presence, much less getting his permission for them to be there.

But there was one thing I remembered very clearly from that night. When Declan told us the names of the clan leader and his new mate, I'd been stunned. Not by the fact the Northern California clan leader died in a fight with the female Alpha of the Texas clan. Not even by the fact the Michael Jennings tried to kill the Texas clan leader. No, I'd been shocked by the identity of the female Alpha. I knew her. We'd grown up together, been best friends. I'd mourned when she ran away and blamed myself for not being there when she most needed me. Now my fate might very well rest in her hands. Would she remember me? Would she be able to forgive me for failing her?

With that came memory of the local clan leader's name. Kincade. Obviously Chief Kincade was a relative. Whether that was good or not, I didn't know. I only hoped the clan leader and his mate were morning people. Unless I was very wrong, we'd be at their place long before the sun was up. Then I'd have to hope Declan did as he promised and filled the clan leaders in on my mission and why it was so important I be allowed to work in the Texas territory. If not, well, Volk would be the least of my worries.

And I still hadn't had any coffee.

CHAPTER TWO

An hour later, I knelt on the floor, waiting for what happened next. Instead of taking me to the county jail as he'd told Dispatch, Coyote Springs Police Chief Jim Kincade drove me to a secluded ranch. This was the Texas of so many TV shows and movies: vast open spaces, no nearby neighbors and lots and lots of cattle and horses. This particular ranch house lay half a mile or so back from the road, hidden from view by rows of trees. There was absolutely no way a casual observer would see anything they weren't supposed to.

It was, in short, the perfect spot for our kind to conduct the sort of business we didn't want the normals knowing about. Unfortunately for me, I was the focus of that business and I was doing some mighty hard praying just then.

A man who bore a strong resemblance to Jim Kincade sat a few feet away. I guessed he was a few years younger than the police chief. He wasn't as muscularly built, but there was no mistaking the power that emanated from him. It hit me the moment he entered the house and I hadn't been surprised when he'd been introduced as Matt Kincade, Alpha of the Texas clan and Jim Kincade's brother.

That had been a few minutes earlier. Since then, the Alpha had taken his seat in what appeared to be a well-worn but comfortable chair. Then he asked his brother to fill him in. Once he had, Matt Kincade leaned back and studied me with an expression that gave nothing away. For my part, I'd done what any self-respecting shapeshifter would do in the presence of someone stronger than she: I'd stayed quiet, head bent, and tried not to think about how badly I hurt—or about what easy prey I'd be if the Alpha decided to deal with me in a very permanent manner.

The sounds of someone else entering the house reached me a split-second before another wave of power washed over me. Another alpha? My white tiger, that proud and always confident creature, tried to take control. She recognized a stronger female and knew she should to show submission. But I wouldn't. These weren't my Alphas. My allegiance was to Declan and Eileen and no one else, not yet.

Head bent, I listened as the newcomer entered the room and moved purposefully toward the clan leader. As she did, it took every ounce of my self-control not to whimper. I tried telling myself it was because of the pain but I knew better. The woman had to be the clan's female Alpha. Her power rolled over me. It was all I could do not to drop to my belly and submit. Instead, I focused on the tips of her scuffed black boots.

"Jim, go ahead and tell her what you told me." Matt Kincade's voice was deep, almost as deep as his brother's. And, like his expression earlier, it gave nothing away.

Much as I wanted to glance up and get a good look at the newcomer, I didn't. I studied the floor and waited. They'd get to me soon enough. Hopefully by then I'd have the answers they wanted.

"The short version is, I received a call from the rookie on my squad, reporting that he'd just seen a murder. I rolled and found he'd taken her into custody. His story was that as he turned into the alley behind the hardware store, he saw her lifting a decapitated head in one hand. He hit his overheads then and was out of the squad car fast enough that she couldn't get away.

"I knew the moment I got to the scene that she's one of us." He paused, and I glanced to my right, to where he stood next to me. His expression was taut, his concern clear. "I also scented others of our kind, but the scent was fading. All I can say for certain is that I didn't recognize their scents."

"What did you do?" the woman asked.

"I secured her in my SUV. Then I checked the alley. I didn't find anyone or anything, but I could tell there'd been a fight there. Fortunately, there was no body – human or otherwise. Whoever else had been there worked fast and cleared at least that much away. Then I sent the rookie back to the station to write it up and said I'd transfer her to County. That's when I called Matt."

"You're sure there's nothing in the alley that can lead back to us?" the woman wanted to know.

Curiosity finally got the better of me and I dared a quick glance in her direction. Standing next to his chair, her hand resting lightly on the Alpha's shoulder, was a dark-haired woman. Dressed in jeans and a black tank top, her hair pulled back in a braid, her clan markings were a beautiful tapestry from her left wrist to past that shoulder. Her expression was troubled as she listened to the report. Then she looked at me and, for one brief moment, the world stopped.

Breaking all the rules of protocol, I stared at her in disbelief. I'd known, at least intellectually, there was a good chance we'd cross paths, especially after my "arrest". But it was still so hard to believe. The last time we'd seen one another had been ten years ago. We'd been best friends. I'd held her as she cried after her parents died – No, after they'd been murdered. Then she'd run away, and I hadn't seen or heard from her again.

Until today.

Now she stood before me, her power as an alpha almost as strong as the clan leader's. Never had I been in the presence of another female of our kind who exuded such natural power. I'd heard of the clan leader from Oklahoma, Irene Walkinghorse. She was a legend among our people, not only for her strength but also for her foresight and leadership. It was obvious that her granddaughter, my childhood friend, was much like her. I hoped that bode well for me.

"As sure as I can be without better light and more time to check it out." Jim rubbed a hand over his face, his frustration clear. "Matt, Finn, I can't promise anything. I'll be able to handle the guys in the department. It's easy enough to explain away what the rook thought he saw. It's just a few weeks before Halloween and that means there are pumpkins everywhere, even in the alley. I'll figure out a way to say he saw one and simply made a mistake. The thing is, I want to do it in such a way it doesn't ruin him as a cop. He's got potential and that's something the public needs."

"You know we trust you to do what's best, Jim."

Matt Kincade got to his feet and moved to stand in front of me. As he looked down, it felt as if he was gazing into my very soul. Instinct had me dropping my gaze, showing that I recognized his dominance over me. I'd never challenge Declan, at least not publicly. I sure as hell wasn't going to challenge the Alpha so many of the others were looking to for guidance on many of the issues facing our kind.

"Your name and clan."

I swallowed hard, knowing the next few moments would determine my future, if not my life. "Maggie Thrasher, Northern California clan."

"What happened in that alley?"

"Wait!" Her voice was sharp. My heart raced, and my breath caught as I heard her take a step forward. It was all I could do to stay where I was. Part of me wanted to go to my childhood friend, to beg her to believe me. Another part, the part that always felt I'd failed her, wanted to run and hide. Before I could do either, she stood before me. Her touch was gentle as she lifted my face so I looked up at her. "Maggs?" Disbelief filled her voice.

I nodded. The lump in my throat kept me from saying anything for a moment. "I can't believe it's you, Meg."

"It's Finn now." She gave me a quick smile that disappeared the moment she looked at Jim Kincade.

"Release her." When he didn't instantly do as she said, looking instead to his brother, her expression darkened. "I said release her!" she snapped and her power rolled over us. Only her grip on my chin kept me from falling to my belly. God, had she always been this strong and I'd just been too young and inexperienced to realize it?

"Finn!" Now it was the clan leader who snapped.

"No, Matt." She released her hold on my chin and turned to him. I couldn't see her face, but I could see the tension in her posture. "I know her. God, we were best friends a lifetime ago. She's no threat to us."

"We don't know that, Finn." Now it was Jim who spoke. "She was hunting another shapeshifter."

"Maggie, is this true?"

She turned back to me, her expression hard. I looked at the floor and nodded. I knew what she'd gone through a year ago. Hell, I doubted there was a shapeshifter in the U.S. who didn't know what happened. She'd spent years on the run. After her parents' deaths, deaths we now knew were murder, she'd come face-to-face with the man responsible. Michael Jennings had murdered her parents so he could usurp them as clan leaders. Once he had, he tried claiming Meg – no, Finn. I needed to remember that – as his mate despite the fact she was underage even by our laws and grieving the loss of her parents. When that hadn't worked, he cornered her at her home and tried to rape her. She fought back and managed to escape.

She'd been on the run since then – until the afternoon Matt Kincade rescued her from the trackers Jennings sent to bring her back, no matter what. It all culminated when Jennings shot Matt. From what Declan told us later, Finn had challenged Jennings then, killing him before a gathering of not only her new clan but clan leaders from many of the U. S. clans as well.

"It is." I drew a breath and tried to find the right words to explain why I'd been here. "My clan leader, the new Alpha of the Northern California clan, sent me after a renegade. He assured me he would inform the local clan leaders that I was in your territory and why."

"He did." Matt's voice was soft but gave nothing away. "And I gave him permission for you to hunt as long as you did nothing to draw attention to our kind."

"Matthew!" Finn's outrage was clear. "Why didn't you tell me who the tracker was?"

"Finn." He reached out and, much as she had done with me a few moments earlier, lifted her face so she looked at him. "I'm sorry. I didn't think it was important. After learning that most of those who had been in the clan when you were there left under Jennings' rule, it didn't occur to me you might know the tracker."

Much as I did not want to get between the two Alphas, I wasn't going to be able to kneel there much longer, at least not without pitching forward on my face. My left thigh had gone from throbbing painfully to screaming in agony. The wound was bleeding again. If I didn't bind it up soon, I'd pass out from loss of blood.

"Please." I shifted positions slightly and fought to keep from groaning in pain. "We did leave. But after Finn defeated Jennings and Declan took over, he asked those who left to return if they wanted. A number of us did."

"We can discuss that and everything else after she's been treated." Finn waved her hand at me, concern and frustration clouding her expression. "Damn it, are the two of you blind? Even if you are, can't you smell the blood? She's injured, badly unless I miss my guess."

The men looked from me to Finn and back again. For my part, I held my breath. The sooner someone uncuffed me, the better. If I did fall on my face, I'd like to at least be able to try to break my fall.

"How badly are you injured?" Matt asked.

"I've been hurt worse."

Probably not, but I wasn't going to admit it in front of strange shapeshifters. I'd learned early on as my clan's only female tracker never to show weakness. Ours was still a fairly patriarchal society, at least my clan was, and I'd been put into a role usually reserved for men. That meant I'd had to prove myself, to them and to the clan, more than once. Just earning the rank of tracker meant fighting the others of that rank and proving I was just as strong and cunning as were they.

"I want Stefan to have a look at her," she said to her mate before once more turning her attention back to me. "He's our clan's doctor and he's patched all of us up more than once."

"Thank you."

"Soon." Matt held up a hand before Finn could protest. "We have to be sure, Finn. You know that." He waited until she nodded reluctantly. She obviously didn't like it. I probably wouldn't either had our roles been reversed.

"Then get on with it. She won't be able to tell us anything if we don't get her wounds treated and soon." Finn stood defiantly before him. God, they must have explosive arguments and I had no doubt the make-up sex was just as explosive.

For a moment, Matt didn't say anything. I couldn't imagine Eileen ever standing up to Declan like that, and especially not in front of a non-clan member. Of course, Finn had been headstrong as a kid and more than a bit protective of her friends. That clearly hadn't changed over the years.

"Jim, free her." Matt smiled at me, a smile that was both welcoming and full of warning at the same time. I was welcome to stay, at least for the moment, but I would play by their rules. Message received.

I hissed slightly as cramped muscles protested their sudden change in position. Then, instead of taking the time to stretch and get the circulation going again, I did what any other shapeshifter with an ounce of common sense would do. I dropped to hands and knees, lowering myself so my belly touched the ground. I wouldn't roll onto my back in full submission, my tiger wouldn't let me, but I would show submission to the dominance of the clan's two Alphas.

Finn moved once again to stand before me. Her hands were gentle as they lifted me first to my knees and then to my feet. Without a word, she slid an arm around my waist and helped me to a chair. Then, before I could react, she twisted her fingers in the ripped fabric of my jeans and tugged, tearing the material even more and exposing my mangled thigh.

My stomach pitched, and I swallowed against the bile that rose in my throat. The muscle of my thigh was torn, ripped, chunks of it gone. Even though it had scabbed over some earlier, it was bleeding again. One part of my mind told me I'd been lucky. I hadn't bled out so that meant the feral had missed the artery. But I needed medical treatment soon. As it was, it would be days, perhaps even weeks, before I completely healed. Our kind might heal faster than a normal human, but it still took time, especially for a wound a serious as this appeared to be.

Her expression troubled, Finn reached out to touch first my cheek and then my forehead. "Matt, call Stefan now. She's feverish."

I shook my head, fear replacing pain.

"It's all right, Maggie. He'll know what to do." Finn held my hand between hers and I knew she was worried about me. Hell, I was worried about me. But, more than that, I was worried about what Volk might be doing even now.

"Maggie, she's right." Now Matt knelt at his wife's side. "You're under my protection now. As Finn here can tell you, I take my responsibilities very seriously. I look after my own, even when they might not want me to." The grin he gave her spoke volumes. Obviously at some point in their past, he'd tried to protect her, and she hadn't appreciated it. "I know you want to tell us what happened, and we need to hear it. But you need to be treated first. It won't take him long to get here."

He was right. I didn't want to wait to tell him what I could. I might not be able to go after Volk again just now, but Matt could at least warn his people so they wouldn't fall victim to him or to his ferals. But, just then, I wasn't sure I could tell him enough to make him understand the danger before passing out. Damn it, why had I been so foolish as to go after that bastard Volk without back-up?

"Now, let's get you into the guest room and settled while Matt calls his uncle." Finn climbed to her feet and motioned her brother-in-law forward. "Jim."

He nodded and, before I could protest, he swung me up into his arms. Normally, such action would have me twisting and turning until I was once more standing on my own two feet. But not this time. Sure, I was hurt and hurting and really didn't want to try to walk on my injured leg after seeing the damage the feral had done to it. But there was more to it, something I hadn't noticed before. Something I really didn't want to notice now.

Instead of struggling, I rested my cheek against Jim's chest and wrapped my arms around his neck. When his arms tightened, I breathed deeply. The scent of him, that crisp grasslands aroma filled me. It called to my tiger and she was suddenly purring loudly in the back of my mind. Lust rose unbidden and I gasped.

No and no and no again.

I did not need this sort of distraction, not while I was on the hunt.

But I wasn't on the hunt, not right now at least. And I'd always had a weakness for a man in uniform. . ..

No, that was just reaction talking. Nothing more. I'd come close to dying tonight, twice if you counted the fact that Matt Kincade could have demanded my life in forfeit. Add in my injuries and the fever and, well, Jim was a man in uniform.

"Easy," he said softly as he gently settled me on the mattress in what I assumed was the guest room. "You're safe and I promise I'll go back to the alley and see what I can find. Besides." Now he gave me a lopsided grin, one that didn't quite touch his eyes. "I need to make sure neither Snyder nor any of the others go back and find something they shouldn't. In the meantime, I want you to promise to stay here. You'll be safe until I get back."

"Be careful." I reached for his hand, holding it tightly. I couldn't let him go without giving him some sort of warning about what he might find. "I killed a feral tonight, but he wasn't the main threat. That would be Volk."

"Volk?" Finn's voice cracked like a whip as she quickly crossed to the bed. "Not Joshua Volk?"

I nodded. I'd forgotten that she'd recognize his name.

"Finn?" Matt looked from her to me and back, his confusion clear.

"Volk joined the clan a year or so before my parents were murdered. Young as I was, even I knew there was something wrong with him. He was too smooth, too slick. It was like he had to be everyone's best friend. But there was something evil about him. You had the feeling that if you scratched below the surface of his perfect appearance and manners, you'd find a monster.

"You remember, don't you, Maggie? He tried to talk his way into being one of the mentors for the younger members of the clan who were just beginning to shift. One of them —" She paused and closed her eyes, her expression troubled – "Randy Henson went out with him. They disappeared for more than two weeks. Randy's folks were frantic, and my parents had the entire clan out looking for them. When they finally returned, Volk looked like he'd just walked off a photo shoot set. But Randy – God, Randy looked like he'd been through hell. His eyes were wild, and he wouldn't go with anyone but Volk." She moved to stare out the window, her hands fisting at her sides and beating against her thighs.

"Matt, Jim, you saw what Jennings was like. He was nothing compared to Volk. In those two weeks he'd torn the humanity from Randy. With the next full moon, Randy shifted." She turned, and she was now as pale as I felt. "He couldn't control the shift. No one, not even my father could control him. No one but Volk, that is. Volk tried to tell us he'd done nothing to Randy, that this only proved he – Volk – was the stronger alpha in the clan. When my father refused to step down in his favor, Volk ordered Randy to attack."

Tears ran down Finn's cheeks as she spoke. I didn't realize until I felt my own tears dripping onto my hands that I was also crying. God, I'd forgotten – or had at least tried to forget – that terrible night. After what happened to Finn's parents, then Finn running away and everything else that led to my family leaving the clan, I had forgotten. But not now and never again.

"I don't know how they did it, but my parents and their closest advisors managed to get Randy under control. He'd been badly injured in the fight, so badly even being one of us wouldn't heal him completely. He was left crippled and you know what that's like for one of us." She scrubbed her hands over her face and drew a deep shaky breath before continuing. "By the time the fight was over, Volk was gone. My parents put out a warning about him and ordered him killed if he returned to clan territory. That was the last I heard of him."

"Dear God." Jim's voice was soft with disbelief and yet I heard the anger running beneath it. "You're sure it's the same guy?"

"Unfortunately." Now it was my time to tell what I could. "After Finn killed Jennings – and good going there by the way. He deserved to die and I'm glad it was by your hand. – and the other clan leaders offered the Northern California clan to Declan, he sent out word to those of us who had left after Jennings took over. We were welcome to return. He did it to show the other clans that he wasn't going to perpetuate the injustices that Jennings committed. But he also did it because he knew he was going to have to clean house and wanted loyal clan members he could count on.

"As I said earlier, a number of us returned. Not everyone. Most of our parents have settled into their new lives and clans. But there were a number of younger members of the clan who returned. We were glad to be able to go back home. Besides, by going to what was basically a new clan, we wouldn't have to spend years proving ourselves and our value to the clan. We would be able to do so immediately, especially since Declan made it clear everyone had to prove they had the good of the clan at heart.

"Believe me, Declan was as good as his word. He cleaned house. He spoke with the various pride and pack leaders as well as those of our kind in the area who had refused to join the clan under Jennings. Any of those who willingly went along with what Jennings had done, especially where Finn and her family were concerned, were banished. But it wasn't a smooth process and Volk wound up right in the middle of it.

"It didn't take long for Declan to discover that Volk had been using ferals to hunt normals as well as our own kind. Before we could confine him and bring him before the pack and pride leaders to hear the charges against him, Volk disappeared. That was less than a month after Declan took over the clan.

"I hadn't returned to California yet, so I'm not exactly sure of the timeline. What I can tell you is Volk showed back up several weeks later and all hell broke loose before he disappeared again.

"Since then, Declan's had our trackers, me included, looking for him. Our orders were to locate him, kill any ferals he might have and return him to the clan for justice. If that proved impossible, we were to kill Volk as well."

I paused and glanced up at Matt, trying to read his expression. I'd hate to play poker against him. While his brother stiffened in anger when he heard the charges against Volk, the Alpha merely nodded. Whether that was because he already knew the story or he'd simply guessed it from what he'd seen and heard, I couldn't tell. Frankly, I didn't care as long as he believed me.

"I've been on Volk's trail for close to six weeks now. I followed him here from Phoenix. Each stop along the way, I've been a day or two behind him. This was the first time I came within striking distance.

"But our intelligence failed. I didn't know he had any of his ferals with him. If I had, I'd never have gone after him alone. Unfortunately, I didn't know and when I finally cornered him in the alley, he had the feral attack while he stood back and waited. I'd just dispatched the feral when the officer pulled up. I really hope Volk's used the time to get out of here, out of your territory, but I doubt it. This was the closest any of our people have come to him and I cost him one of his own. He's not going to just slink away."

In fact, unless I missed my guess, it meant he'd be coming for me. That was most definitely not a pleasant thought. Making it worse, I knew he wouldn't care who he hurt to get to me.

"You're sure you finished the feral?" Finn asked.

"I am" I ducked my head as I felt a blush of embarrassment heat my cheeks. I'd been a fool not to anticipate Volk would have had at least one feral with him. At least I'd been a lucky fool. I was still alive. "By the time I realized that SOB wasn't alone, the feral had shifted. Luck was on my side. I managed to kill it and had just beheaded it when Snyder arrived. I don't know what he thought he saw –" Although I had a pretty good idea. – "but if he'd searched, he would have found a wolf with its head lying a good six feet from its body. Still, I'm glad he didn't go down the alley. Volk would have killed him."

"God, you were lucky." Jim shook his head as he looked down at me. "And I owe you an apology. I was so shaken to find a tracker in the area, one who'd just killed another of our kind, that I didn't pay attention to what my senses were telling me. But, damn it, why didn't you tell me you were injured?"

Why indeed?

I looked at him, not quite sure how to respond. It had been a long time since anyone had worried about me being all right. The life of a tracker was often a solitary one. Even when we were with the clan, we were apart. Many of our own kind feared us because we were the enforcers, the ones to carry out the final judgment of the clan leader. Add in being the younger sister of the clan leader's mate and, well, there weren't a lot of guys lining up outside my bedroom door because they knew what Declan would do to them if they should ever hurt me – and that was only after my sister finished with them.

"Because I didn't realize I'd been hurt as badly as I had been." And that really was the truth.

For a moment, he just looked at me, as if unsure whether to believe me or not. Then he gave a quick nod before looking at his brother. "Matt, I need to get back."

"Call Stefan on your way out."

"I will."

"Jim, don't try to find him on your own. Promise me." I grabbed his hand and held it, doing my best to relay just how dangerous such action would be.

"Don't worry." He used his free hand to brush a lock of hair back from my face. "I'll take Tamara or Danny with me. Both of them can more than take care of themselves and any trouble we might run into. You get some rest and do whatever Stefan tells you."

I nodded, wishing there was something I could do to dissuade him. He smiled and then he was gone, closing the door behind him.

"Declan did talk with me before the shit hit the fan, Maggie," Matt continued. "So you don't have to worry about that. And, while you're here, you are one of my own even if you aren't a member of my clan. I promised Declan I'd help you and look out for you." Now he reached out and touched my forehead, much as Jim had a moment ago. As he did, I felt him exerting his will, soothing my tiger and, in turn, soothing me. "I know you want to be out looking for Volk. But you can't face him injured. You know that."

He waited until I nodded reluctantly.

"Until you are healed enough to return to the hunt, my people will look for him for you. If you want to call Declan and confirm it with him, go ahead. I'm confident he'll tell you we have some of the best security and surveillance people available."

"Thanks, the offer is enough." There was no way I'd insult either Matt or Finn by calling Declan in their presence. Of course, as soon as I could, I'd be calling to check in and if, by some chance, Declan asked what was going on, I'd tell him.

"Just try to relax now. Finn will stay with you until Stefan gets here. We'll talk some more later."

"Don't move." Finn pinned me with a firm glance before

following her husband to the door across the room. "Call Danny and tell him what's going on. And let Declan know. And find out why the hell he had her working on her own." Even though she spoke softly, her anger was clear. A moment later, she returned to the bed and, with gentle hands, helped me undress. "Stefan will be here before long. Believe me, you'll feel better after he's seen you."

I nodded, praying she was right.

CHAPTER THREE

"Maggie, if you're up to it, Matt needs to ask a few more questions before you get some rest."

Finn stood next to the bed. She spoke softly, almost gently. But the look she sent her mate was anything but. She did not approve. I didn't need to ask to know why. Before leaving a few minutes ago, Stefan told both of us he wanted me to rest. To Finn, that didn't mean answering yet more questions. Even so, I understood. Matt had more to worry about than me. All those in the clan looked to him for protection. He also had to worry about the normal in the area. That meant, he needed to know everything I could tell him. After seeing what Volk could do, I understood, even if it did leave me in the position of choosing between helping Matt and Finn or obeying my clan's Alpha.

"I promise this won't take long, Maggie," Matt said as he pulled a chair up next to the bed.

"Ask your questions. I understand."

"You're sure it was a feral?"

At least he got right to the point.

"I am." When he said nothing, I knew I needed to continue. "I don't know if you've ever seen one for yourself, Matt, but one you have, you never forget. They are wilder animal than human and rabid wild animal at that. It doesn't matter if they are shifted or not."

I sat up some and smiled slightly as Finn helped arrange the pillows behind my back. The look she gave me reminded me of Stefan's instructions. Until morning, I wasn't to even think about getting up. Even then, he'd prefer it if I stayed in bed. When I'd started to protest, he'd waved me to silence, reminding me he'd put in more than two dozen stitches to close the wound in my thigh and even more in other wounds that marked my body. Then he'd promised Finn he'd be back later to check on me. His parting comment had been to Matt, telling his nephew to make sure I stayed where I was.

"We haven't had any ferals in the area since before I took over leadership of the pride several years before I became clan leader." Matt frowned, his concern clear. "Are they traveling with Volk?"

"They are. At least that's the only conclusion that makes any sense after what happened back home." I paused, trying to find the best way to explain. Neither Finn nor Matt were part of my clan, but they were now in the middle of our war with Volk. Declan might not approve but they needed to know more about why I'd been hunting the man. "When he tried to take control of the clan, Volk sent his ferals after Declan and the rest of us without a thought for them." Or us, for that matter. "When the fighting was over, we believed we'd killed all the ferals. At least we'd hoped so. But we knew there was a chance some of them escaped with Volk. That's why Declan said he was warning all the other clan leaders to be on the lookout."

Something he failed to do, based on Matt's questions and Finn's quick intake of breath. Damn him.

"I'll be honest. One thing that's worried me is that Volk would find others to join him. He always seemed able to. I still don't know what he did to Randy. None of us do. Somehow, he turned Randy and I have to believe he's done it with others as well. What else could explain how he keeps finding ferals to follow him?"

"She's right, Matt." Finn sounded troubled, as she should be. She'd seen what Volk was capable of. "Let me put it this way: if we could turn normals into one of our kind by attacking them, Volk would have gone on a spree to do just that years ago. He makes Jennings look sane. That's why my parents were so determined to stop him."

"At least Volk isn't an alpha." God, I didn't want to even think about the trouble he could cause if he was as strong as Declan, much less Matt. "I'm not sure he's even close to being one. However, he is one of the most charismatic people I've ever met, normal or shapeshifter. He has what my mother calls the gift of the gab. Worse, he somehow manages to get people to tell him their deepest desires or fears and he uses that to his advantage.

"As I said earlier, he believed he should be clan leader after Finn killed Jennings. It didn't matter that he'd never risen to the rank of pack leader. Just like it didn't matter that he wasn't an alpha. He'd convinced himself that he would be the best to lead us and nothing was going to stand in his way. When he failed to defeat Alex Buchman to lead one of the smaller packs in the clan, he challenged Declan. He wouldn't listen when the leaders of the various packs and prides pointed out he had no standing to challenge for clan leadership. He refused to back down. That's when we discovered just what a snake Jennings had been nurturing and just how much of a mistake Declan had made in not banishing Volk right away."

I swallowed hard as memory of that night returned. I'd just moved back to California. My parents hadn't wanted me to leave Tennessee where we'd settled after leaving California less than a month after Finn ran away. But, with Declan taking over as clan leader and Eileen going with him, I knew the clan needed people who were loyal to the new clan leader and his mate. Besides, I wanted to be able to prove myself as a valuable member of a clan in my own right, not based on who my parents were and what their role in the clan happened to be.

That night, that terrible night, was the first gathering of the full clan since I'd arrived in California. I'd been so excited. Okay, there had been a fair share of nerves as well. Even though Declan and Eileen had been there more than a month, I knew there were still those who resented them as outsiders. because of that, I wanted to be there for my sister and her mate, her husband, and heaven help anyone who said anything against them.

Declan had barely called the gathering to order when Volk appeared, claiming he was the rightful leader of the clan. I had to give it to Declan. He simply looked at Volk, his expression similar to that worn by someone who had just smelled something very bad. Without raising his voice, Declan reminded Volk he'd been given leadership of the clan at the gathering of other clan leaders following Jennings' death. His appointment had been accepted by the clan's various pride and pack leaders. Then, almost casually climbing to his feet, he *suggested* Volk apologize.

For a moment, Volk stared at Declan as if he couldn't believe what he heard. Then he laughed and told Declan and the various pride and pack leaders that they'd underestimated him and his power. Before anyone realized what was happening, Volk tossed back his head and howled. It was a sound I'd never heard from anyone whose animal form was canine or feline. It sent chills down my spine and signaled the beginning of a nightmare I prayed ended soon.

Without warning, a dozen or so of Volk's ferals – shapeshifters more animal than human, no matter what form they were in. Shifted, they were like wild, almost rabid creatures that answered only to their master – charged us. They tore into those gathered, mauling young and old alike.

Declan reacted, rolling all of us with his power as clan Alpha. But he'd delayed too long, too stunned by what happened to act instantly. As a result, half a dozen of our people died. More than three times that had been injured, some seriously. Worse, the delay gave Volk time to flee. I still hear his laughter, taunting and evil, in my dreams.

That night was the first time I'd killed to protect family and friends. All it had taken was the sight of one of the ferals closing in on my three-year-old nephew. I knew the wolf would kill Sean. Unlike Declan, I didn't hesitate. Never before had I shifted as quickly as I did that night. For the first time, I gave my white tiger full control, telling her to do whatever she needed to protect our new clan. I was merely along for the ride and I had reveled in the violence we unleashed against those attacking our clan almost as much as she had.

At the next clan meeting less than a month later, Declan named me tracker. Oh, he refused to let me go searching for Volk until I'd been trained by the clan's other trackers. Then he'd held me close to home, making sure I was ready for this mission. Finally, we got a solid lead on Volk and he sent me, as well as the others, on the hunt. It had been my bad luck to be the one to find the bastard.

"I have to let my pride and pack leaders know what's happening. They need to take precautions to protect their people. More importantly, they will keep an eye out for Volk and his followers." Matt frowned, his expression troubled. Then, seeing how I watched him in concern, he reached out and lightly patted my hand, his expression easing. "Don't worry, Maggie. I'm not going to send you home. This is your hunt and I understand why you, or someone else from your clan, needs to finish it. However, you aren't familiar with our territory. I'll assign some of my own trackers to work with you, but this is still your hunt. You have my word."

"Thank you." What else could I say?

"But I insist you do as Stefan said." Finn pinned me with a firm look and then smiled as she reached for my other hand. "Maggie, I'm asking as your friend. Please get some rest like Stefan said. You're in no shape to go after Volk yet. Besides." And now she grinned. "I remember your sister. When we were kids, she always said you were her pesky little sister, but she always blamed me when you and I got into trouble. Believe me, I don't want to have to tell her I didn't take care of you now."

I grinned at the image of her doing just that. Eileen had always been protective of me, even when I had been that "pesky little sister". Not that I liked being told what to do. Still, Finn and Matt were right.

I needed to heal up before going after Volk again. I'd learned the hard way not only that I couldn't underestimate him but that I needed to be at my peak before going head-to-head with him again.

"I'm not going to argue, Finn. I'll admit I want to get right back on the hunt, but I'm not foolish. Injured as I am right now, I wouldn't be much of a challenge for Volk and, believe it or not, I really would like to live to a nice old age, something he'd make sure I wouldn't have the chance to do." But there was one thing I did need to do. I may have promised to stay in bed, but this was important. I carefully changed positions, ignoring the pain that grabbed at my thigh, and lowered my forehead first to Finn's hand where it rested on mine and then to Matt's. "Alphas, while I am in your territory, I will abide by your word. My arm is yours and I will give my life to protect you and yours. As long as you don't ask me to betray my own clan, I am yours to command."

Matt lifted my face so I looked him in the eye. Respect and understanding were reflected there. "All I ask right now is that you get some rest so Stefan doesn't tear strips out of my hide." Now he grinned, his affection for his uncle clear. "When Jim gets back, we'll discuss what needs to be done next. Until then, rest."

"I will," I promised. "But first I probably ought to call my sister."

Finn grinned, understanding what I left unsaid. By calling Eileen, I could not only reassure her that I was all right, but I'd be able to let her know what happened without having to face Declan's disappointment or disapproval. "Tell her I said hello," she commented as she handed me her cell phone. A moment later, she led Matt to the door. "Once you've finished your call, go ahead and shift. You'll heal faster and, if you're anything like me, feel better." She smiled once more and closed the door behind them, giving me privacy to make my call and then shift.

I woke, senses alert. Ears flicked as I listened to the sounds around me. Soft voices, male and female, from nearby. A sniff and the scents confirmed what my ears told me. Alphas. Not my Alpha and his mate, but my protectors. I was safe. They would not let Volk near me, at least not until I was healed. Maybe not even then.

I moved slightly on the bed, a sharp stab of pain in my left rear leg reminding me of the fight with the feral. A soft growl deep in my throat sounded as memory returned. That one was dead. But there were others. There were always others and would be until I found and killed Volk. Until then, he and the ferals would continue to be a danger to all our kind.

I needed – no, I wanted – to return to the hunt but couldn't. Neither the tiger nor the human liked that.

A soft sound, not really a sound, more like a hint of one warned me I wasn't alone. I lifted my head slightly and sniffed again. This time I purred in satisfaction. He was there and close, closer than the Alphas. The room smelled of him.

"Shh," a voice said. His voice. "Rest some more."

His hand ran over my head, fingers scratching behind one ear. I rubbed my head against his palm. This was one I could trust.

This was one I wanted and, when this was over, I'd have.

"You really are a beauty." Admiration filled his voice, as it should. In this form, I was beautiful and powerful. "But you need to rest some more. Stefan will be here in a couple of hours. You'll have to shift back then. Sleep now."

I shook my head and my muscles gathered. Then, as pain ripped through my injured leg, a soft mew, more like a kitten than a grown tiger, escaped. Damned feral. I should have fought it shifted.

The mattress dipped as he stretched out at my back. His body molded itself against mine and one arm draped over me, holding me down. It was more symbolic than an actual attempt to confine me. Shifted, even injured, I was stronger than his human form. But the message was clear. I needed to rest in order to heal and he planned to make sure I did.

He might not be an alpha, or at last not *the* Alpha, but he certainly knew how to act like one.

"Relax, Maggie, and rest." His voice soothed, his breath tickling the fur of my neck. "I made sure there was nothing in the alley to betray what you'd been doing there, and Tamara has her people, our trackers, looking for Volk now. I'll tell you everything else later."

That was enough – for now.

But later, oh later he'd better be prepared because I had plans for him.

CHAPTER FOUR

"Your wounds are healing nicely, Maggie," Stefan said as he closed his medical bag. "I'm not going to lie to you. Your thigh will take time. I don't want you putting any weight on that leg for at least forty-eight hours." He held up a hand to stop the protest he must have seen forming on my lips. "I know you want to get back on the hunt. But you need to be healed first. You know I'm right."

Now he looked at me, his expression serious. For the first time, I saw the familial resemblance between him and his nephews. It was something about his eyes. They had that same mixture of concern and determination I'd seen in both Matt and Jim. Stefan might be as small and non-descript as they were tall and memorable but, in that moment, I didn't doubt he was just as strong as were they.

"Matt and Finn told me some about why you're here and how you were injured. I know you are hunting one of the monsters our kind sometimes becomes. Worse, you are hunting ferals and you learned the hard way just how dangerous that can be. But what you might not know is that we may be able to help with more than just the hunt."

"What do you mean?" My frustration at being hurt and unable to immediately return to the hunt for Volk disappeared as I waited for Stefan to answer.

"I'll leave most of the story to Finn. It's hers to tell. But when Jennings sent that last group of trackers after her, they were armed with Tasers as well other weapons that could have seriously injured Finn—or worse. After she'd been injured, we discovered the barbs of the Tasers, as well as the blade used on her, had been treated with a drug that slowed Finn's metabolism down, preventing her from healing as she normally would.

"When I first saw her, it was an hour or so after Matt rescued her. The Taser barbs were still embedded in her back and she had a knife wound in her side. The drug they'd been tainted with had her weak as a kitten. I removed the barbs, treated her wounds and took blood samples. Then I sent everything to a lab I trust, one that often works for our kind, and had them analyzed. We have the drug's formula now."

Hope flared. If what he said was true, it might give me the edge I needed against Volk and the ferals. I'd already learned Volk wouldn't let me near him unless it was on his terms. That meant I'd have to fight my way through his ferals. The only way to do that would be to do it quickly enough he didn't have the chance to escape. But even with the advantage Stefan seemed to be offering me, it wouldn't be enough. I needed help. But, first things first. I needed to know more about this drug and I needed to know why Declan hadn't known about it. This wasn't the sort of thing one clan leader should be keeping to himself.

"I'll talk to Finn and Matt about it." And I'd be doing it damned soon, even if it meant disobeying Stefan's orders about not putting weight on my injured leg. There was no way I could stay off my feet now, not when he'd just dangled a very tasty metaphorical carrot in front of me.

"I'd prefer it if you stayed in bed for the next few days." Again, he held up a hand to forestall my protests. "But I have a feeling you are every bit as stubborn as Finn. We won't even talk about how stubborn

Matt and Jim can be. There is a pair of crutches on the floor next to the bed. Just remember, your thigh is held together with more than two dozen stitches and tape. You rip it open again and it will be weeks, not days, before you're healed. If you get up, your foot isn't to touch the ground. Understand?" He pinned me with such a firm look I dropped my eyes and nodded.

He patted my hand and left the bedroom, closing the door behind him. There was a murmur of voices a few moments later. I didn't need the acute hearing of my tiger to know he was reporting to Finn exactly what he'd told me. That meant I needed to move fast – well, as fast as I could on a pair of crutches – if I wanted to get out of bed and be dressed before she could protest.

Pain lanced through my thigh as I swung my legs over the side of the bed. That settled at least one thing. I'd have to use the crutches. If simply sitting up sent pain arcing through me like that, I didn't want to think what standing would do.

I stood, carefully balancing on my good leg, my right hand anchoring me to the side of the bed as I bent to retrieve the crutches. By the time I hobbled across the room to the small half-bath, I wasn't sure getting up was such a good thing. But I'm stubborn and I didn't have time to waste staying in bed. Even though Eileen had been worried enough about me when I'd talked with her earlier to tell me to do what the local alphas said – and to take care of myself – she'd also stressed the need to get back on Volk's trail as quickly as possible. None of our other trackers were in the area. It would take time for them to get here, time in which Volk and his ferals could disappear again. We didn't dare risk that.

I didn't have any choice. I had to be up. If Matt and Finn wouldn't put their own trackers after Volk, I'd have to figure something else out. I'd been so close. Damn it, as close as I'd come to be killed, I'd been that close to getting Volk. It's foolish, but I wanted to be the one who finally catch and deal with that bastard. It was bad enough that he put all our kind in danger with his ferals – and, unless I missed my guess, hunting of normals. Attacking our clan and turning the ferals loose on children earned him a death sentence. I wouldn't let him harm anyone else.

"Would you mind telling me just what in the hell you think you're doing?" Finn may have spoken softly as I emerged from the bathroom but there was no mistaking her disapproval. Disapproval? She was furious. Everything about her, from the way she stood just inside the room, arms crossed over her chest, one toe tapping the floor to the way she looked at me, confirmed it. In that moment, she reminded me of her mother whenever she'd catch us doing something we shouldn't have been. Those had been good times —unlike now.

"I can't stay in bed, Finn. I have a job to do."

"You can, and you will get your ass back in bed or you'll find yourself stuck there even longer." One finger stabbed the air in the direction of the bed. I considered, for one brief moment, disobeying. But I was starting to shake as weakness returned. So, giving my best impression of a broody teenager, I obeyed.

"Finn!" I protested as she took the crutches from me and set them against the wall across the room, well out of reach.

"Maybe that will keep you in bed – where Stefan said you were supposed to stay." She pinned me with a firm look and then smiled, shaking her head. "Look, Maggie, I'd have tried it too, which is why I figured I'd better get in here before you did yourself damage. If you promise to be good and stay there, I'll go get you something to eat. I'll even bring you something to wear. You're still smaller than me, but I think you can wear some of Sharon's things."

Sharon? Who was Sharon? My cat reared up in my head, growling as a flare of jealousy raced through me. What the hell was happening to me? What did I care if Jim was married or involved with someone? We'd just met.

If Finn noticed my reaction, she gave no indication. Thankfully. There was no way I wanted to try to explain it to her. Hell, I couldn't explain it to me. I didn't even want to think about it. I had more than enough to worry about without that complication. Still, Finn could answer at least one question, hopefully without asking any I didn't want to deal with.

"Sharon?" Thankfully, my voice didn't crack nor did anything other than simple curiosity fill it.

"Matt's and Jim's sister."

I wasn't relieved. No, really. And my stomach didn't unclench. No, none of that happened. At least not that I was going to admit to, even to myself. Still, as I pulled my legs onto the mattress and leaned back, I relaxed, and my cat resumed her slumber in the back of my mind. Then, after promising to stay where I was, I watched as Finn left the room. She returned a few minutes later carrying a tray and my stomach growled as I smelled what I bet was a perfectly grilled steak.

Finn settled the tray on the bedside table and then helped me sit up a bit more. A moment later, I took the plate from her. With a smile that I hoped told her how much I appreciated the food, I dug in, pleased to know my guess was right. The steak was a perfect medium rare and marked with precise grill marks. The baked potato was huge and filled with butter. I could have lived without the green beans, but I ate them anyway, pretty sure Finn would have *suggested* I clean my plate.

As I ate, we talked. At first it was a little awkward, at least for me. How could I apologize for not being there for her all those years ago?

"Maggie." Finn's hand closed over mine and she waited until I looked at her. "What's wrong?"

"Finn, I'm sorry." I could barely choke out the words.

"For what?"

"I wasn't there for you, Finn. I should have been, but I wasn't."

For a moment, she looked at me, her expression troubled. Then she smiled and gave me a quick hug.

"Maggs, I'm glad you weren't there. Jennings would have used you against me and you know that. I'm sorry I left without saying goodbye and I'm sorry I didn't get in contact with you later. But Aunt Jane and my grandmother told me I needed to stay off the grid as long as Jennings still controlled the clan and they were right. I'm just glad it's over and we finally have a chance to get to know one another again."

She meant it. I could hear it in her voice. When had she become the adult of the two of us? She'd always been the one to lead us head-long into trouble. Always with the best of intentions, of course, but usually with unforeseen outcomes that often met with parental disapproval. Now she was a clan alpha and, judging from what I'd heard from others of our kind, very well respected. She'd certainly come a lot farther than I had.

Thankfully. She deserved it.

With that out of the way, we spent the next hour just talking. It was so clear Finn way happy in her marriage to Matt and in her role as Alpha. Her face lit up as she talked about spending time with her grandmother and others of the family she'd been cut off from for so long. There was no mistaking her satisfaction to know she was the one to deal with Michael Jennings and rightly so. He'd taken her life from her, forcing her to leave family and home. He would have done even worse if he'd managed to get his hands on her again.

"Finn, it really is good to see you again." I grinned and squeezed her hand. God, I'd missed her so much.

"I missed you too, Maggs." She pulled the sheet up over my legs and sat back, studying me. "But you're tired now. I want you to get some rest. We'll talk more after you do."

"But—" We still hadn't discussed Volk and what her people were doing to find him.

"I know what you're going to say." She shook her head as I opened my mouth. Habit and respect had me closing it with a snap. She might be my childhood friend, but she was also her clan's female Alpha. "I promise we'll fill you in after you rest. Just know we have people out looking for Volk even as we speak." She reached out and switched off the bedside lamp. The dark that settled over the room surprised me. It was obviously later than I thought. "Give a shout if you need anything."

With that, she got to her feet and left the room, closing the door behind her. With the crutches still across the room, I didn't have much choice. I settled back and closed my eyes. Maybe I'd be healed enough to get out of bed come morning.

And maybe pigs could fly.

The smell of coffee brewing tickled my nose and light streamed across my face. Groaning, I pulled the sheet over my head. Too late. I was awake. The throbbing in my thigh followed by an undeniable urge to get to the bathroom confirmed it. I tossed back the sheet and carefully sat up. As I did, I noticed the crutches leaning against the wall next to the head of the bed, within easy reach. Obviously, someone had checked on me during the night. Probably Finn, judging by the stack of clothing resting on the edge of the dresser.

Five minutes later, I once more sat on the edge of the bed. The short trek to the adjoining bathroom had almost done me in. If possible, my thigh hurt worse this morning than it had the day before. I ran a hand across my brow and closed my eyes. I needed to get up and find out what happened overnight. I simply wasn't sure I could.

Sitting there, I pulled on a tee shirt and then a pair of loose sweatpants, carefully easing them over my injured thigh. Finn had been right when she insisted I shift just as she'd been right to make me rest even when I hadn't wanted to. As badly as I hurt, I didn't want to think what it would be if I hadn't shifted for those few hours yesterday. Beneath the bandages, raw skin and ragged edges had scabbed over. My various injuries looked as if days had passed instead of a little more than twenty-four hours. Even so, and like it or not, Stefan was right. I needed at least a week, maybe more, before the leg would be close to healed enough for me to be up and about. Returning to the hunt would take longer, at least if I wanted to keep my head attached to my body should I find Volk again.

Damn it, the feral had managed to hurt me worse than I first thought. God, I'd been lucky. A little deeper, a little more to the inside of my leg and the femoral artery would have been severed. I'd have bled out quicker than I'd have been able to heal.

Maybe I should send Officer Snyder one of those cookie bouquets. Seems he might have saved my life after all.

I looked at my boots where they rested against the wall a few feet away. As I did, I heard Mom's voice in my head telling me it was only polite to put on my shoes before leaving the bedroom. I was a guest here, after all. Besides, as a tracker and member of another clan, I needed to do my clan leader proud. But the thought of trying to pull on the boots caused me to blanch. The leg hurt enough as it was. I didn't want to do anything to add to it.

Well, nothing more than getting out of the bedroom and finding someone who could tell me what was going on and if they'd discovered anything that might help lead me to Volk.

Carefully, moving slowly because I remembered Stefan's warnings about putting any weight on my left leg, I stood. Pain lanced through the leg from the movement and, for one brief moment, the room swam around me. Sweat pricked out on my forehead and my right hand closed about the bedpost, holding on for dear life. I waited, praying I didn't fall on my face, until the room quit spinning and my stomach no longer lurched. Then, gritting my teeth and telling myself I would not throw up, I would not pass out, I reached for the crutches and tucked them under my arms. I slowly moved into the hallway, careful not to let my left foot come close to the floor.

God, I hoped I'd find the kitchen before I fell on my face.

I'd only taken a couple of steps when Jim Kincade stepped into the hallway from what I assumed was another bedroom. He wore a pair of jeans and nothing else. For a moment, I thought he hadn't seen me. Then he turned, concern lighting his eyes before he shook his head and moved quickly to stand before me.

"What the hell are you doing out of bed?"

"I need to know what's going on." I swallowed hard as another wave of pain washed over me. I would not let him know how badly I hurt. I wouldn't.

He looked down at me, searching my expression. Without a word, he took the crutches from me and tossed them back inside the bedroom. Then his left arm went around my waist. Before I could react, his right arm went under my legs and he swung me up in his arms. The look on his face as he glanced down at me was enough to keep me from protesting. He might not be an alpha, but he was as bossy as one.

At least he didn't try to take me back to bed. Instead, he carried me into the kitchen. With his right foot, he pulled a chair out from the round table at the far end of the room. As he did, the cook in me sighed in wonderment. The kitchen was large and airy. The appliances were almost new and top of the line. Obviously, someone loved to cook as much as I did. Hopefully, they had more of a chance to indulge themselves. One of the downsides to being a tracker was that I wasn't home as much as I wanted to be.

"Do not move. Don't even think about moving."

Jim pinned me with a firm look before crossing to the cabinet near the refrigerator. A moment later, he returned with a tall glass of orange juice that he placed before me on the table. It was quickly followed by a mug of coffee. I shook my head when he offered milk and sugar.

"Finn will have my head when she finds out you got out of bed and I don't want to think about what Stefan will do," he said as he opened the oven.

The enticing aroma of cinnamon filled the air. My mouth watered, my stomach growled, and I leaned forward, hoping to catch a glimpse of what was inside what I now recognized as a convection oven. There was no way, absolutely no way, a can of sweet rolls would produce that heavenly scent. The final proof that someone – could it actually have been Jim – had baked homemade cinnamon rolls.

He moved with the ease of much practice as he popped the rolls out of the muffin tin and began drizzling icing over their tops. Then he turned, and one eyebrow lifted as he caught me watching him. Damn if I didn't feel a blush spread across my cheeks. But who could blame me? After all, there aren't many things sexier than a man dressed only in faded jeans, the top button open and learning he can bake.

I licked my lips and took a sip of coffee. As I did, he set the rolls on the table and then sat opposite me. Without a word, he reached for one of the rolls and took a bite. Icing dribbled from the corner of his mouth. I swallowed hard and put a firm hold on my cat. All she wanted was to reach over and lick the icing from his chin. Since it sounded like a pretty good idea to me, I needed to think about something else and quickly. I bit into my own cinnamon roll and then moaned. It was every bit as good as it looked.

"I take it you approve." A grin touched Jim's lips as he reached for his own mug of coffee.

"God, this is wonderful." I took another bite. "I make a pretty good cinnamon roll, but you've got me beat hands down."

"I like to cook." He grinned and lifted one shoulder in a shrug. I managed, barely, not to ask why some woman hadn't snapped him up. Partly because that would reveal way too much of my own thoughts just then and partly because I didn't want to find out that there was a woman who had snatched him up. Just because I hadn't seen one yet didn't mean she wasn't out there waiting for him.

"Any news about Volk?" That's what was important. I had to remember that.

"Nothing solid yet. Matt has our people checking for him and we're keeping an eye out for reports of any missing people or unusual deaths. My guess is that he's going to go to ground for a few days, at least as he decides what his next move will be."

"He's patient. That's the one thing I am sure about where he's concerned." I reached for my mug and frowned. It was empty. Seeing it, Jim leaned back and snagged the coffee pot. I smiled in appreciation as he gave me a refill. "My concern is that he'll leave the area until he figures out what he's going to do."

For a moment Jim didn't say anything. He just sat there, looking at me. His finger ran along the rim of his mug. He was thinking and thinking hard. I could almost hear his brain working. But I couldn't read anything from his expression.

"Maggie, we're going to need to know everything you do about Volk. You know that, right?"

I nodded. I did know it, but that didn't mean I was ready to. How could I when Declan hadn't given me permission to tell them everything. But then, Jim had made sure only that our kind were safe from discovery in the way he handled our first meeting. Then there was the fact he seemed more than willing to help me find Volk. I couldn't, in all good conscience, let him go hunting that bastard without knowing as much as I did.

But, unless we were both wrong, we had some time before I needed to tell him everything I knew or suspected. Probably not a lot of time, but enough for me to contact Declan and try to convince him of the need to let Jim and the others know what we did. I just hoped Declan agreed because I didn't want to disobey my Alpha. The consequences would be painful at the very least. He could decide to ban me from the clan. I didn't think he would, but if he felt it would keep my disobedience from undermining his position, he'd do it and Eileen wouldn't try to stop him.

Like most of our kind, I didn't want to live without my clan. That meant I couldn't go against Declan's orders. Hopefully, Jim and the others would understand and give me the time necessary to convince him to see it my way.

As if reading my mind, Jim leaned forward and placed his hand on mine where it rested on the tabletop. "But you need to get your Alpha's approval before you say more."

It wasn't really a question. Not that I'd expect it to be. Jim knew the way clan politics operated. He probably understood it a hell of a lot better than I did. Relieved he understood, I nodded again. As I did, I hoped he wouldn't try to press the issue, at least not yet.

"Until then, I think you're right to look for any of our kind who have gone missing. The same with any unusual deaths. When we started looking into Volk after he attacked the clan, we quickly realized he'd obviously been planning it for some time. We knew by then that he'd been hunting normals without Declan's approval. The only reason his activities hadn't triggered the attention of law enforcement was he was smart enough to do it in the wild and the kills were always solo hikers or runaways. It was easy enough for officials to write the deaths off as unfortunate animal attacks. There are still enough of those around our clan's territory that no one was too concerned, although a few reporters were starting to note that there seemed to be more of late than usual.

"The ferals killed when they attacked the clan were identified as lone shapeshifters who had gone missing from our territory and the surrounding area. One of them disappeared more than five years before the attack. The only conclusion is that Volk's keeping them with him, managing to keep them under control somehow. We just don't know how."

"I'll make sure Matt knows. He can get word to the neighboring clans so they can be on the lookout as well." He reached out and once again covered my hand with his. "I want your promise that you'll do as Stefan says. I know you want to return to the hunt. But you can't, not until you're healed. Right now, you'd be the one being tracked and, whether you want to admit it or not, easy prey for him."

I wanted to take offense at what he said but couldn't. He was right. I didn't like it and, frankly, it scared me to admit it. But injured as I was, I wouldn't even be able to make a run for it if I came across Volk or one of his ferals. Even shifted, my injuries were serious enough to hamper me. Instead of trying to bluff and tell him I was all right, I turned my hand over so our palms touched and wrapped my fingers around his hand, giving it a quick squeeze. As I did, that almost electric shock ran up my arm. I gasped and looked at him, not sure whether to be relieved or scared to see a startled look in his eyes.

Oh . . . my.

"I - um - I need to get ready for work." He let go of my hand and shoved his chair back from the table. The look he gave me as he did had my stomach doing flip flops. I so didn't need this but was it wrong to at least think about what he'd be like in bed?

"I'll clean up. It's the least I can do since you baked such wonderful rolls."

"Not this time." He cocked his head and waited, as if expecting me to object. The memory of him tossing the crutches back inside my bedroom returned and I sighed. I could no more clean the kitchen than I could get back to my room without them. Damn it.

"Is there anything I can do to help?" God, I hated feeling helpless, much less useless.

"You can try to convince your alpha to let you tell us everything you know about Volk. Then you need to rest. Finn will be over before long to check on you. She'll stay until I get home."

"Jim, I hate to ask it, but can someone go by my motel and get my things?" I knew there wasn't a chance in hell they'd let me go, at least not until I'd had a few more days to heal. Not that I blamed them. I'd be a handicap to anyone with me should Volk or his ferals find me.

"Sure." Now he smiled with a hint of apology. "I should have thought of that before. Sorry."

"Don't worry about it. I just get bored easily and I've got a couple of books with my stuff."

"I'm sure I can find you something to read before I leave. After work, I'll run by your motel and get your things." He looked at the clock as the chime sounded. Seven. "I need to finish getting ready. Do you want to stay in here for a bit or go into the den or what?"

For a moment, I considered asking him to help me into the den. Then I changed my mind. If I was going to have some time on my own, I'd shift and rest. The more time I spent shifted, the faster I'd heal. Even though the house was well off the beaten path, there was no reason to risk someone coming to the door and seeing a white tiger through the front window.

"If you don't mind, the bedroom. After I talk with Declan, I'll shift and rest until Finn gets here."

And, hopefully, not think too much about how I'd felt when our palms touched.

"Damn it, Declan, they need to know!"

I tugged at my hair with my free hand and gritted my teeth. At times, my Alpha was one of the most stubborn, short-sighted men I'd ever had the misfortune to know. He was so worried about not showing weakness, either within the clan or to other clan leaders, that he didn't always think about the consequences of his actions – or inactions. The fact I was confined to bed and damned lucky to be alive was proof of that. Not that he seemed to care just then. No, he was too worried about keeping clan secrets. Damn it, why couldn't he understand Volk presented a danger to all our kind?

The fool.

"You have your instructions, Maggie. Don't disobey me on this."

God, I hated that smug note in his voice.

I blew out a breath and tried again. Somehow, I had to make him see sense.

"Alpha." He might be my sister's mate, but I needed him to think of me as one of the clan's trackers right now and not as Eileen's little sister. "Volk is dangerous. Our clan learned that bitter lesson at great cost. I have confirmed he still has ferals with him. That means he presents a danger to the other clans, specifically to the Texas clan and those surrounding it right now. The clan leaders here deserve to know what sort of an enemy they are facing."

"I said no." I pictured him pulling himself up to his full height and trying to stare me down. It didn't matter there was more than fifteen hundred miles between us. Declan did not like being questioned or challenged. "I mean it, Maggie. You are to tell them only what I've approved. Nothing more." His tenor voice was sharp with an anger that matched my own. That wasn't good. There were others at risk now beyond our own clan.

"Then at least send the other trackers here to take up the hunt while I heal."

"No. They have their own leads on Volk to run down. You blew it when you let him get away. Now they have to clean up because you failed the clan."

My anger spiked, and my tiger stirred. We had not failed the clan. To hear Declan say that I had was too much. My grip on the cell phone tightened and my jaw clenched. There was a wave of pain, as if every pore on my body was suddenly alive. That was not good. I hadn't been this angry, this out of control since I first started shifting. I closed my eyes and concentrated. I would not shift now. I wouldn't give Declan the satisfaction of knowing he'd pushed me that far.

"You're wrong, Declan, just as you're wrong in not sending the others and just as you're wrong in not telling the clan alphas here what they need to know. But you are my Alpha. I won't disobey. However, if Volk hurts or kills an innocent here or elsewhere because you tied my hands, that will be on you." Before he could say anything else, I ended the call.

Damn him! I understood he needed to secure his position as Alpha, but that didn't mean he could ignore his duty to all our kind. He'd been Alpha of the Northern California clan for a year. He'd already solidified his position, at least in everyone's eyes but his own. Only his own self-doubt prevented him from realizing the prides and packs were loyal. He also should have figured out that the other clan leaders were there to assist when needed. Asking for help didn't show weakness, especially when it meant protecting all our kind.

Most of all, damn Volk and his ferals. I wanted, I needed to be out of bed and pacing, thinking about how to end Volk once and for all. But I couldn't. I was stuck here, too wounded to do what was necessary.

I tossed the cell phone onto the bedside table. It landed with a loud *thunk* and then skittered across the top. It hit the wall before falling to the floor. Angry as I was, I didn't care if it had broken. I had a feeling Declan – or more likely Eileen at his behest – would be calling back before long to put me in my place. I loved them both, but right now I didn't like Declan much and I sure didn't need this shit. I was the one who'd seen up close and personal what Volk was capable of. I knew he was still in the area, not off in some other part of the country. I'd become his next target by not dying in that alley and that thought of facing Volk again scared the hell out of me. If Declan couldn't understand that, to hell with him.

"Maggie?" Finn looked inside the room, her expression concerned.

"Go away."

For a moment, she stood there studying me. Then she stepped inside and closed the door behind her. Without a word, she moved to where the cell phone had fallen. She picked it up and then turned it over in her hand, shaking her head to see the crack across the screen. Great, Declan would expect me pay to replace the phone. That didn't help my mood one bit.

"I take it you finally got hold of your clan leader." She spoke softly, nothing in her voice betraying her thoughts.

"I did." I bit out the words. There was no sense trying to hide my anger. Even if she didn't see it, her cat would smell it radiating off of me.

"And I'm guessing from the way you just destroyed your cell phone that it didn't go well." She placed the ruined phone on the table and sat on the bed at my side. "Don't worry, Maggs. Matt told me at lunch he had a feeling Declan was going to drag his feet."

I looked at her, my brows knitting in confusion. "How?"

"Declan didn't take your call right away. Worse, he didn't immediately return it, something he should have done. You were injured and could have been killed. Not only did he fail to return your call, but he hasn't reached out to Matt or me to check on you. So Matt is going to have a *chat* with him." Before I could protest, knowing Declan would think I'd gone crying to Matt, Finn held up a hand. "Don't. This is exactly the sort of conversation any decent Alpha would have when another clan's tracker had been injured in his territory. If that doesn't work, then I'll talk with your sister."

I couldn't help it. I smiled slightly at the thought of the *talk* Finn would have with Eileen. My sister had been jealous of Finn when we were kids because Finn's parents were our clan alphas. She thought Finn received special treatment none of the rest of us received. What she hadn't realized was the only special treatment Finn received was that the entire clan watched over her, ready to make sure she knew if she wasn't living up to her potential. It was like having dozens and dozens of proud but demanding parents. How I wished her folks had lived to see the woman she'd become.

"Declan's a good Alpha, Finn, really." And he usually was, even when he pissed me off so much.

"But he's still learning his way and is unsure of his hold on the clan since it is new to him. He wasn't brought up in the Northern California clan and he has to make sure the taint of Jennings is erased forever," she completed for me. I nodded. She was absolutely right. "We understand all that, Maggs. But he has to understand that he can't let those insecurities endanger the rest of us." Now she smiled and stood, motioning for me to lay back. "It's late and Stefan will be here early in the morning to check on you. Why don't you get some rest?"

I was tired, but I needed to know a couple of things first. "Have you heard anything new? Anything about Volk or the ferals?"

"No, sweetie. I'd let you know if we had." And she would. I knew that. Something told me that she didn't play games now any more than she had when we were kids. "In fact, Jim called a few minutes ago to let us know he was on his way home. He said to tell you that he's seen nor heard anything to make him think Volk is doing anything more than hiding and trying to figure out his next move."

I didn't like knowing that bastard was still out there and quite likely planning his vengeance against me. But at least no one else had been hurt. Now, if only I could figure out some way to convince Declan to come clean with Finn and Matt before all hell broke loose.

If not, I'd have to choose whether or not I disobeyed my Alpha in order to protect all our kind.

"Now lie back and get some rest. I'll wake you when dinner's ready." Finn gently helped me lie back. As she pulled the sheet about my shoulders, she bent and pressed her lips to my forehead. When she straightened, she smiled down at me, affection reflected in her eyes. "Don't worry about Declan or anything else. You're safe and you're going to be all right."

God, I wanted to believe her. But so much could go wrong and so many lives could be lost.

Damn Volk and damn Declan for being so stubborn.

CHAPTER FIVE

"**D**amn it, Finn. There's no reason I can't sit in the den for this."
Of course, it's hard to make that point when your doctor's staring daggers at you and all but daring you to try to get out of bed. To add insult to injury, Finn didn't say a word. Instead, after looking at Stefan and seeing him give a slight shake of his head, she reached for my crutches. Not only did she move them out of reach, but she took them out of the bedroom altogether. The message was clear: I'd do as I was told, whether I liked it or not.

"Maggie." Stefan smiled slightly and patted my hand where it rested on top of the sheet covering my legs. "If I had my way, you wouldn't put either foot on the ground for the next three or four days. But I have a feeling you're too much like Finn to sit still for that. However, I must insist you stay in bed now. You've been up too much already today."

To make sure I understood, he pulled the sheet away from my injured leg and gently, carefully removed the bandages covering my thigh. I hissed as he did, a mixture of pain, frustration and stomach-churning fear. More than twenty-four hours had passed since the feral tried to chew my leg off. I expected to have healed more by now.

Sweat dotted my brow as Stefan cleaned the thigh. My fingers dug into the mattress. How they didn't poke holes in it, I'll never know. Bile burned my throat and I swallowed against it. Seeing the torn skin, the ragged edges of muscle that still looked to be missing pieces and I no longer felt so strongly about getting out of bed. In fact, I might not get out of bed for a week or two.

Except duty called and I had my orders from my Alpha.

"Maggs?" Finn gently touched my cheek, waiting until I opened my eyes and looked at her.

"I'm all right."

She didn't say anything for a moment. Instead, she moved around the bed. The mattress dipped as she gently sat next to me. A moment later, her arm went around my shoulders and she pulled me close. It seemed natural to rest my head on her shoulder, much as I used to when we were kids, spending the night together and talking about our deepest, darkest secrets. Now I held my secrets—well, my clan's secrets—close even as I accepted Finn's reassurances and protection.

God, I had to find a way to keep from failing her a second time.

"No, you aren't. But you will be." She gave my shoulders a squeeze and turned her attention to Stefan. "You're right about one thing," she told him. "Maggs is a lot like me. She's going to fret and possibly do something stupid if we try to keep her in bed for too long. If she's careful and promises not to get out of bed without someone helping her and she also promises not to touch that foot to the floor, can she get up tomorrow?"

Stefan didn't answer right away. Instead, he continued working on my thigh before rebandaging it and turning his attention to my other injuries. When he finally looked up, he sighed and gave a slight nod.

"If there is someone with her and if she doesn't go any further than the kitchen, bathroom or den." He waited until we both assured him we understood. "But, until morning, you are not to get out of bed unless someone carries you."

I didn't like it but, after seeing my damaged thigh, I knew I had no choice. "Promise."

Okay, I sounded like a sulky teenager. I'm not too proud to say I felt like one just then. I've never liked anyone, not even my parents, telling me what to do.

"As for this meeting you have planned, Finn." Now he turned his attention to her and she all but squirmed under his gaze. Not that I blamed her. Stefan might appear unassuming and almost harmless, but I learned quickly he had a spine of steel and he didn't hesitate to let you know what he thought about something. I liked that and was glad Finn and Matt had someone like that in the clan to help advise them. "One hour and not a minute more and that only after she's had something to eat."

"Agreed." She gave my shoulders another squeeze and then carefully slid off the bed. "While Stefan finishes checking you, I'll go see what Jim left in the slow cooker for dinner."

Half an hour later, Finn watched with a critical eye as I leaned forward so she could place another pillow behind my back. I might be under strict orders not to move from the bed but, by God, I'd not meet with clan Alphas flat on my back. Besides, I felt better after two bowls of some of the best chili I'd ever eaten. My injuries throbbed but the pain, thanks to another pain pill, no longer reached had me wanting to scream. Hopefully by morning, I could convince Stefan I no longer needed to stay in bed.

Not that I'd lay money on it.

Once I leaned back, Finn looked at me, her eyes missing nothing. Then she gave a slight nod as she settled the sheet at my waist. To my surprise, instead of taking one of the chairs Jim pulled up next to the bed, she remained standing, her hand resting on my shoulder. The implication was clear. I wasn't to even think about moving from where I was. But there was more. She was sending a message to Matt and Jim that she wasn't going to let them push me. Still the protector, even now.

When no one said anything, I fought the urge to sigh. They were leaving it to me, trusting me to tell them what they needed to know. Unfortunately for all of us, my hands were tied. At least after a point. I hoped they understood just as I hoped Declan came to his senses before long. Otherwise we faced a danger even worse than Volk. We faced our existence becoming common knowledge. Sooner or later, one of his ferals would shift in public and then all our careful plans, all our attempts to stay in the shadows would be for naught and the proverbial witch hunts would begin.

How in the hell had I managed to get myself in the middle of it all?

For the next ten minutes, I detailed how I had tracked Volk to North Texas. I should have expected the trap. He hadn't made much of an attempt to hide his movements. That should have been my first warning. Volk was anything but stupid and he certainly wasn't careless. He'd proven that in California. Then I'd been foolish enough to follow his trail into that alley. Talk about stupid. It could have been a scene right out of a slasher film. All that had been missing was the ominous soundtrack.

What he hadn't expected, and what probably saved my life, was for me not to play by the rules. Most trackers carry no weapons in another clan's territory, at least not until they have checked in with the local clan leader. Our kind learned long ago that prevented a number of problems. There were no misunderstandings that a new shifter might be in town with ideas of taking power for him or herself. There were no concerns that one clan might be after another clan's territory. Volk obviously expected me to follow true to form. Fortunately for me, I'm a suspicious soul and had weapons with me, weapons I hadn't hesitated using to stay alive.

"Maggs, why were you searching for Volk alone?"

I heard the mixture of worry and outrage in Finn's voice. Not that I could answer. That was one of the things Declan forbade me from explaining. Unfortunately, I needed to say something, and I had a feeling Finn would know if I lied.

"I hadn't had a chance to call in reinforcements yet." Which was the truth, at least part of it. "I wanted to make sure I wasn't following another dead end before sending for the others."

They knew I was holding back. I saw it in their eyes. But, to my surprise, they didn't condemn me. Whether Finn had told them what she'd seen when she walked in at the end of my call to Declan or not, I didn't know. I didn't care. What mattered was they respected me, if not my Alpha, enough not to push—yet. And I knew it was only a matter of time. If one of their people was injured, or worse, before Declan came to his senses, Finn and Matt would demand answers. The question was if I would give them to them.

"Maggie spoke with her Alpha earlier," Finn said, as if reading my mind.

"I see." Matt didn't say anything else. He didn't need to. Not when his frustration shone on his expression. "We won't push, Maggie." Frustration gone, he smiled and leaned forward to clasp my hand. "I gave you my word as clan leader earlier. We will help you with this hunt. You aren't alone now."

Which only made me feel worse. Matt and Finn owed me nothing. In fact, they could demand I leave their territory immediately because my encounter with Volk and the feral caught the attention of a normal. Things could have gone so much worse than they had, and our existence could have been exposed. But they didn't make the demand. Instead, they treated me better than my own clan leader did.

Damn Volk and damn Declan.

"Matt's right," Jim said. "Our trackers are on alert and looking for Volk. We've contacted the neighboring clans as well." When I opened my mouth to protest, he shook his head, his expression serious. "Don't worry, Maggie. We didn't mention your or your home clan. But they needed to know."

I nodded. I couldn't do much else, not when he was right.

"Tamara, the head of our trackers, will have a full report to Finn and me by morning," Matt said. "Finn or I will go over it with you as soon as we get it. I promise."

"Thank you." Hopefully, he understood I meant for more than that.

"Maggs, you don't have to thank us. We'd help you even if we didn't have the clan to protect." Finn carefully sat on the edge of the mattress. A moment later, she gave me a hug.

And they would. Even as a girl, Finn had been the protector. I had no doubt Matt was the same. Then, seeing the look on Jim's face, I knew he'd do whatever it took to deal with Volk, whether I wanted him to or not. He might not be an alpha, but he viewed the area as his territory, probably because of his role as sheriff. One thing for certain, I didn't have to hunt Volk on my own any longer.

I wished I felt better about it.

"You need to get some rest now." Finn stood and looked down at me for a moment. Before I could start to squirm, she seemed to make up her mind. "Jim will you help her into the bathroom?"

"Of course."

"I can do it on my own if you'd get me my crutches." I didn't whine, but it was close. Finn thought so too because she grinned and shook her head. "Nope. Stefan made it clear he didn't want you to risk putting any weight on your leg."

"And we'd better get on our way home," Matt said. "Tomorrow's going to be a long day."

"Why don't you stay the night?" Jim suggested. "Your room's ready for you."

"Thanks, big brother." Matt clapped Jim on the shoulder and then smiled down at me. "Get some rest, Maggie. We're here if you need anything."

Ten minutes later, Jim settled me back on the mattress. He watched, his eyes dark with concern, as I found a comfortable position. Then he pulled the sheet over me. "Do you need anything?"

"No, thanks." Well, I needed to be healed and I needed to be back on the hunt, but that wasn't going to happen soon. No sense whining about it—yet.

"My room is next to yours. Just give a shout if you need

anything." Then he glanced over one shoulder, as if making sure no one could overhear. "I'd bring your crutches back in, but Finn would have my head. Promise you won't try to get up on your own."

"I promise."

He gave me one last look and then said good night. As the door closed behind him, I slid down in bed, exhausted. My thoughts swirled. Images of Volk and the feral mixed with memories of the attack on the clan. Then there was that odd electrical spark whenever Jim's hand touched mine. I shifted positions slightly and bunched the pillow under my head. A moment later, much to my surprise, my eyes closed and sleep descended.

Pain and something else woke me. For a moment, I lay still. Through barely opened eyes, I saw darkness alleviated only by the faint glow of the clock next to the bed. 2:37. Much too early to be awake. I started to settle back and then stopped. I wasn't alone. Someone else was in the room with me. My heart beat faster and I forced myself to lie still. I couldn't let whoever was there know I was awake. I needed time to think, to figure out how best to respond.

I shifted slightly in bed, hoping whoever was there would think I was simply changing positions. A sniff and my lips curved up slightly. My pulse pounded, but not from fear. Most definitely not from fear. The tingling between my legs and the tautness of my nipples were another thing. Not that I was going to think about that.

He was there. I probably shouldn't be surprised. He'd been as adamant as Finn that I not try to get up by myself.

I reached out and switched on the bedside lamp. Jim sat in the wingback chair by the window, his head bowed until his chin touched his chest. He wore a pair of cut-offs and a tee shirt. A stubble of beard shadowed his jaw. Sleeping.

My tiger roused and rumbled in satisfaction. This is where he belonged. Well, it was almost where he belonged. As far as she was concerned, he needed to be in my bed and we most definitely did not need to be sleeping. Well, we'd disagree there. At least for the moment. I was still too hurt to have that sort of fun. Besides, I didn't need to be distracted by anything until I found and killed Volk and his ferals.

Still, he didn't need to sleep sitting up. He'd already shared my bed once. Sure, I'd been shifted then and he hadn't, but that didn't really matter. Not to our kind.

"Jim." I spoke softly. The last thing I wanted was to wake Finn and Matt.

He started, waking instantly. Without a word, he was out of the chair and across the room. As he knelt next to the bed, he reached out to touch my cheek, my forehead. Concern clouded his expression. "Are you all right? Do you need another pain pill?"

"I'm fine." And I was. It didn't matter that my thigh throbbed, not with him so close. "Why are you sleeping in the chair?"

"I wanted to be here if you needed anything."

"And if I decided to do something foolish like get up?" I grinned as he ducked his head.

"Something like that," he admitted.

"You don't have to sit there all night, Jim. I'm not going to get up. I promise."

The look he gave me spoke volumes. He didn't believe me. Considering how I'd tried to sneak into the kitchen that morning, I couldn't blame him. I wouldn't believe me either.

"Then at least share the bed. You need to your rest if you're going to work in the morning."

For a moment, he hesitated. A slight blush darkened his cheeks. Damn, he was cute. He was also as unsettled by what was happening between us as was I. For some reason, that made me feel better.

"Are you sure?"

I nodded. "Jim, we're both tired." Hell, he looked exhausted. "You have a job you need to be rested for. I'd never forgive myself if something happened to you because you exhausted yourself trying to make sure I didn't do anything foolish." I shoved up into a sitting position, gritting my teeth against the pain, and motioned to the other side of the mattress. "So come to bed and get some sleep. Please."

Without a word, he stood. I watched as he pulled off his tee shirt. Doing my best to ignore the desire that flamed deep inside, I waited as he slid under the sheet at my side. Then I switched off the lamp and settled back. But I didn't object when he drew me close. Instead, I rested my head on his chest and welcomed the sleep that came.

CHAPTER SIX

"You bitch!"

Declan's voice filled the bedroom, waking me. At the same time, his hand closed about my arm. I gasped, pain arcing through me, as he hauled me out of bed and to my feet. Before I could react, his free hand connected with my cheek in a resounding backhand. My head snapped back and I saw stars. The sound of flesh striking flesh was sounded as loud as his shout. Ears ringing, pain from the blow and from my injured thigh threatened to send me under.

"Is this how you pay me back for bringing you into the clan?"

Another blow and warm blood flowed from my nose. My tiger roared in anger. No one treated us this way, not even our Alpha.

Before I could answer, the bed shifted. I sensed more than felt someone suddenly standing next to me. Another set of hands grabbed me and pulled me free from my Alpha's grasp. I don't know how he did it, but somehow Jim was suddenly between Declan and me. I didn't need to see his face to know Jim was angry. No, he was furious. It radiated off of him. His panther was so close to the surface, I could see it rippling across his skin. For good or ill, my tiger approved.

"You will keep your hands off of her and get the hell out of my house." Jim's words were clipped, his tone deadly.

"Get out of my way, cub." Declan shoved against Jim, trying to move him out of the way. Jim stood his ground. "She's mine. A member of my clan, even if it appears she let her libido override her duty."

"Declan!" I struggled to move around Jim, hissing in pain as I did. I was damned if I'd let that sort of accusation go without response.

"I told your sister you'd disobey me." His voice was thick, and I cursed mentally. He was as close to shifting as was Jim. I needed to diffuse this situation before it exploded.

"Damn it, Declan, listen to me."

I swayed as I slipped from Jim's grasp and once again tried to move around him. My thigh screamed in pain as I put weight on that leg. I ignored it, or at least I tried to. I couldn't give in to the pain any more than I could give in to the fear suddenly coursing through me. Declan was my clan leader. He could do almost anything he wanted to me. Worse, if Jim hit him, he could demand justice from Matt. I couldn't let that happen.

"I said get out of my way, *cub*." He spat out the last word like an epitaph.

"Jim, no!" I grabbed his arm and held on for all I was worth. I wouldn't let him strike Declan. Not in the mood my Alpha was in. I had to get this focused back on me and quick.

"Goddamn it, Declan!" I took a painful step forward and jammed my forefinger into his chest. It was insubordinate but not nearly as much as slapping him would have been. "Have you lost your fucking mind?"

"No, but it is clear you have." He grabbed my wrist and, before I could react, he twisted my arm behind my back, turned me and shoved me onto the bed. I couldn't hold by my cry of pain as my thigh connected with the wooden footboard. Pain threatened to send me to my knees. The smell of blood, my own blood, filled the air. If I hadn't torn out the stitches, I'd be surprised.

"Jim, no!"

Matt's command filled the room even as his power rolled over us. Jim froze for a moment. Then he shook himself. As he turned to me, I gasped. I had no doubt that if Matt hadn't appeared just then, he'd have gone for Declan. It wouldn't have mattered that Declan was Alpha of the Northern California clan. The fact that he had stormed into the bedroom and attacked me was all that mattered to Jim. Hell, just then, it was all that mattered to me. Declan had gone too far and, I wasn't sure I dared trust him to be my Alpha any longer.

Growling, his eyes glowing like his cat's, Jim knelt next to the bed. His hands were gentle as they helped me sit up. When I tried to avert my face, he reached out and grasped my chin. He tilted my head this way and that, hissing to see where Declan had struck me. But his touch was immensely gentle as he ran his fingers lightly over my bruised cheek and swelling nose.

"I'm all right," I said softly before he could ask.

"No, you aren't." He stood and turned back to Declan and Matt. As he did, Finn slipped by him, her arm going about my waist as she helped me to my feet and away from the bed. "Matthew," he growled.

"Get your ass dressed, Maggie. You're coming with me," Declan snapped. Instinct had me stiffening. He was my Alpha. I had to do what he said.

"The hell she is," Jim countered, once more stepping between us. "In case you haven't noticed, she's been seriously injured and, thanks to you, her wounds have reopened. Or hadn't you noticed in your desire to punish her?"

Declan ignored him and turned to Matt. "Call your cub off, Kincade. I'm here to deal with one of my own."

I've never appreciated being talked about when I'm standing – or sitting – right there, but this time I knew better than to get in the middle of a couple of angry shapeshifters. I just hoped Matt could deal with the situation before it got any worse.

"Deal with her?" Jim motioned to where I sat in the wingback chair he'd been sleeping in not too many hours earlier, Finn standing protectively at my side. "Don't you mean punish her?"

Finn's quick intake of breath was followed by her dropping to her knees at my side. Before I could react, she'd grabbed my chin and was examining my face much as Jim had just moments before. When she stood, she glared down at me, her anger as palpable as Jim's.

"You do *not* move from that chair, Maggie." She waited until I swallowed and then nodded. Then she strode across the room to stand at her mate's side. "He struck her, Matt. Her cheek is already bruising and her lip's cut. I'll bet my next paycheck that he broke her nose. Worse, the wound in her thigh has torn open."

"None of which is your concern," Declan countered. "I told her not to betray the clan and what do I find? I find her sleeping with *him*." He jabbed a finger in Jim's direction.

I couldn't help it. I laughed. The absurdity of the situation couldn't be denied any longer. Much as I wanted to throw Jim down on the ground and have sex with him, I hadn't. I'd remembered I was here for one thing and one thing only: to deal with Volk and the ferals. Yes, we'd shared a bed, but only to sleep in. Something I was sure my male counterparts wouldn't be condemned for.

Once more, I carefully pushed myself to my feet. Sweat pricked out on my forehead and my breath hissed out in pain as I did. But I would do this standing. If it cost me my clan, so be it. But Declan was acting the fool and embarrassing himself and me in front of two of the most powerful alphas of our kind.

I swiped a hand under my nose and my upper lip curled back painfully to see the blood. "You're right, Declan. I was sleeping with Jim. *Sleeping*, nothing more."

How could I ever trust him to be my alpha when he'd been so willing to misjudge me?

"Jim knows me better after only a couple of days than you do after knowing me for years. He knew I was likely to try to get back on the hunt, injured as I am, because I have a duty to the clan to find and kill Volk. He was sleeping in this chair–" My hand patted the back of the chair to make my point –"when I woke and saw him. I asked him to join me in bed because he's doing everything he can to not only keep me safe but to find Volk and the ferals so no more of our kind are hurt."

"I wasn't talking to you, Maggie, so keep your mouth shut."

"The hell I will!" God, did he treat Eileen this way?

"Maggie, submit!"

His command caught me off-guard as his power washed over me. Even as my knees buckled and I started to drop to all fours, part of my mind registered that he wasn't nearly as strong as Matt. Or as Finn, for that matter. Then a hand closed over my arm, holding me upright. This was bad, very bad.

"How dare you?" Declan roared, closing the distance between us. Yes, us. Jim stood next to me, his hand on my arm, supporting and protective. "She is a member of my clan and is mine to command."

"Jim, no." I spoke softly, my fear for him clear. "He's right."

"But it isn't right, Maggie." He looked down at me and I could see his concern. Then, as he looked past Declan to Matt and Finn, his expression changed. God, I wished I knew what he was about to do. "Matt, Finn, you can't let her go with him. Please."

"They can't stop us," Declan said confidently.

"Actually, we can, if we feel there is reason enough to," Matt corrected. "And, right now, I'm inclined to do as my brother asks if for no other reason than you broke into his house and accosted someone under our protection." His eyes flashed and Finn nodded in agreement.

Declan looked from them to Jim and me and frowned. This wasn't going the way he expected. Or at least not the way he wanted. Well, too fucking bad. He'd caused the situation and now he could figure out how to get out of it with at least some shred of dignity. But, in the meantime, I was bleeding again. I could feel the blood running down my thigh. Damn it. The stitches had been torn open and that was not good.

Worse, I knew what was going through his mind. Or at least

thought I did. He had told me not to tell my protectors everything we knew about Volk. For whatever reason, he'd decided to come here personally to make sure I didn't. But that didn't explain why broke into the house and then into my bedroom and it sure as hell didn't excuse him striking me.

"Alpha, I did not disobey you." I reached out and gently removed Jim's hand from my arm. I took one, two painful and halting steps toward Declan. Then I slowly sank to my knees, hissing in pain as I did. "I told them only what you said I could and admitted I had to await your approval before saying anything else. They neither condemned your decision nor pressed me to disobey."

The hiss turned to a gasp as I tried to climb to my feet. Before I could, Jim was there, his hands gentle as he helped me stand. "I have held true to my oaths to clan and as a tracker. Can you say as much?" Now I glared, allowing my anger and hurt to shine through. Let him think about that for a moment.

At least he had the decency to look a little abashed.

"Clan leaders, will you give us a moment alone?" I wasn't sure I wanted to be alone with my brother-in-law, my Alpha, just then, but what I had to say didn't need witnesses.

For a moment, Matt hesitated. Then, after looking at me as if weighing his options. He nodded. "Of course." He motioned for Finn and Jim to come with him.

Jim hesitated. "Maggie?"

"I'll be all right." At least I hoped I would be. I waited until he left the room, closing the door behind him. Then I looked at Declan, no longer trying to hide my anger. "All right, *Alpha*, what the hell did you think you were doing?"

"I'm trying to protect our clan," he snapped. "Something you've obviously decided isn't all that important."

"Bullshit." I was shaking I was so angry. I also needed to sit but wasn't about to just yet. I wanted to be on my feet for this discussion. "This was all ego on your part and you ought to know it." I realized I was rubbing my injured cheek and forced myself to stop. "You hit me

—twice and without reason. Eileen might let you get away with a lot of things, but do you think she'll take kindly to that?"

He paled slightly at the thought of what my sister would say – or do – when she found out he'd actually struck me. It wasn't as if he'd done so in the Circle or after hearing evidence against me and rendering judgment. This had been done in anger, not something any good Alpha should ever do. But was he calm enough now to realize just how close he had come to stepping over a line he'd never be able to step back from?

"As for protecting the clan, that's all I've ever done and you know it. I gave up everything to join the clan when you asked and then again to become your tracker. You failed me by not making sure I had accurate information on Volk. You failed our kind by not telling the other clan leaders everything you know about that bastard and the ferals. Now you've made yourself look the fool in front of two of the most well-respected Alphas by your actions this morning. If anyone's weakened the clan, it's you."

I was furious. I didn't care what consequences I'd face for my insubordination when I returned home. Declan had to understand he couldn't keep worrying about appearing weak. If he kept it up, he'd undermine his position as clan alpha and he'd have no one to blame but himself.

"God." He rubbed his hands over his face. "Sit down before your drop." As if understanding that I wouldn't sit until he did, he dropped onto the edge of the mattress and waited as I returned to the chair. "I overreacted and I apologize. The clan leaders will also get my apology. I came to discuss Volk with them. You were right. We need to let them know all we do and, I hate to say it, you don't know everything."

Hearing that, I felt as if I'd just taken a punch to the stomach. He'd sent me out hunting the renegade and hadn't told me every-thing? Which one of us was the bigger fool: me for trusting him or him for not trusting me enough to tell me everything I needed to complete my mission?

My hands fisted, and my anger built. I'd come close to losing my life and for what? To learn he'd held information back from me?

Damn him!

"Declan, get out. Go talk to Matt and Finn. Be honest with them at least. It would be best for both of us if you don't try to talk to me for a while."

"Maggie."

"Alpha, you are my clan leader. I honor the position. But right now, I'm royally pissed at the man. Go."

I dropped my head into my hands, my heart breaking. For the first time, I had an inkling of what Finn must have felt when she left the clan. When an Alpha breaks trust, it turns your world upside down. I wasn't sure I could ever forgive Declan, not as my Alpha and that worried me. If I didn't trust him, could I continue being part of the clan?

I waited until I heard him leave the room. Then I got to my feet and limped into the bathroom. I cursed and cried with each step. Even if I'd had my crutches, it wouldn't have helped. The damage had been done. Now all I wanted was a shower to wash away the emotions of the last few minutes. Hopefully, the sound of the water beating down on me would drown out the sounds of the conversation between the alphas as well as the voices in my head. Then I'd rebandage my thigh. Hopefully, by then Declan would be gone.

Finn waited for me when I opened the bathroom door. Her expression thunderous, she slid an arm around my waist and took on most of my weight. It didn't surprise me to hear her growling or to scent her panther. Angry as she was, I was amazed she hadn't shifted. Maybe one day, she'd teach me that level of control.

"Don't," she snapped as she settled me on the edge of the bed and I started to say something. "I'm not mad at you but I will be if you start making excuses for him."

I had no doubt who she meant.

Ten minutes later, after a call to Stefan, she helped me into a pair of shorts and a tee shirt. Without a word, she moved to the bedroom door. After calling for Jim, she turned back to me. For the first time since I'd emerged from the bathroom, her expression softened.

"Maggie, you are not to set a foot, either foot, on the ground until Stefan's seen you. He'll be over later, after we deal with this situation. I swear, if you don't promise to do as I say, I'll knock you out and tie you to the bed."

Part of me wanted to object but I knew better. Declan's manhandling had torn out most of the stitches Stefan put in. I hurt all over and, adding insult to injury, my face throbbed where he'd hit me.

"I'll do as you say, Alpha."

She let out an exasperated sigh and crossed to the bed. "Maggs, I'm not mad at you and you don't have to take that submissive tone with me. But I am worried about you, more so now than before."

Before I could respond, Jim appeared in the doorway.

"Carry her into the den. We need to deal with this," Finn said simply.

"She needs to rest." He didn't challenge her but he did let her know he didn't approve.

"Uh, *she* is sitting right here." I really do hate being talked about as if I wasn't present.

"Hush." Finn moved to where Jim stood and placed a gentle hand on his arm. "I wish we could let her rest. But we have to deal with this, Jim. Matt and I can't let what happened go unchallenged."

His mouth thinned but he lowered his head in acknowledgement. Not long after that, he carried me into the den. Once he'd seated me on the sofa, he lifted my legs onto the cushions. With a slight smile, he draped an afghan over my legs. Then he lowered to sit on the arm of the sofa at my shoulder.

"Maggie, we've been talking with Declan and we have some questions for both of you." Just like when I first met him, there was nothing in Matt's voice or on his expression to betray what he was thinking. Finn was another matter. Her expression darkened once more, and her eyes sparked angrily as she looked at Declan. Maybe I should have stayed in my room. I sure as hell didn't want to get in the middle of a power play between the Alphas.

"Alpha?" I'd show Declan the respect of rank in front of the others, but nothing more.

"Answer their questions."

Oh, he was pissed. This was most definitely not good.

"Maggie, how much training have you had to be a tracker?" Matt wanted to know.

That wasn't what I expected him to ask and I had a feeling he wasn't going to like my answer. "A couple of months. But that doesn't include the martial arts training I've had since I was fifteen or the fact that my dad taught me weapons from the time I was old enough to hold a gun."

"Who trained you?" Finn asked.

"Some of the elders in the clan."

"Were they trackers?"

"N-no. At least not actively." I could see where this was going and didn't want to throw Declan under the bus. I understood the reason he needed to get the four of us he named trackers trained up as quickly as possible after Volk's attack. But we hadn't been trained as well as we would have been if Declan had just reached out to some of the other clans for help.

"What sort of proving did you have to do to show you were ready to start tracking Volk?"

I didn't answer right away. I knew the moment I did that there'd be trouble. Jim was already tensing at my shoulder. He didn't like what he heard and made no attempt to hide the fact. Then, seeing how Finn watched, understanding reflected in her eyes, I knew I had to say something. Well, Declan had told me to answer their questions.

"I had to fight the other trackers, prove I could defeat them one-on-one and hold my own against the group."

Jim growled and shifted restlessly at my back. But at least he hadn't gotten to his feet. That had to count for something.

"Have you ever had to track anyone or act as enforcer before then?" Matt leaned forward, elbows on his knees and his chin resting on his fists.

"No, sir. Until the night Volk and his ferals attacked, I never considered becoming a tracker. That night changed everything. That's when I swore I'd make them pay for what they'd done. They betrayed the clan and killed our own. Worse, I knew Volk would continue until our existence was revealed to the normals. We aren't ready for that. So I answered our Alpha's call for volunteers to track the renegade and his ferals."

Even now, knowing what I did, I'd have done the same thing. Volk had to be stopped.

"What sort of training did you get?" Matt reached for Finn's hand, pulling her down to sit on the arm of his chair. She looked so angry and outraged. Funny someone who wasn't my Alpha seemed to care more for me than Declan, my clan Alpha and brother-in-law, did.

"Tracking, fighting, that sort of thing."

I'd barely closed my mouth when Jim all but erupted off the arm of the sofa. He stalked across the den to where Declan sat near Matt and Finn. I didn't need to see his face to know how angry he was. The fear reflected in Declan's expression was enough. But I had to give it to Declan. A moment later, he had himself under control and he stared up at Jim with an almost bored expression.

"Jim!" I couldn't help it. I had no right to try to stop him. He wasn't of my clan and I had no claim on him. But if he laid hands on Declan, his life could be forfeit.

"That's all the training you gave them—gave her?" He stared down at Declan. For the first time, I realized he wore only his cut-offs. The muscles of his back rippled and his hands fisted at his sides. "You sent out four members of your clan, naming them trackers, without properly training them?"

"We did train them!"

"You didn't come close to training them!"

I could have sworn he wanted to say more but he didn't. Instead, he turned to Matt and Finn and bowed his head in unspoken apology. Damn, the man had more self-control than most shifters I knew. It wouldn't have surprised me if he'd taken a swing at Declan. I knew he was angry enough, outraged enough to. But he didn't. Instead, he moved back to where I sat and, with a nudge of his hip, had me changing positions so he could slip onto the sofa and then settle me so I rested against him. Protective, possessive and, unless I missed my guess, a way to keep him from doing something extremely foolish.

"He's right, Declan," Matt said. "You should have asked for help. You sent sheep out to the slaughter and we're all lucky Volk didn't kill Maggie."

"What was I supposed to do?" Declan's frustration was clear from his tone of voice to the way he threw his hands into the air. "We're a new clan. Asking for help would be to admit weakness. I couldn't risk that. I wouldn't risk another clan deciding our territory was theirs for the taking."

"It wasn't a risk. Matt offered you any help you needed when you were named clan leader. So did my grandmother as well as the clan leaders from Colorado and Oregon/Washington. Instead, you let ego put not only four of your people but all of our kind in danger." Finn's disgust was clear.

"That's not fair!"

"Not fair!" Jim started to get up only to stop when I hissed in pain. He leaned back and his arms once more went around me. He held me close and I had a feeling it was as much to let me know he wasn't going to let anything else happen to me as it was to keep himself from going after Declan. "What's not fair is sending untrained members of your clan after a renegade you know has ferals under his control. What's not fair is failing to inform the local clan leaders that your tracker isn't trained and not telling them everything you know about the renegade."

"Kincade, I don't need to sit here and be attacked by this cub," Declan spat.

"Cub!" Jim roared.

This time he did get to his feet. I wouldn't have stopped him even if I could and there was no way I could. A wave of power rolled off of him that surprised me. I looked at Finn and saw her smiling in approval. What the hell was going on? How many damned alphas was I in the presence of?

I licked my lips and wished I was anywhere but there. I'd realized pretty much from the beginning that Jim had the confidence of an alpha. But he hadn't *read* alpha. Now there was no doubting exactly what he was. Oh, he didn't have the power his brother did, not even the power of Finn. But he was most definitely an alpha. Hell, in most clans, he'd be recognized as pride leader. The fact he hadn't sought out his own pride but had chosen – and it had to be a conscious decision – to support his brother first as pride leader and then as clan leader, told a lot about the man. He wanted what was best for our kind, even if it meant forgoing personal glory. That really was something I could admire.

But there was more. As he stood there, all but vibrating in anger and looking like he was about to give Declan the dressing down he so richly deserved, my cat stirred. I could see her stretching and preening. This was a shapeshifter worthy of us. She had no doubt about it. Neither did I just then. Lust rose and I wanted nothing more than to go to him and love him right there. It didn't matter others were around. He was mine and I wanted them to know it.

This was what I'd been unable to find in any of the other shapeshifters I'd been around. Here was a man who was confident in himself and his role, who took care of those around him and who was as dedicated to both normals and our kind as well. Strong and caring, what a heady combination. But that was not what I needed to be focused on right now. Somehow, I had to defuse the situation before it got out of control.

But how?

Before I could find an answer, Matt looked at his brother. That was all. He just looked. Jim took a step back and breathed deeply. I watched him relax his fisted hand, one finger at a time. Then he turned and, looking a little sheepish, moved back to the sofa. Without thinking about how Declan would react, I held a hand out, hoping Jim accepted it. When he did, I pulled him toward me, leaning forward so he could resume the seat he'd vacated a few moments earlier. Then I drew his arms around me, holding them there, letting him know through touch that I appreciated what he'd just done.

"Declan, you owe Jim an apology." My voice was firm. I didn't care what penalty I'd pay when I returned home. He'd been out of order. This wasn't his territory and he continued to insult the clan leader's brother, the man who very probably had saved my life.

"Maggie–"

"No, Declan. I'm sorry, but you do." Damn, I'd pay dearly when I got home. No alpha liked being called out for any reason and especially not by a female who was, at best, a beta. But it had to be done. He couldn't put his ego ahead of the good of our people.

For a moment, he didn't say anything. The muscles of his jaw clenched, and he looked like he wanted to stare a hole straight through me. I swallowed hard. I'd gone too far and I knew it. Then Jim's arms tightened around me. He nuzzled my hair and I relaxed. At least as long as I was here, I was safe.

"She's right," Finn put in. "If for no other reason, you broke into Jim's house and then entered Maggie's bedroom without permission. You are lucky we think you an ally. Otherwise, I'd have called you out for striking her. She is wounded and has done nothing to embarrass or betray your clan."

But you have.

Finn hadn't said it but the implication was clear. Judging from the way Declan's expression darkened, he knew it. Now, would he be man enough to own up to it?

"You're both right." He sat back down and sighed heavily. "I've been a fool and I owe everyone here an apology, especially you, Maggie. I've shamed myself and my clan by my actions."

"Declan, I know how difficult it is to lead a clan in transition. Part of me understands why you didn't ask for help and why you took the actions you did when you sent your trackers out. However, a truly strong leader knows when to ask for help." Matt waited and I held my breath, praying Declan accepted what he said.

"I realize that now. I let my ego get in the way. I assure you it won't happen again." He rubbed a hand over his face and then looked at Jim and me. "I apologize to both of you as well. I knew you were just sleeping, Maggie, even as I accused you of betraying your duty to the clan. You'd never betray us. You were the first to step up and volunteer to protect the clan by going after Volk. I never should have doubted you and I never should have laid hands on you."

I nodded. I'd accept his apology because I could see he believed what he said. But he'd shaken my trust in him. That would take longer to win back.

"As for you." Declan looked at Jim and it was clear he wasn't comfortable. Not that I blamed him. He was having to apologize to another alpha, one he probably hadn't realized was an alpha until just a few minutes ago. "My apologies."

"Accepted." Jim extended a hand and I held my breath until Declan accepted it. Relieved, I relaxed some, glad when Jim's arms were around me again. Apologies might have been made, but there was still too much tension in the room for my liking.

The next few hours were little more than a blur as Declan, Matt and Finn discussed Volk and the ferals. Sitting in the protective cradle of Jim's arms, I was stunned to hear how much information Declan had received about Volk, especially about what he'd done before Declan took over the clan, that he hadn't passed on to me or the other trackers. There had been so many more deaths, deaths Volk was undoubtedly responsible for. It truly was a miracle the cops hadn't shown up at the clan's doorstep to find out what was going on.

"Is there anything else you can tell us that might help locate Volk?" Matt asked.

"Not that I can think of." Declan stood and stretched. As he did, Matt and Finn climbed to their feet. "I'll let you know if I hear anything else. I promise."

I didn't doubt that he meant it. He'd be a fool not to, especially after the last four hours. Without actually condemning him, Matt made it very clear that his actions had been irresponsible. Finn had been a bit more direct, but then she always had been one to speak her mind. At least it was over. I was exhausted, mentally and physically. Worse, the pain from my injuries hadn't eased. All I wanted was to get food and some rest. I'd worry about what happened later.

"Maggie, can we talk privately?" Declan asked after saying his goodbyes to Matt and Finn.

For a moment, I considered. Part of me wanted to refuse. But I couldn't. I nodded and looked over my shoulder to Jim, hoping he understood. He looked at me and then nodded. A moment later, he slid out from behind me and, before I could try to stand, he'd swung me up in his arms and carried me into the bedroom, not bothering to wait to see if Declan was coming.

"Thank you," I said softly as he settled me on the edge of the bed.

"Are you sure?" He pointedly ignored Declan as he entered the room.

"I am."

"I'll be right outside the door." His hand lightly caressed my bruised cheek before he straightened and walked past Declan and left the room.

I carefully lifted my legs onto the bed and settled against the headboard. Declan continued standing near the door, staring at his feet. He seemed embarrassed and unsure what to say. Too bad he hadn't felt that way when he burst into the bedroom earlier. A lot of heartache would have been prevented if he had.

"You had something you wanted to say?"

There are times when being the Alpha's sister-in-law had advantages. This was one. I could be less than respectful and get away with it. I wondered if he knew how lucky he was that I was injured. Otherwise, I'd not just be sitting there, waiting for him to speak.

"I was out of line. Part of it was because I was too damned proud to ask for help. Part was because your sister and I have been worried about you since we found out you'd been hurt. That's really why I came out. I did need to talk to Matt, but it was more important was making sure you really are all right. Finding Kincade in bed with you just sent me over the edge. I'm sorry."

"As you damned well should be." When he started to speak, I shook my head. He'd had his chance, now it was my turn. "Declan, you are my sister's mate, her husband. You are my Alpha. But you acted like a fool today. You not only embarrassed me in front of two alphas who can wipe the floor with both of us without ever breaking a sweat, you struck me. Then you tried to force me to submit in front of them when I had done nothing except show my loyalty and obedience to you as my Alpha. That hurts even more than my face where you hit me. It's going to take time to get over all of that. Time you are going to give me."

He didn't look happy about it and he certainly didn't apologize. Instead he nodded and stared at some point over my head. "You'll have it. Just take care of yourself and come home once this is over."

At least he knew better than to say or do anything else. Instead, he turned and left the room, closing the door behind him. Why did it feel like he was closing the door on one part of my life?

A few minutes later, there was a soft tap at the door. Before I could call out, it swung open and Finn slipped inside. As she closed the door behind her, she looked at me and shook her head. Then she was across the room and sitting on the edge of the bed next to me, tilting my head some so she could examine my face.

"Are you all right?"

"No. I'm pissed." And that was putting it mildly.

"Good." She grinned at me, clearly approving of my reaction. "I know he's your brother-in-law, but that man is an idiot and a lucky one at that. Does he realize how close he came to losing one or more appendages when he hit you?"

"I doubt it." Just as I doubted he'd let me return to the clan without making sure I understood I failed him as my Alpha. "I don't know what surprised me more, that or when he tried to force me to submit in front of you and Matt." I dropped my face into my hands, wishing the last few hours would disappear from memory. "Finn, I'm sorry I brought this to your territory."

"You didn't do anything, Maggie." She waited until I looked up at her. "You did your pride and your clan proud today, much more than your clan leader did."

I sighed, knowing she was right and wishing she wasn't. Declan had a lot to learn about being a strong leader. Hopefully, he'd figured that out today. Otherwise, it wouldn't be long before either the other clan leaders decided to remove him or another alpha challenged him. Our entire clan would lose then.

"Enough of that. I want to talk to you about something else," Finn continued.

She changed positions, pulling her legs onto the mattress. A moment later, she leaned against the headboard at my side. As she did, I remembered all those times when we were kids and had done much the same thing. We'd sit on her bed or mine and talk and talk until we fell asleep. We'd been so close back then, almost like sisters. Damn but I'd missed her. I hadn't had another friend like her.

"When Matt rescued me that day in the parking garage, I didn't know what to think. After so long of avoiding our kind, in a period of minutes I'd been stalked by Jennings' trackers and then rescued by another shapeshifter. Once Stefan got the Taser barbs out of me, treated where I'd been knifed and the drugs wore off, I couldn't deny how I was drawn to Matt. Hell, even if I'd wanted to, my cat wouldn't let me. She was all for knocking him down and having my way with him then and there. I'd never felt anything like it before."

I looked at Finn and she grinned. My cheeks flamed and wondered how many more surprises the day was going to hold.

"I'm guessing you've been experiencing pretty much the same thing where Jim's concerned."

What could I do? I nodded.

"At least you admit it, which is smart considering I had sensed your feelings."

Damn it. If she'd managed to sense it, had Jim? My blush spread, and I had a feeling if I turned much redder I'd burst into flame.

"Probably not." I looked at Finn in surprise. Had I said it out loud? She grinned and gave my hand a squeeze. "Maggie, he's just as confused as you are. Add in a very healthy dose of protectiveness after Declan's foolishness and Jim isn't thinking straight. He doesn't even realize he outed himself as an alpha today. Believe me, you probably realize more about what the two of you feel than he does.

"But, I want you to know one thing. The Kincade brothers are good men. They take care of their own and, if Matt is any example, they are excellent lovers. You could do a lot worse than Jim."

"Finn–"

"Don't worry, Maggs. I'm not going to say anything to Jim or even to Matt. Besides, there's no rush. You need to heal and then we need to find Volk and deal with him and his ferals. Until then, you aren't to worry about anything."

Finn shifted and, before I knew it, she'd helped me stretch out. Her voice was soft but firm as she told me to rest. Suddenly tired – besides, I'd had enough of arguing with alphas for one day – I did as she said. Maybe when I woke, I'd find that all this had just been a bad dream.

Later, when I did wake, I glanced at the clock next to the bed. I'd been asleep a couple of hours. I felt better but the slight throbbing in my cheek and nose told me it hadn't been a bad dream. At least my thigh no longer screamed in pain. Judging from the way it felt, I knew Stefan had treated it while I slept. Before I could worry about it too much, a soft breath sounded at my back. Reaching behind me, I felt the soft fur of a large jungle cat. My tiger purred loudly, possessively in the back of my mind and my nose told me what my sleepy mind hadn't yet figured out.

Turning, I smiled to confirm my suspicion. A large panther lay next to me, its dark fur gleaming in the light coming in through the window across the room. He was so beautiful. Sleek and strong.

Carefully, I turned onto my side so I faced the panther. My hand caressed its ears and down its powerful neck. With a soft *prrow*, it opened its eyes. I had no doubt who the panther was in human form, not when those eyes locked into mine.

I didn't think. For once I just acted. Smiling, knowing it was right, I sat up and stripped. Pain arced through me as I released control. After all, I'd heal faster shifted. The fact there was a gorgeous panther to impress had nothing to do with it.

Absolutely nothing at all.

CHAPTER SEVEN

"**A**re you sure you don't want some more eggs or something?" Jim asked as he cleared away his dishes.

I leaned back and shook my head. If he kept feeding me like this, I'd have to start working out, injured leg or not. Not only was I eating more than usual because I needed to heal but he was a damned good cook. If I were honest, I'd have to admit he was better than me. But that was just because I was out of practice. Besides, if I had a kitchen like this one with all its shiny new appliances, I'd be back to my old standard pretty quickly.

"No thanks." I handed him my plate and watched as he put the dishes in the dishwasher. "It was great."

He smiled and then turned his attention back to cleaning up the remains of our meal. As he did, I took advantage of the opportunity to just watch him. When I'd awakened, I'd been alone in bed. But I could tell that he hadn't been up for long. His side of the bed was still warm and his scent hung heavily in the room. Then I'd heard the shower down the hall. Even though my tiger hadn't liked it, I'd taken control and shifted back to human form.

Just in time for Stefan to arrive. He'd had more than a few words to say as he set his bag next to me on the mattress. Without looking up, he ordered Jim to tell him exactly what happened. It didn't matter Finn and Matt already had. He wanted to hear it from Jim. There were a few muttered comments about Declan and idiots unwilling to ask for help, but that was it. At least until he finished checking my thigh. Then he'd looked at me, his expression grim.

"I won't speak ill of your Alpha, Maggie."

He didn't need to, not when he sounded ready to shift and fight.

"However, I do expect you to follow my instructions now." He pinned me with a firm look. "Your Alpha managed to tear out most of your stitches. I replaced them while you slept but the damage was done. Add to that he broke your nose and damned near broke your cheek. You are not to touch that foot to the floor for another two days minimum—and I will be back to check on your tonight. I want you to shift and stay shifted as much as you can. But your tiger needs to understand it is to rest and not be up and about. If you can't impress that on her, you are to remain in this form."

"Yes, sir."

"Good." He closed his medical bag with a snap. "As for you." He turned his attention to Jim. "If anyone else lays a hand on her, you are to bring me that hand. I don't care if it is still attached to their body or not."

Jim's grin told me he had absolutely no problems obeying that particular order.

That had been half an hour ago. Since then, Jim settled me at the kitchen table. I'd watched as he cooked breakfast. For the first time since before Declan's arrival, I saw my crutches. They leaned against the wall at the far end of the kitchen. Part of me was tempted to try to convince Jim to get them for me. Then, remembering Stefan's instructions, I knew better. I needed to do everything I could to heal so I could return to the hunt. Volk was somewhere out there and I needed to find him before he killed again.

"Jim, has there been any news?"

"No, and right now I'm looking at that as good news." He

returned to the table, coffee pot in hand. I watched as he topped off our mugs before placing the coffee pot on the counter top. Then he slid back onto his chair opposite me.

"God, I hope you're right, but I can't help worrying."

He reached over and rested his hand on top of mine. "I know. Part of me feels the same way. But if you're right and he is going to try to come at you, I want you healed. If he did somehow manage to get past me, I want you able to get away and you can't if you're still forced to use crutches."

The very thought of Volk or one of his ferals coming after Jim made my mouth go dry. I pushed the image out of my mind before he realized just how much it bothered me. I needed to change the subject, but to what?

"What about Officer Snyder? Despite everything, he probably saved my life." Just as Jim's arrival had probably saved both of us.

He smiled, obviously pleased I was worried about his rookie. "He's taken some ribbing from the others in the department about what happened, but not too much. The fact I'm supporting him and reminding the others that they've all made mistakes. He'll take some more ribbing from the guys but, in a way, this made him one of them."

"Good." I sipped my coffee, savoring its rich flavor. He really did make a mean cup of joe. "Jim, we haven't talked much about that night."

"I figured you'd talk when you were ready – or when your Alpha gave you permission to."

My Alpha. Was Declan still my Alpha? I wasn't sure any more. That was just one of the questions I'd have to answer when the search for Volk was finally over.

"I picked up Volk's trail the day before all this started. Everything pointed to him coming here. So I'd checked into a motel and got some rest. I'd been scouting the town when I thought I caught scent of a shapeshifter. It didn't dawn on me it could be anyone but Volk. That's how I found my way to the alley. When Volk appeared with the feral, it caught me off-guard. I was a fool to have gone there alone and I know how lucky I am to be alive." It was hard to admit but it was the truth.

"Maggie." He reached across the table and tilted my face up so I'd look him in the eye. "You were lucky, but you also proved you are a warrior. If you weren't, you'd have been killed. If you'd been trained properly, we'd probably not be having this conversation because you'd have dealt not only with the feral but with Volk as well. I'm firmly convinced of that."

"Maybe, maybe not. Anyway, what did you tell your department about me?"

"That was actually pretty easy. I didn't find anything in the alley to support Snyder's claim and you had no wants or warrants out on you. So, I released you after making sure I knew where to find you if necessary." Now he smiled and leaned back. Then he turned serious again. "After everything that happened yesterday, I didn't get by your motel to get your things. Do you feel up to driving there with me? Afterwards, if you're up to it, I'll take you by Tamara's and introduce you and let you see how we search for someone. I think you'll be impressed."

The thought of being able to get out of the house, especially if it was with him, had me grinning. "Sounds good. Would it be possible to swing by the alley? I'd like to retrieve my gear."

Now he grinned. "I'd wondered what you'd done with it. I know Snyder was too spooked to do a good search of you, but I did and you weren't carrying anything remotely close to a weapon. I didn't find anything in the alley either. So, what did you do with your gear?"

I shook my head, smiling. "I'll show you when we get there."

"Then let's get dressed and on our way."

More than glad to finally have something to do, I cast a glance across the kitchen to my crutches. Jim shook his head. A moment later, he lifted me in his arms and carried me toward the bedroom. As he set me on the edge of the bed, he promised we'd take the crutches with us. But I had to promise not to do anything foolish. Then he moved to the closet, rummaging inside to find something for me to wear. As he did, I smiled slightly. I might not be back on the hunt, but this was better than nothing.

"Finn was right," he said as he helped me into the passenger side of an ancient pickup I assumed was his personal vehicle. "Sharon's clothes are a pretty good fit on you."

Only the memory of Finn explaining that the mysterious Sharon was his sister kept my jealousy from flaring. As he slid in behind the steering wheel a few moments later, there was no denying the elephant in the truck with us. The scent of him filled the cab and I fought the urge to reach over and rip his shirt open. I wanted to run my hands over his skin. I wanted to feel him against me, inside of me. I wanted to shift and have him hunting with me.

God, I just wanted him.

"Jim." I licked my lips and drew in the scent of him. When he reached for my hand, sparks seemed to flow between us. Then he lifted my hand and pressed it to his lips.

"Maggie, I swear when this is over we are going to have to figure out whatever this is between us." His voice was rough with desire.

Thank God he felt it too. It would have been so very embarrassing to find out he was clueless.

"Yes." I looked at him and a warm feeling spread through me as I thought about what we could do with some time alone. Lust and a man in uniform and I could be a very happy woman. "So, let's get this done quickly. I don't know how much longer I can wait."

"That makes two of us." He grinned wickedly before turning the key in the ignition.

Forty-five minutes later, we parked outside the door to the motel room I'd rented a week before. A thin layer of dust covered the outer door. That reassured me. There was nothing to show anyone had tried to get inside. Hopefully that meant Volk hadn't come looking for me.

At the door, Jim took the keycard from me and slid it into the lock. He didn't need to tell me to wait outside while he checked the room. A few moments later, he reappeared in the doorway and motioned me inside. I nodded and, taking a firm grip on the crutches, stepped over the threshold.

And exhaled in relief to see nothing had been touched. Of course, it was difficult to tell since the bed was in disarray and the bathroom counter was strewn with different items. It was nothing but a mess, but it was my mess. So, unless Volk had someone watching the room, he hadn't found out where I'd been staying. That meant he didn't have a network here – yet.

"Is everything okay?" Jim asked as he glanced around.

"Yeah. I left a mess thinking I'd be back to grab some sleep before checking out." I moved to the small closet and reached inside. My backpack rested on the luggage rack. Setting my right crutch off to one side, I reached for one of the backpack straps and then tossed it onto the bed. "It won't take me long to pack up."

"Give me your credit card and I'll go check you out while you do." When I looked at him in surprise, he simply cocked his head to one side and extended his hand. Sighing, I dug the card out of my pocked and gave it to him. "Don't open the door for anyone but me," he added before slipping outside, closing the door behind him.

By the time he returned, I'd managed to stuff most of my things into the backpack. The rest I'd tossed into a plastic bag I'd found in the closet. I took one last look around the room to make sure I hadn't forgotten anything.

"Ready?" He shouldered the backpack and reached for the plastic sack.

"Yeah." I reached for the crutches and carefully stood. "Any trouble with the front desk?"

"Nah. The clerk seemed to think you'd found yourself someplace better to stay." He grinned and I snorted out a laugh. Well, the clerk was right there. "Where to now?"

"The alley?"

Hopefully, he wouldn't ask how I felt. I knew he'd take me back to his house the moment he realized I was hurting again. Under better circumstances, I'd agree. But I wanted to get to the alley and retrieve my gear before someone found it—assuming they hadn't already.

"All right. Then I'll take you to Tamara's. You can work with her while I go into the station for a while."

"Sounds good."

Half an hour later, Jim parked at the mouth of the alley. I waited as he hurried around the truck. As I opened the door, he reached inside. His hands closed around my waist and he effortlessly lifted me out. With my hands on his shoulders, I balanced on my uninjured leg. Then he handed me my crutches and stepped back.

I stood there, studying the alley where I'd come so close to losing my life. As I did, I lifted my head, sniffing. All the smells you'd expect were there: spoiled food, dirt, urine assailed me. But there was no hint of any shapeshifters in the area except for Jim and myself. That meant Volk and his ferals hadn't been there for at least twenty-four hours. So far, at least, my luck appeared to be holding.

But for how long?

"Walk me through what happened," Jim said as we moved slowly away from the truck.

"Okay." I let my mind go back to that night. "I got a hit on Volk's credit card from a gas station on the outskirts of town. He'd filled up and bought some things that afternoon. I figured I'd better get a lay of the town and thought doing it that late wouldn't lead me into trouble. After all, Volk had been travelling that afternoon. So he'd be resting, right?"

Hearing myself say it, I knew how foolish I'd been – and how lucky.

"Anyway, as I was walking down the street, I caught scent of one of our kind. I should have remembered the adage about curiosity killing the cat because it almost did. I ran headlong into Volk and the feral. Thankfully, I'd surprised them as badly as they had me. Then the feral was on me, Volk telling him to kill me. I didn't have time to shift. So I fought the best I could. I didn't even know I'd been hurt until after I'd killed the feral and your rookie showed up. Then all I cared about was getting the hell out of here before Volk decided to finish the job the feral had started."

"Why would Volk take the feral's body with him?"

"I don't know unless he wasn't willing to risk your clan finding out he was in the area."

After what happened last year with Michael Jennings, that made sense. Matt had proven that he and his clan were willing to stand up against shapeshifters who endangered our kind. But it went beyond that. The outcome of the clan meeting where Finn killed Jennings after he'd wounded Matt had been a meeting of many of the clan leaders in North America. That's when Declan had been named the new Northern California clan leader. But it was also when many of those same clan leaders pledged to work closer together, finally realizing that failure to do so could lead to our discovery by the normals before we were ready. All of which could explain why Volk had removed the feral's body. Frankly, just then I really didn't care why he'd done it.

"And what did you do with your weapons and other gear? I can't imagine you managing to behead the feral with your bare hands."

I grinned. No, I hadn't been able to do it with my bare hands. I'd barely been able to do it with my broad axe. Fortunately, I'd stunned the feral with a roundhouse kick to the temple. There's a reason why I tend to wear steel-toed boots. The feral went down and I grabbed my axe from where it had hung from my weapons pack. For the first time in my life, I was glad for all the gym work I'd done to strengthen my upper body.

"When you checked the alley, did you check the roofs?" I asked.

Jim looked at me, at the roofs on either side of us and then shook his head. "You're telling me that you managed to toss it on top of one of the buildings?"

"Yep."

"Right or left?"

Damn, which one was it? Everything had happened so fast that night. I'd frozen in place when the squad car's headlights first hit me.

There'd been one brief moment when the movement of the car had taken me out of the path of the light before a spotlight focused on me. In that time, I'd not only tossed the feral's head away from me and scrambled as far from the immediate are of the fight as possible but I'd also tossed my gear away.

I closed my eyes, remembering. The feral's head had been in my left hand. It had been a wolf, a scrawny but determined wolf that came close to killing me. The fact it hadn't been well fed and therefore not in the best condition was probably all that had kept me alive. But if the head had been in my left hand, that meant the axe had been in my right. I pictured where I'd been in the alley and the motion my arm would have taken as I tossed the axe away. The backpack that held my other weapons and gear had followed. There'd been the sound of metal hitting concrete, but it had been faint, almost covered by the sounds of the squad car engine. Then Snyder had piled out of the car, yelling for me to stop and put my hands up.

I nodded and opened my eyes. "That one." I pointed to the two-story brick structure on the right that looked like it had been built around the time of World War II.

After telling me to wait there, Jim trotted down the alley. I watched as he stopped under a rusty fire escape. Tall as he was, he still barely managed to close his hands around the bottom rung of the ladder when he jumped. With a metallic screech, the ladder slowly lowered. As soon as it locked into place, Jim began climbing. When he disappeared over the edge of the roof, I waited, my heart beating a little faster.

A few moments later, he reappeared. The backpack was slung over his left shoulder, the axe hanging from the loop on the right. After checking to make sure no one was watching, Jim swung his leg over the edge of the roof and quickly came down the fire escape. Once he made sure the ladder was once again secured in its upward position, he trotted to where I waited.

"Yours?" He grinned as he swung the backpack off his shoulder and held it out for me to inspect.

"Yeah." A quick look inside had me sighing in relief. Everything was still there: knives, my gun, spare ammo and more.

"Then let's get out of here." As he helped me back inside the truck, I could tell he wanted to say something.

"What is it?" I asked finally as we drove off.

"I don't know whether to skin you alive for not telling me about this arsenal or be glad no one else found it. Then there's the fact I'm relieved to know you weren't completely unarmed." He turned the truck north and we headed out of town. "Then there's the fact I'm damned glad you didn't use the gun. That would have been harder to explain away."

"I might not be trained as well as I should be, but I'm not stupid."

Far from it, in fact. If Declan had known what sort of weaponry I kept with me, he really would have blown a gasket. His instructions to all of us had been to carry nothing that would cause the cops to look twice if we should be stopped for any reason. I'd disobeyed. Hell, I'd done it without a second thought because I knew I'd need every possible advantage if I came across Volk or his ferals.

"No, you're not stupid." We stopped at a red light and he looked across the cab at me. "Maggie, I'm not criticizing. Far from it. I'm glad to see you took precautions. But the cop in me is relieved none of the troublemakers in town found your kit."

I nodded, understanding. I should have told him about the backpack and everything else sooner, but I'd had other things on my mind —like staying alive.

CHAPTER EIGHT

"So, Maggs, what did you think?"

Finn pulled the Mustang out of the warehouse parking lot. What did I think? My brain was a muddle of questions and impressions. Maybe, in a year or two, I'd be able to process everything I'd seen and heard today. But for now, all I knew for certain was that this clan was very different from either of the two I'd been associated with so far.

It was more than the clan having its own high-tech security firm. Spending the last few hours with Tamara and her people had been eye opening in a number of ways. The first was the sheer vastness of resources the clan had. Tamara had shown me how they were searching for Volk, keeping track of his credit cards, hacking into security cams and using facial recognition to locate him. There was one employee, not a shapeshifter but married to one, who was pouring over crime reports and missing person's reports from around the country to see if a pattern could be found that would help us figure out what Volk was doing. Others checked in with the clan's trackers currently out in the field.

While all that made me feel like I was standing in the middle of some Hollywood spy movie, what really hit was something I'd noticed earlier with Finn. She wore her clan markings proudly. Her tattooing was a work of art. Of course, only one of our kind would realize what the inking really meant.

It had been the same with those I'd met at the security firm and that surprised me. Both the Northern California clan and the Tennessee clan, the only ones I was familiar with, had cautioned their members not to be too open with their markings. So their tattooing tended to be small and usually not where anyone but the closest of friends and family would ever see.

"I think I don't know what to think."

Finn chuckled before clicking on the turn indicator and changing lanes. "That's exactly how I felt the first time Matt brought me here. But the techie in me loved it and, after all I'd been through, I was glad to know someone of our kind understood how important it is for us to keep on top of security."

I nodded, my mind a whirl. Finn was a techie? That was a surprise. When we'd been kids, she'd been determined to be an artist when she grew up. She'd spun tales about how she'd go to Paris to study and have her first gallery showing in New York. Was that a dream she'd been forced to give up because of Jennings?

"I have to agree." And I was glad to have those resources looking for Volk.

"So what's bothering you?"

I glanced at her, surprised. "What do you mean?" Nothing like answering a question with another question.

"C'mon, Maggs. It's been a long time since we've been together, but I know you. You're worried about something. So give."

I leaned my head against the seat back and closed my eyes. I couldn't deny that she was right. I was worried. But how could I explain it so she'd understand? More importantly, how could I do it so she wouldn't interfere?

"Finn, you remember what Volk was like when we were kids." I turned my head and looked at her. When she nodded, I continued.

"From what I've gathered talking to those who stayed in the clan after Jennings took over, Volk returned pretty quickly. He became Jennings' enforcer and was pretty much left alone to do whatever he wanted. If possible, he got worse than before."

"Tell me." Finn glanced to the left and merged onto the freeway. For a moment, I wondered where we were going. Then I realized we were headed back to Jim's.

"There were more cases like Randy Henson, only they didn't end like his did because Jennings didn't try to stop the ferals. As long as Volk didn't openly use them against clan members, Jennings turned a blind eye. So, every couple of years, one of the youngsters would go off with Volk and come back *changed*."

"God." Finn shook her head. "I'm more glad than ever that I killed that bastard."

"Me, too." And I was. In his own way, Jennings had been worse than Volk. Hell, I wished I'd been there to see her do it.

"But that doesn't explain why you're so worried."

"Finn."

"Maggie, tell me."

"You're not going to take no for an answer, are you?"

"Nope." She gave me a quick grin before returning her attention to the road.

"I screwed up the other night. By killing the feral but not Volk, I painted a great big target on my back. As soon as he figures out where I am, Volk's going to come after me and he'll kill – or worse – anyone who gets in his way." There, I'd said it. I'd said it before but never in quite that way. Maybe now she'd understand why I had to get back on the hunt just as soon as possible.

"Maggie, I'm glad you realize it. I hope you realize something else. You aren't on this hunt alone any longer. You have the strength of my clan behind you."

"Finn–"

"Hang on."

There was frustration in her voice as well as determination. She flicked on the right turn indicator and then checked for oncoming traffic. The engine roared as she hit the accelerator and sped ahead of a car, exiting the freeway. A moment later she pulled into the parking lot of a fast food restaurant and parked. She twisted in her seat to look at me and I swallowed hard. This was not my friend from childhood. This was a female alpha, the only female alpha I'd ever met. I was going to have to do some fast talking if I had any hope of getting her to understand.

"Finn, look."

"No, you look." When I opened my mouth to protest, she simply glared and I snapped my jaw shut. "I don't know what the hell Declan thought he was doing sending you after Volk without proper training or information. Well, I do, in a way. But you have to understand that the moment Volk entered our territory, he became our problem as well as yours. You've seen some of the resources we have, resources we'll use to find and defeat him. I promise we aren't going to try to stop you from fulfilling your mission, but you will do it with our help."

I sighed. She didn't understand. Or she wasn't letting herself understand. Either way, I had to try to get through to her.

"Finn, I appreciate it, but I will not stay where I put anyone and especially not anyone you care for in danger." There, I'd said it. Maybe now she'd understand.

Her lips twitched up in a smile and she chuckled. When she reached out and patted my hand, I wondered what was so funny. Fortunately for both of us, she decided to explain. "Maggs, don't you think I felt much the same way when I realized it was Jennings' thugs Matt had rescued me from? Even after I realized he was my mate, I was willing to give him up. I thought I'd be protecting him. What I didn't understand was that he wasn't about to let that happen. Between him and my grandmother, they made me understand that running wasn't the answer. I had supporters here, protectors, people who cared about me. That was strength and I'd be foolish not to draw upon it.

"You need to realize the same thing. We might not be your clan, but we are your friends. We also know what a danger to all our kind Volk and his ferals are. There is no other clan in this part of the country save my grandmother's that is better equipped to deal with Volk. So don't worry. Let us help you and together we will bring Volk and those who follow him down."

She had a point. I'd be a fool not to use all the weapons at my disposal in this hunt and this clan made for a very powerful weapon. "All right. But as soon as I'm able to get around on my own, I need to get back to the hunt."

"And you will. Until then, you can work with Tamara. That's the first line of attack anyway. We need to find out where Volk is before we take the fight to him."

Like it or not, Finn was right. Besides, I was suddenly too tired to argue. "Thanks, Finn. I promise to be good."

"I know you will, whether you like it or not." No longer the alpha, she gave me a cheeky grin that reminded me of better times when we'd been kids. "Now, let's get you home. Stefan's going to have my head for letting you overdo."

"Tell you what, I won't tell him you let me overdo and I'll even rest when we get back to the house as long as food's involved somewhere along the line. I'm starved."

"Food is handled, and I'll hold you to the rest of it."

With that, she backed out of the parking space. It wasn't long before we were back on the freeway and speeding away from town.

Later, I slipped into my bedroom and closed the door behind me. Finn hadn't lied when she said food had been handled. What she hadn't told me was I'd soon be meeting Sharon Kincade, Matt's and Jim's sister. Nor had she told me that the small woman, even smaller than me, was a spitfire who was every bit as protective of her brothers as they were of her. It hadn't taken long for her to start "getting to know me" – which was just a polite way of saying interrogating me.

Fortunately for my sanity, Finn had quickly put an end to it, telling Sharon we'd have plenty of time "to talk" after I'd rested.

Then she'd reminded her sister-in-law that Stefan would be over in an hour to check my injuries. That had quickly shut the younger woman up. It was clear that, like her brothers, she cared a great deal for their uncle and had absolutely no desire to get on his bad side.

That was definitely something to keep in mind.

Placing the crutches against the wall, I dropped onto the edge of the mattress and carefully toed off my shoes. I unbuttoned my jeans – well, Sharon's jeans – and wiggled them over my hips before dropping them to the floor. The plaid shirt I'd been wearing followed. Wearing only a white tank and panties, I stretched out, doing my best to ignore the sounds of Finn and Sharon working in the kitchen, laughing and talking.

Sleep was close when I sensed more than heard the bedroom door open. A slight smile touched my lips as I scented Jim. I lay there, eyes closed, as he closed the door behind him. A moment later, his hand lightly touched my forehead and then my cheek where Declan had struck me. Then, before it could withdraw, I reached up and grasped it.

"I was hoping you were getting some rest. Finn said you were tired." He sat on the edge of the mattress, looking at me closely.

"I am." I knew better than to lie. He'd see through it. Besides, there was nothing to gain by denying the obvious. I had overdone that day. "But it felt good getting out of the house and I learned a lot talking with Tamara and then Finn."

He nodded and then looked at the closed door as his sister's laughter filled the air. "Sorry I wasn't here to introduce you. She give you any trouble?"

I had no doubts he meant Sharon. Nor did I doubt he'd have something to say to her if I told him she'd been a bother.

"Nah. Finn cut the interrogation off before it could get started." I smiled as he groaned. "Jim, it's okay. She's just worried about you. Believe me, my sister would be doing the same thing if our situations were reversed."

Well, maybe not, but I'd like to think so.

"Stefan will be here soon. Then we'll eat. I hope you don't mind but Matt and Finn, as well as Sharon and Danny, will be joining us. We sort of make up Matt's inner circle."

"Jim, why would I mind? This is your place. I'm grateful for all you've done for me."

He shifted slightly, turning so he could take my face in his hands. There was a hunger in his eyes that had me swallowing hard before my tongue reached out to lick my lips. My hands closed over his, holding them there. Something flashed in his eyes – desire? – and my breath caught. God, I wanted him.

"I don't want your gratitude, Maggie," he rasped. He bent and his lips brushed against mine. I moaned. I think I moaned and then I leaned into him. Then the sound of Sharon laughing again filled the air and he pulled back, cursing. "There are times when I want to kill my little sister," he growled, his cheeks darkening with embarrassment.

Interesting. I hadn't expected that. Most males of our kind, especially alphas, weren't shy. Hell, shyness wasn't exactly normal for any of us. Because it is easier – and a lot cheaper – to strip before shifting, nudity among clan members is part of our lives. Many of our kind have no problem sharing partners or engaging in sex with others looking on. We aren't exactly inhibited. Maybe that's part of the animal in us. But there was no doubt Jim was embarrassed and, judging from the way the front of his pants tented, very frustrated.

Well, that made two of us.

"You could tell them to leave and come back in a couple of hours." I leaned into him, nuzzling his neck. God, he smelled so good. But he had on too many clothes.

"Or I could just cuff you to this bed and make sure you don't go anywhere until I can have you." His hands closed around my waist and he pulled me onto his lap.

I nipped his neck and he gasped slightly. Then his hand cupped my breast, fingers teasing the nipple through the thin material of the tank top. "Promises, promises." His mouth followed his hand, suckling through the cloth. The hand that had been at my breast found its way between my legs.

"We will finish this later," he rasped as the sound of a car door shutting reached us.

But he didn't let me go, not yet. Instead, his mouth crushed against mine, his tongue forcing its way through my lips. I held him close, fingers digging into the flesh of his back, his shoulders. If I could have crawled into him, I would have. Instead, I returned his kiss, and be damned with anyone who interrupted us.

"We'd better," I said as someone knocked at the door. "You'd better."

"*We* will." He nuzzled my neck one more time and then called out for the newcomer to enter.

Stefan stepped inside, took one look at us and smiled in approval. Then, with a jerk of his head, he motioned for Jim to get out. For a moment, I thought he'd argue. Instead, Jim gave me a quick hug before settling me back on the mattress. As he stood, I could see him squaring his shoulders. Fortunately, I managed to choke back my laugh. I had no doubt that the moment he left the bedroom his sister and Finn would jump him. They'd smell me on him. Even if they didn't, his desire hung thick in the air.

Poor Jim. Those two women were going to tease him mercilessly.

But that left me with his uncle, a man he clearly adored and respected. I swallowed hard as Jim left. Before I could say anything – not that there was much to say. Stefan would have to be dead not to realize what he'd interrupted – he smiled and patted my hand.

"It's about time that boy found someone."

With that, he reached for his bag and began his examination.

CHAPTER NINE

We watched the tail lights of Finn's Mustang disappear up the drive, the last of the three cars leaving the ranch. A light breeze ruffled my hair and I lifted my face, sniffing. There was rain in the distance. I could smell it, just as I could smell the horses in a nearby pasture. I caught the scent of a coyote, a real coyote, and smiled as it howled. From the distance came an answering howl. Was its mate calling a response?

Jim's hand closed around mine, our fingers twining. Without a word, he helped me back inside. He moved slowly, shortening his stride to match mine. A slight smile touched my lips even as I said a silent thank you to the now absent Stefan for agreeing that I could be up with the aid of crutches. He still wanted me in bed so this was a victory.

Jim led me through the den to the back of the house. He opened a door off the short hallway leading to the kitchen. Inside was what could only be his study. A floor to ceiling bookshelf filled one wall. Across from the door was a dark wooden desk. Its surface was littered with papers and books. To the right of the desk was a secondary work station. A large monitor showed various views of the property, including drive leading to the house.

"Sit here." Jim pulled his desk chair next to the chair at the work station. He waited for me to comply before he took his seat. "After what happened with Declan, I want you to see that you are safe here." He pulled a keyboard in front of him and then sighed. "Maggie, I screwed up the other night and didn't set the security system. I promise it won't happen again."

His fingers flew as he entered a command sequence. I watched the monitor as the upper right quadrant showed the gate sliding shut. Jim entered a second command and then looked over at me. "The gate's locked now and an alarm will sound if anyone tries to get inside. There's one tone if someone tries to force the gate open and another if they try to climb it." Another command and the images switched again. "There are cameras all around the property. I don't have motion detectors because of the wild life. I'd never get any sleep." He grinned and I felt myself responding.

"But there are alarms on all the outbuildings and motion detectors inside here. There are also breakage detectors on the windows and doors." He paused and I knew he was waiting for me to respond. So I nodded, impressed. "The system's armed and no one can get close to the house now without us knowing."

"You said there are motion detectors. Will they go off if I decide I need a drink of water in the middle of the night?" I had a vision of being scared witless as some loud siren sounded the moment I stepped outside my bedroom.

"No." He grinned and gave my shoulders a quick squeeze. Apparently, he approved of my question. "I have the motion detectors on the doors and in areas of the house, like the basement and attic, where no one should be at night."

"Thank goodness. I'd hate it if you shot me because you thought I was a burglar."

"I think I could figure out the difference." He turned his attention back to the console and tapped in another command sequence. "In the morning, we'll set you up on the system. I want you able to come and go as you like."

"Jim."

My voice caught. Throughout the evening, we'd flirted with one another. Despite the knowing glances from his sister and Finn, he'd never been far from my side. When he was close enough, we were touching, whether it was holding hands or our knees touching under the table. But now that we were alone, this was real and I suddenly wasn't sure what to do.

He didn't say anything. Instead, he stood and kicked his chair aside. Before I could react, he'd lifted me in his arms. My crutches clattered to the floor as he shoved the desk chair out of the way. He ignored them as he carried me out of the room.

"You can say no," he said softly as he paused before the door I'd seen him come out of just the day before. "But you'd better do it now."

I swallowed hard. My heart beat a mad rhythm in my chest. No was the last thing I wanted to say. Instead, I reached up and licked the side of his neck and the line of his jaw, nipping his chin. He grinned down at me and pushed open the door. A moment later he carefully set me down, holding me for a moment. Then he stepped back, his eyes hungry.

"Strip." His voice was rough with desire.

I balanced on my good leg, my head cocked to one side in a conscious imitation of him. "You first." Two could play the domination game.

The corners of his mouth twisted up and the look he turned on me sent my pulse pounding. He hadn't touched me yet and I was already wet. I didn't need to look down to know my nipples were taut. I could feel them straining against my bra. What was it about him? I'd never reacted like this before.

"I can smell you." He took a step toward me.

I sniffed and my tiger purred in satisfaction. I wasn't the only one whose arousal filled the room. "And I can see you." I nodded to the erection tenting his jeans.

"I mean it, Maggie. If you don't want this, tell me now."

His hands fisted at his sides and I could see him taking control. God, what kind of man was he? Most of our kind would have already thrown me across the bed and taken me, no matter what I said I wanted. My body was betraying me, if you could call it that, and yet he still wanted to make sure I knew I had a choice.

"I'm here, aren't I?"

"Say it. Say you want me as much as I want you."

I stepped forward, the pain in my thigh a distant annoyance. Before I'd taken a second step, he was there. His arms pulled me close, his mouth crushed mine. My hands grasped his shirt and pulled it free from his jeans. I needed to feel him. I needed his skin against mine.

I needed him.

His hands were rough, demanding as they went from shoulders to breasts to waist. My head fell back as his lips ravaged my throat. The feel of his teeth scraping my chin before he ducked his head to my right breast sent me wild. My fingers twisted in his hair, holding him there. But it wasn't enough. It wasn't nearly enough.

As if reading my mind, he straightened. His arms lifted me and a moment later he gently laid me across his bed. When I reached for him, he grabbed my wrists. He pinned my hands above my head and looked down at me, desire radiating off of him.

"Say it," he repeated.

"Jim." It was barely more than a breath. I couldn't think, couldn't do much more than feel and just then I wanted to feel him inside of me.

"Say it, Maggie. I want to hear you tell me you want me as much as I want you." He bent down and buried his face in the crook of my neck. His legs held mine between them when I tried to open up for him. I twisted, nipping at his ear, his jaw. He growled and moved his head out of the way. He wasn't going to give me anything until I said what he wanted.

"Yes, damn it. I want you." It came out in a rush and I tried to lean up. I wanted my mouth on his, his hands on me.

He grinned down at me and then ran his lips over mine. He shifted slightly and I felt him grasp both my wrists in one hand. His other ran down my hair to my blouse. His fingers worked quickly, but not quickly enough, to undo the buttons. Finally, he pulled the blouse from my jeans. My breath quivered and my heart skipped a beat or three as his fingers found their way under my bra.

"You have on too many clothes," I panted.

"I'm getting you undressed first." He grinned as I groaned and ground against him. "Patience, Maggie."

"I don't want to be patient."

He leaned back, looking down at me. He was up to something and it wasn't what I wanted. Damn him.

"I'll tell you what. If you keep your hands right here and don't move them while I undress you, then you can undress me."

There was a catch. I knew it but I didn't care. I wanted him naked and I wanted him naked now. "All right."

He kissed my cheek and released my hands. As he did, his eyes gleamed with approval. Then he leaned down, his lips close to my ear. "Move only when I tell you to or when I move you. Nod if you agree."

I'd have agreed to just about anything to have his hands on me, so I nodded.

His hands were gentle as they lifted me just enough to slip the blouse from my arms. Then he returned my hands to where they had been over my head near the top of the bed. His right hand snaked under me and I felt him fumbling with the catch of my bra. A moment later it he pulled the ends out from under me and gently lifted the cups off my breasts.

His hands kneaded my breasts as he planted a kiss between them. He shifted slightly and his tongue flicked my left nipple. At the same time, his hands worked to unbutton my jeans. I arched into him as his hand slipped inside the denim. I could feel his smile as his fingers began to stroke.

I moaned in protest when his hand withdrew. His breath tickled as he chuckled softly. Then he began easing my jeans over my hips. When he came to my injured thigh, he lightly kissed the bandage, promising to be careful. Eyes closed, teeth clenched, hands fisted, I shook my head. I didn't want careful. I wanted him, and I wanted him now.

"God, you're beautiful." He knelt there, his knees on either side of my legs, and looked down at me.

"And you still have too many clothes on." I wanted to reach for him, to pull him down. Hell, I was ready to rip his clothes off. But I remembered the challenge. He didn't have me completely undressed yet. My bra still hung from its straps across my chest. But if he didn't busy soon. . . .

"Shh." His finger rested against my lips. I could smell my juices on it. I twisted my head slightly and nipped the finger, holding it between my teeth and growling. He grinned. Then he caught my clit between thumb and forefinger and I forgot everything else. "Like that?" His breath was soft against my throat. Then his tongue lathed my jaw. As it did, he gently slid a finger inside me and started pumping.

"God, yes."

I could feel my climax building. Panting, I reached for him. I wanted our first time together to *be* together. Then, without warning, his fingers were gone and I was writing in frustration. When I looked up at him, he shook his head, a slight smile on his lips.

"I told you not to move your hands." He cuffed my wrists in his right hand and returned them above my head. Then he stretched out, pinning me under him. Still holding my hands, he reached over to the bedside table. His left hand pulled open the drawer. There was no mistaking the sound as he produced his handcuffs. "Now I'll just have to make sure you don't have another chance to distract me until I finish undressing you."

I lay there, watching, as he secured one of the metal cuffs around my right wrist. He fed the other cuff through the metal bars of his headboard before securing my left wrist. Then he used the pointed end of the key to double lock the cuffs so they wouldn't tighten.

His hands moved down my extended arms to my shoulders. "Tell me what you want."

"I want you." I might not have the use of my hands any longer, but that didn't mean I was helpless. I wrapped my legs around him, ignoring my wounded thigh. "I want your scent on me and I want you in me." I tugged against the cuffs. "God, I want you."

"Good, because I want you too." Holding my face between his hands, he kissed me. Then he sat up and pulled his shirt over his head. It was exquisite torture not to be able to touch him. "I want to pleasure you, Maggie. Will you let me?"

I tugged on the cuffs again, making sure they rattled against the headboard. "I can't exactly stop you." But I smiled. I wanted him to know I wasn't mad. Hell, I was far from it. I'm not what most would consider kinky, but there's nothing wrong with a little role playing from time to time.

"No, you can't." He cupped my bruised cheek with his hand and I rubbed against it. "But I don't want to hurt you." His eyes flicked to my bandaged thigh.

"You won't." I trusted him and wanted him to know it.

For an eternity, he tortured me with his hands and mouth, bringing me to the brink of climax before backing off. My hips bucked and my fists clenched. If anyone else had been in the house, they'd probably have thought wild animals had taken up residence. My cries were matched by his satisfied chuckles. Never had anyone been able to make me feel this way. I wanted not just release. I wanted him and I wanted to give him release. I wanted to be with him, one with him and I wanted it now.

He blew on my clit and a long shudder ran through me. Every nerve tingled and it would take only the lightest of touches to send me over the brink. He knew it. He had to have known it. But he didn't give me the release I needed. Instead, he kissed the inside of my right thigh, nipping and licking his way upward before turning his attention to the other thigh.

I lifted my head and looked into his eyes. Lust looked back at me. Good, maybe he would finally give me what I wanted. If not, well, we both knew I could get out of the cuffs without much trouble. But I didn't want to shift. I wanted to stay human and love him.

"Please." It was barely a whisper, but a lifetime of emotion was in it.

He moved up my body. His hands were gentle as they removed the cuffs. For a moment, he massaged my wrists before studying them, making sure I hadn't been bruised. His lips kissed a ring around first my right wrist and then my left. Finally, he lay back at my side and guided my hands to his waist.

My time.

Finally.

I sat up and, careful of my injured thigh, straddled his legs. His chest rose and fell with each breath. That breath caught as I ran my hands across his abdomen. He lay there, his eyes on my face, as I worked to undo his jeans. I didn't need to say anything. He lifted his hips and then one leg at a time so I could pull his jeans down. I grinned to see he'd been commando under the denim. His erection left no doubt that he was as aroused as was I. Well, I could do something about that . . . in time.

I blew a soft breath across the head of his cock, watching as his eyes closed. He groaned as my tongue ran along the back of his shaft. Precum leaked from the tip. His hands fisted on the sheets. Good. He was giving me the chance to play with him much as he had me. Most guys wouldn't worry about that. They'd want to get their rocks off and then, wham, bam, thank you, ma'am.

I took him in my mouth, my tongue teasing. Slowly, I went down on him, taking him deeper and deeper. As I pulled back, he tensed. His breath quickened and I knew he was close. But not yet. Not yet.

I licked my way up his abdomen. Every nerve in my body was

alive as I stretched out on top of him. I reached for his hands, linking fingers. He was mine. Mate and lover for however long it lasted.

"Now." I kissed him as if sealing the deal.

His arms went around me, and he shifted until I lay on my back. His mouth still on mine, he used his legs to spread mine. Ready, I wrapped my legs around him, opening for him. Then he was in me and the universe exploded as my already overly-sensitized system overloaded.

I woke not to the smell of freshly brewed coffee or even the singing of birds. No, there was pounding followed by the sound of a doorbell. As I opened my eyes, I glanced at the clock on the other side of the bed. Six thirty. Who the hell could be pounding on the door at this hour and why wouldn't they go away? Jim and I had loved one another most of the night. Now all I wanted was to sleep some more.

Memory of Declan bursting into the bedroom returned and with it came concern. Then I remembered Jim showing me the security system the night before. Since alarms were sounding, whoever seemed intent on beating down the front door must have the code to at least get through the gate. But why in hell were they here so early?

Before I could sit up, Jim's arms went around my waist. As another round of knocking began, he cursed softly. His lips brushed mine before he slid out from under me. He sat up and looked around. A moment later, he stood and hurried across the bedroom to where I'd tossed his jeans the night before. Damn, that man had the finest ass I'd ever seen. What a shame he had to cover it up.

"Stay there. I'll be right back." He paused at the bedroom door and shook his head. "All right! I'm coming!" he yelled and stomped off as whoever it was leaned on the doorbell.

"About damned time, Jim. I was about to break the door in."

Hearing Finn's voice, I groaned, praying nothing had happened overnight.

"You and what army?"

Oops, that wasn't good. He sounded as pissed as I felt. That wasn't the way to greet Finn. But, damn it, what the hell was she doing there?

"Back down, Jim. It's obvious I woke you." There was a hint of warning in her voice. "But if you'll remember, you asked me to be here this early. You have a briefing in less than an hour with your cops."

Damn. That meant no fun and games for us this morning.

I tossed back the sheet and sat up. Before I could get out of bed, the door opened and Jim appeared. The look on his face was priceless. It was a mixture of sheepishness and frustration. Not that I blamed him. I felt pretty much the same way. Then I thought about Finn and felt my face flaming. She'd know the moment she saw me what had happened.

Crap!

"You heard?" he asked as he dropped onto the mattress at my side.

I nodded.

He sighed and pulled me onto his lap. I wrapped my arms around him and nuzzled his neck. "Stay with Finn today, sweetheart." He must have felt me sigh because he chuckled softly. "I know. She's going to give you hell but remember one thing. She only does that to people she cares for. Besides, it's nothing compared to what Matt and Sharon will do to me once she clues them in."

Well, that did make the day a little more palatable. "When will you be home?"

"As long as nothing happens, I should be home by six. I have to meet with the city council this afternoon and then with the mayor."

"Sounds like fun." Not.

"If you really think so, you're strange." He kissed me and then set me on the mattress. "I need to get dressed now. Why don't you try to get some more sleep?"

"There's no sense in putting off the inevitable. I'll go face Finn, while you're still here to keep me from killing her if she gets to be too much of a pest."

Now, if my stomach would quit doing flip-flops.

"Where're your crutches?"

I thought for a moment and then sighed. "In your office."

He stood and quickly crossed to his closet. He looked inside for a moment and then tossed a Cowboys football jersey at me. A pair of navy shorts followed. When I just stared at him, he moved to my side and pointed out the drawstring on the shorts. Well, at least they wouldn't fall off of me. At least I hoped they wouldn't.

By the time I was dressed and Jim had returned with my crutches, the aroma of coffee brewing filled the air. I waited until I heard the sounds of the shower running in the adjoining bathroom before leaving the bedroom. One thing I knew for sure: I wanted Jim there when Finn realized we'd slept together. I just didn't want him in the room when she started asking questions.

And, unless I was horribly wrong, she'd have lots of questions she'd want answered. So, being the brave shapeshifter that I am, I turned left as I entered the hallway and moved as quickly to the guest bedroom and its shower as I could on my crutches. Maybe soaking my head would wake me up enough to be able to face my childhood friend without becoming a babbling idiot.

CHAPTER TEN

I knew before I emerged from the bathroom that I wasn't alone. I didn't need my heightened senses to tell me who waited in the bedroom beyond. Not when my tiger whimpered in the back of my mind. I pictured her dropping to her belly, snout to the ground. Hell, if I was honest, I'd like nothing better than to hide in the bathroom until Finn decided to go away. But I couldn't.

No, I wouldn't. I hadn't done anything wrong. What happened between Jim and me had been something we'd both wanted. There was nothing to be ashamed of. Besides, unless I'd been very wrong the day before, Finn approved of the way the two of us had flirted with one another. Still, I couldn't deny the realities of our situations either. I belonged to another clan and was here only until I finished my mission – or until Declan called me home.

The thought of being forced to leave so soon had me baring my teeth. A growl sounded deep in my throat. Even as it did, I stared at my reflection in the mirror over the sink in surprise. I'd been angry with Declan before. Hell, after his sudden appearance and accusations, I'd been more than mad. I'd been pissed. But never before had I actually considered disobeying him. That I was now scared me.

Much as I wanted Jim – I couldn't bring myself to say love because I had no idea if I did love him. I wanted him. God, how I wanted him. But was it just a case of over-active hormones or was it something more? I didn't know, and I couldn't stand here debating the issue while Finn waited in the room beyond.

Well, I couldn't hide in the small bathroom forever.

I wrapped a large navy blue towel around me and drew a deep breath. Time to face the music.

"Sit!" Finn's voice brooked no disobedience. Her power rolled over me and it was all I could do not to drop straight to the floor. Fortunately, she jabbed a finger in the direction of the bed, her intent clear.

"Finn," I began softly as I dropped onto the edge of the mattress.

She started to answer and then shook her head frowning. Almost instantly I felt her power pulling back. As it did, I blew out a shaky breath, relieved. Then I watched as she moved to kneel before me. Her hands were gentle as she pushed back the towel and peeled away the bandaging covering my injured thigh.

I watched as she worked, pleased to see how much better the jagged wound looked. Except where the stitches had torn out when Declan shoved me, it looked as if it was at least week old. Pink skin peeked out from the scabbing. I found myself hoping it meant I wouldn't scar, at least not too badly. But, if I did, it would be a reminder not to be so careless the next time.

If there was a next time.

"It's looking a lot better today, Maggs." Finn leaned back on her heels and smiled. As she did, the last knots in my stomach unwound. Maybe she wasn't pissed with me for sleeping with Jim after all.

I nodded.

"Stefan wants it left open some today. So I won't put a new dressing on it until we're ready to leave."

I blinked. Okay, I hadn't had my coffee yet, so conversation wasn't easy. Hell, thinking wasn't easy, especially since I'd just caught the scent of Jim hovering in the hallway. Lust rolled over me and I felt my cheeks heat. Finn's chuckle didn't help any. Instead, she almost flowed to her feet and hurried to the door, reaching out and grabbing him by the arm before he could slip away. I didn't know whether to laugh or what to see his face flaming as bright red as mine felt.

Finn stood there, a grin on her face, as she looked from one to the other of us. Then she laughed and guided Jim to the bed. Her hands on his shoulders had him dropping onto the mattress at my side. Without conscious thought, I reached for his hand. The moment our palms touched, I relaxed. Better, I could feel him relaxing. Good. Very good.

"Jim, I know you need to get going, but I have something to say." Finn looked down at us, her expression softening. Did I actually see approval in her eyes? "Both Matt and I are pleased for you two. Well, Matt will be when I tell him. It's been obvious to the two of us from the moment we saw you together that you were meant for one another. We aren't going to push – not much at any rate – but we will do whatever we can to help you find a way to make this work."

For a moment, I couldn't say anything. As Jim squeezed my hand, I realized he was a surprised by Finn's announcement as was I. More than that, he was going to leave it to me to say, or not say, something. Typical male.

"Thanks . . . I think." What else could I say? Especially when my whole body was starting to hum just sitting next to Jim, holding his hand.

Finn grinned even more, if possible. Then she pulled Jim to his feet and pushed him toward the door. "Go to work. We're going to have a little girl talk and then run some errands."

He looked over his shoulder, his expression uncertain. "Maggie?"

"Go on." I didn't mean it. Not really. I didn't want to be alone with Finn when she looked at me like a cat looks at its prey. But I couldn't ask him to run interference for me when he had work to do.

He nodded and then surprised both Finn and me. Before she could push him out the door, he twisted and stepped to the side.

Finn's delighted laughter filled the room as he hurried back to the bed. His hands closed over my arms and he lifted me to my feet. Fortunately, he held onto me as we kissed because damn that man can kiss. My muscles melted and my arms went around his neck. By the time we separated, we were both breathless.

"Call me if you need me," he said softly, burying his face in my hair.

"I will. Now go. I can handle Finn."

I think.

For a moment, he just held me. Then he kissed me again. The look he gave Finn was priceless: a mix of warning and resignation. He obviously knew his sister-in-law well enough to realize she planned to grill me mercilessly about what we'd done last night but he hoped she'd respect our privacy. If she was anything like she'd been when we were younger, there was fat chance of the latter. But I could hope.

Without a word, Finn moved back to stand in front of me. Before I knew what she planned, she reached out. A quick flick of her wrist and the towel I'd wrapped around me dropped to the floor. As my mouth opened in protest, she simply arched one eyebrow. Frustrated, not sure what to do or say, I stood there, torn between embarrassment and frustration.

"Maggie."

Finn's voice was soft, troubled as she turned me this way and that. She was obviously looking for something but what? Had she expected me to suddenly grow wings or something after having sex with Jim? Or was it something else, something darker? Had she worried he'd might have hurt me? Surely not. She wouldn't have left us alone if that were the case.

"Maggie, why aren't you wearing any clan markings?"

Not quite sure I heard her right, I didn't respond. Damn it, why couldn't this have happened after I'd had coffee? At least then my brain would be working. Between lack of sleep and residual lust for Jim as well as a definite lack of caffeine, thinking was like moving through mud – slow and treacherous.

"Huh?" Okay, not the best response but the only one I could come up with just then.

Finn looked at me and then smiled, understanding dawning. Without a word, she crossed to the closet and rummaged inside. When she returned, she held my robe in one hand. I stood there, still not sure what to think of her question, as she helped me into it. Then, she pressed the crutches into my hands and left the bedroom, calling over her shoulder to join her in the kitchen.

"You'll feel better after having some coffee and food."

God, I hoped she was right.

"Now," she said as she placed a mug of coffee on the table before me. "I'd like you to answer my question. How can you be a clan tracker and not wear that clan's markings?"

I didn't answer right away. The question had thrown me. But what had thrown me more was the concern in Finn's voice. As I sat there trying to figure out how to respond, I found myself once again studying the beautiful tattoo she sported. It really was no wonder she seemed to favor tank tops. Her markings were nothing short of works of art. I could see how the tattoo artist had paid tribute to her parents and to the Oklahoma clan. Nor was I surprised to find no reference to the Northern California clan. After what Jennings had done, and tried to do, I doubted Finn wanted anything to do with the clan.

Then I thought of my own lack of markings. As I grew up, my parents had followed the example set by Finn's mom and dad. They'd chosen not to have me marked. They knew it was likely I'd move on and find another clan once I was grown. It was up to me to decide then if I wanted to show my history with the Northern California clan. After Finn's parents died – were murdered, I corrected – and we left the clan, I'd chosen not to take the markings of the Tennessee clan. They'd been wonderful in welcoming us and making us feel a part of the clan. But it hadn't been home.

And I still hadn't answered Finn's question.

So I explained why I hadn't been marked as a kid and why, when we moved to Tennessee, I hadn't taken on the markings of that clan.

Finn listened, never interrupting. In fact, she seemed to approve of my reasons. But I could see she was still bothered by the fact I wore no clan alliance anywhere and that, in turn, bothered me.

"I understand all that, Maggs." She paused and took a sip of coffee. Was she giving herself time to think, to find the right words for what she wanted to say next? "But you've been an adult by our kind's standards for more than ten years." She waited until I nodded. "You chose to follow your sister and her husband back to the Northern California clan. I know they changed the clan iconography when they took over. The other clan leaders approved the move. So why don't you wear your clan's markings now?"

I bent my head and stared into my coffee mug. How in hell was I supposed to answer her without betraying my clan? No, that wasn't right. I wouldn't be betraying the clan, but I would be showing just what an insecure fool Declan happened to be. Of course, he'd done a pretty good job of that all by himself yesterday. That didn't mean I wanted to add to it. He was my sister's husband and, despite it all, I did like him. I might not agree with everything he did as clan leader, I knew he acted only in what he saw as the clan's best interest.

"I wanted to, Finn, but everything happened so fast when I joined the clan. You have to remember that Volk's attack happened at the first clan meeting I'd attended. Declan had just accepted me, as well as half a dozen others, as new clan members. Then Volk stepped up and issued his challenge. Before we knew what was happening, he'd signaled his ferals and we were fighting for our lives.

"I completely forgot about being marked in the aftermath of the attack. When Declan asked for volunteers to become trackers to go after Volk, I stepped up. Later, when I finished my training, I asked him about getting marked. I remembered your parents making sure their trackers clearly bore clan markings and so did the Tennessee clan leader. So you can imagine my surprise when Declan denied my request."

Finn's eyes flashed angrily and her hand reached over the table and closed over mine. When she started to say something, I shook my head. I needed to finish, to get it all out.

"Finn, he had his reasons. I don't agree with them and didn't when he explained them. But he was my clan leader and I wouldn't disobey him." I leaned back and sighed. I wanted – no, I needed – to tell her everything but I felt torn. Would she understand why Declan had acted as he had, or would she see it as yet another example of why he shouldn't be clan leader? "What he told me was that he didn't want me marked because trackers need to be able to move among the clans and normals without advertising their presence."

"What the hell?" Finn looked at me like I had just sprouted a second head. Not that I blamed her. "Was he thinking he could send you into other territories without letting the local clan leader know?"

"No." I shook my head. I was sure of that much at least because that had been my question for Declan. "He was going to report our presence but was asking clan leaders not to tell their people why we were there. He was afraid if they saw our markings and realized we were trackers, they'd not want to help us."

Finn pushed back from the table and stood. I watched as she paced the length of the kitchen. Her movements betrayed her agitation. Not that I blamed her. Declan's reasoning was short-sighted and potentially dangerous, not only for the trackers involved but also for the local clans we moved through.

Then she looked at me and came to an abrupt stop. Her expression darkened, and I had a sinking feeling in the pit of my stomach that she realized there was more to it. Damn it. Damn it and damn it again.

"Tell me," she said simply, almost gently, as she returned to the table.

"Finn, please." I heard the anguish in my voice. She asked too much.

"Maggie, I need to know. I'm not just your friend right now. I'm my clan's female alpha. You are under my protection. I already have concerns about letting you return to Declan's clan because of the way he broke in here and attacked you." All it took was a look to keep me from interrupting. "Yes, he did attack you. Look in the mirror if you doubt it." Her voice was harsh and I bowed my head in a show of submission.

"But now I see and hear that he refused to let you, one of the clan's trackers, wear clan markings. I desperately want to believe it wasn't so he could be like Jennings and send you into another territory without telling the local clan leader. I'm tempted to believe that wasn't his intention because he did let Matt know you were here. So there has to be more and the fact you look like you want to find a hole to crawl into just proves it."

"Finn." I swallowed and wished that hole she spoke of would open up and swallow me. "He told me he didn't want me to take clan markings because there might come a time when he'd need me to mate with another clan's alpha or beta in order to strengthen our clan."

There, I'd said it and now I waited for the explosion.

I didn't have long to wait. Finn's chair clattered to the floor as she surged to her feet. Her eyes flashed angrily. When her lips peeled back, I saw her teeth elongating. I felt her animal-side pushing for release. I whimpered and fought the urge to drop to the floor as Finn's alpha presence filled the room. Then, as if that was a trigger, she cursed and stalked out of the room. The front door opened and slammed shut and I released a shaky breath. Then I listened for the sound of her car starting, fully expecting her to speed off in search of my brother-in-law.

I was still sitting at the table, wondering whether I ought to call Matt or Jim, when Finn returned. Anger radiated off of her but at least she looked like she had it under control. I waited, knowing she wasn't going to let the topic drop, especially not after the way Declan had acted the day before.

"I'm sorry, Maggie. I should have better control." She busied herself at the sink. I waited as she splashed her face with cold water and reached for a dishtowel. "But to hear how he was so close to acting like Jennings, even if that wasn't his intention, was bad enough. But to learn that he is willing to give you to another, whether you wanted it or not, just to solidify clan politics was too much." She turned to me and I realized she wasn't as calm as I first thought. "Especially not after knowing how he attacked you after finding you and Jim together."

She scrubbed her hands over her face and drew a deep breath. She released it and returned to the table. "The only reason I haven't already told Matt about this is the fact that Declan was upset by the thought of you and Jim being together. His mind went right to you not finishing the hunt for Volk, not to you destroying any chance there might be of finding a mate for you. Hell, it's the only reason I haven't called him out. We don't force our females into mating with men – or women – they don't want to be with." She all but ground out the words.

"Enough, Finn!" It was out before I could stop it. Her eyes flashed and, for one brief moment, I wondered if I'd gone too far. I knew better than to act that way to an alpha, much less the clan Alpha, even if she was my childhood friend. But, damn it, I liked the situation no more than she did and if any of us had a right to be angry it was me. "I'll remind you that you are talking about not only my Alpha but my sister's mate."

"Something I haven't forgotten," she assured me.

"I also know why Declan said what he did." I scrubbed my hands over my face, suddenly tired. "You don't know what it was like for him that first month after he took over the clan. I wasn't there, but Eileen was on the phone to me every day. She almost despaired as they weeded out those who saw nothing wrong with what Jennings had done over the years. It was as if he'd managed to bring in every shapeshifter who'd ever caused trouble to be one of his enforcers. He rewarded them with pride and pack leadership roles or roles on his inner council. They tried to hold onto their positions through intimidation and threats. I don't know how many of them Declan had to fight. But he finally got them out and he started bringing in new members, doing what he could to shore up his role as clan leader."

I paused, letting Finn digest what I'd said. As she sat back, some of the anger leaving her, I relaxed. Maybe now we could actually discuss what happened and why. I hoped so because her questions had touched a sore spot with me. Being denied the chance to wear the markings of my new clan had hurt. Worse, when I'd tried talking with Eileen about it, she told me she couldn't get involved. Surely, I understood that Declan had to use whatever tools he had at hand to solidify his hold on the clan? Knowing that was all I represented to both my clan leader and my sister had shaken me and I had to wonder if I'd been right after all to follow them to California.

"Maggie, I'm sorry. The last thing I want to do is upset you." Finn reached for my hand and held it. "And I do understand why Declan was desperate to solidify his place as clan leader. I'm not going to say I agree. I know what he was told when the clan leaders met and asked if he would take over the Northern California clan. Every one of us offered him any help he might need. Hell, Matt offered to send Danny and several others from our clan to help with the transition as did my grandmother. Declan turned them down. Now I want you to be completely honest with me."

I nodded, my mouth going suddenly dry.

"I've got one question and it's really pretty simple, Maggs. Would you be interested in joining our clan?"

"What?"

Now it was my turn to stand so quickly that my chair clattered to the floor. That was absolutely the last question I expected her to ask. Join her clan? Leave California and move here? My tiger let me know instantly what she thought of the idea. Her satisfied roar filled the back of my mind. This was, as far as she was concerned, where we belonged. Jim – and his panther – were here. So why was I hesitating?

Finn watched as I righted my chair and was once again seated. "Maggie, please think about it. But know this. I'm asking you to do this because I think you would be a good fit with our clan. It's a strong clan but that doesn't mean we don't need new blood. There's something else. We've missed too many years, years I want to make up for. I've missed having my best friend nearby."

She paused, and a slight grin lifted the corners of her mouth. "Besides, whether you realize it or not, you and Jim are meant for one another. I promise you, Kincade men are loyal and caring and you'll never find another man who'll love you more than Jim does."

Loyalty warred with desire only to be overshadowed by reality. Even if I wanted to join the clan – and, heaven help me, I did – I still had a duty to Declan and the Northern California clan. Besides, just because Finn asked me if I wanted to join the clan, that didn't mean Matt had agreed. The last thing I wanted – well, not quite the last – was to cause trouble between Finn and her mate. When I said as much, Finn gave me a grin I knew all too well. Seeing it, I didn't know whether to laugh or groan. It was clear Finn had anticipated my question and was prepared for it. When she dug into her pocket and produced her phone, all I could do was sigh. A moment later, she handed it to me. Not sure I wanted to know who was on the other end but knowing better than to refuse, I extended my hand and took it from her.

"H-hello?"

"Let me start by apologizing for my wife, Maggie. I have a feeling she's just ambushed you." Humor and understanding filled Matt's voice. He certainly knew Finn well if he realized what she'd done.

"You could say that." Seeing how Finn rolled her eyes, I stuck out my tongue. I know, not very mature but I suited my mood just then.

"Maggie, Finn can be impetuous at times–"

"You think?"

"But this time," he continued as if I hadn't interrupted him, "I happen to agree with her. We'd both be honored if you would consider joining our clan. We won't pressure you. Well, I won't. I can't speak for my mate." There could be no mistaking the humor in his voice at that. "Just know that we'd be proud to call you one of ours. Besides, you'd be doing me a huge favor if you did. It's been fun watching my brother get all tongue-tied and start tripping over himself whenever you're near. It almost makes up for all the teasing I received when Finn and I first got together."

"God, Matt, does everyone know about us?" I blushed furiously, stunned I'd said it out loud.

"Not yet, but all anyone will need is to see the two of you together to know how you feel." At least he sounded like he approved. "So, do me a favor and think about it, Maggie. Know you have a home here if you want it."

"I will, Matt. Thanks."

I handed the phone back to Finn and, as she said her goodbyes to her husband, carefully stood. I needed to think. No, I needed to talk to Jim. That was all I could think of. I'd like to be part of this clan, part of a clan with strong leaders who cared about their people. Part of a clan not struggling to re-establish itself after years of bad leadership. I'd like being close to Finn after all this time. She'd been right when she said we had a lot to make up for. Most of all, I wanted to be near Jim. But if he wasn't committed to seeing where this whatever it was between us was going, I couldn't be here. I couldn't be near him, wanting him and knowing there was no future for us.

God, what had gotten into me? I'd known the man only a few days and here I was thinking about spending the rest of my life with him. I'd heard others of our kind talk about their life mates before, but I'd never really put any credence in it, not even when Eileen told us she'd met her life mate in Declan. It was too much like love at first sight, something I'd always figured was just a fancy way of saying lust at first sight. But now, after meeting Jim, I had to consider the possibility that life mates really existed. But what was I going to do if he didn't feel the same way?

Finn found me in the den a few minutes later. Seeing how she held the cell phone in her hand and how she looked more than a little apologetic, I groaned. What had she done this time? Wasn't calling Matt and making me talk to him enough?

"Don't be mad," she said softly as she handed me her phone. "I'll be in the kitchen. We can talk when you're done."

With that, she left the room. I stared at the phone in my hand for a moment and then lifted it to my ear. I might as well get it over with. All I had to do was think of like removing a bandage. The quicker I did it, the less it would hurt.

At least I hoped so.

"I am so going to kill Finn when I get home," Jim said before I could say anything.

"Only if you let me help."

"God, Maggie, the last thing I wanted was for her, much less my brother, to start pressuring you into anything."

I sank onto the sofa, relieved he wasn't mad at me. But that wasn't enough. I needed to find out what Finn had told him and how he felt about it. "Jim, I know I'm probably going to regret this, but what did she say?"

My heart thudded as I waited for him to answer. It seemed to take forever. Then I realized he was talking to someone else, telling them he'd be there in a minute. "Sorry, sweetheart. As for Finn, she didn't say much. Just that she'd asked you to join the clan and that Matt had also said he'd like you to consider it. Then she said you and I needed to talk. And I am so going to kill both of them when I get home."

Relief filled me. He was as stunned by everything as was I. "Jim, we do need to talk."

"Maggie, I don't want to pressure you but if you don't accept their offer, I'm going to have to turn in my notice here and go with you. So, is your place in California big enough for both of us?"

I laughed. I couldn't help it. The thought of him in my miniscule apartment sent me into fits of giggles. But it was more than that. He wanted to be with me. He was willing to leave his clan and his family in order to do so. That was more than anyone had ever wanted where I was concerned. Maybe there really were life mates after all.

"Not nearly as big as your place nor as nice." But I had to be certain. "Jim, are you sure?"

"More sure than I've ever been before." Another pause and I heard someone in the background. I couldn't make out their words, but I could tell they weren't happy. "Maggie, I'm sorry. I've got to go. But before I do, understand that I want you in my life. If it's here, wonderful. If I have to follow you back to California, I will. All I care about is being with you."

"I feel the same way." God, it felt as if the weight of the world had suddenly been lifted from my shoulders. He wanted me as much as I did him. The memory of what Finn had said about the Kincade men returned and I smiled. Life was about to get very interesting – assuming I managed not to get myself killed by Volk. "Go take care of business, love. We'll talk when you get home."

I leaned back, cradling the phone in my hand. Eyes closed, I blew out a breath. My life had certainly taken some *interesting* twists and turns the last few days. Now I needed to go deal with my childhood best friend. But how?

"Well?" Finn asked a few minutes later.

She stood in the doorway to my bedroom. Instead of returning to the kitchen after talking to Jim, I'd come here. For one thing, I knew she'd be stewing, wondering what we'd said to one another. For another, I needed some time to think. What I was about to do would impact not just me but my sister as well. I hoped she'd be happy for me, but I wasn't sure. She was devoted to Declan, as she should be, and could see this as a betrayal. God, when had my life gotten so complicated?

I finished pulling on my tee shirt and just looked at her. When I didn't immediately respond, she nervously shifted from foot to foot. Good. It served her right.

"Maggie?"

I heard a note of uncertainty in her voice. Maybe it was time to relent, at least a little.

"If I agree, what role will I fill with the clan and which pride will I be a part of?"

"Maggie, we won't make you fill any role unless you want to. As for what pride, I figured you'd want to join the local one. It's the pride Jim belongs to."

"All right." I reached for my jeans and then remembered I needed to rebandage my thigh. "But I owe it to Declan to finish what brought me here. I have to find Volk and deal with him. If you can't accept that, then I can't be part of this clan."

"You haven't changed, Maggs." She grinned and, before I could respond, she was at my side, giving me a hug. "And I'd expect nothing less from you. But this time, you will have trained trackers helping you. So, will you become a member of our clan and wear our clan markings?"

"I have one more condition." When she looked at me suspiciously, I chuckled and waited for her to nod. "No matchmaking. No trying to force Jim and me into anything we aren't ready for."

"That's two demands," she pointed out with a grin. "But I agree. However, I can't promise Sharon will agree."

"Then I'd be honored to become part of your clan, Finn."

There was only one thing to do. I slid off the bed and dropped to hands and knees. If I was to become a member of the clan, I had to admit Finn's dominance over me. I lowered to my belly and rested my forehead on the floor at the tips of her boots. I lay there, waiting. If she accepted me, I'd have one more thing to do. Then, when I saw Matt, I'd repeat it for him.

Finn's hands were gentle as they lifted me to my knees. There was a protectiveness in her expression I'd never seen before as well as approval. One hand ran down my head and I pressed my cheek into her palm. My hands gripped the bottom of my tee shirt and I looked at her, knowing she'd understand my unasked question. She nodded and stepped back, giving me the room I needed.

I pulled the tee shirt over my head and reached behind me, releasing my bra. My shorts and panties followed them to the floor.

Then I dropped back to hands and knees. The moment I eased control, my tiger leapt forward. Pain rolled over me and through me. A cry of pain filled the room. My cry. God, why couldn't shifting be as easy and painless as Hollywood made it look?

When it was over, strength replaced pain. I padded across the room on four paws, doing my best not to favor my injured leg. Stopping before Finn, I dropped to my belly, mirroring the movements my human self had done just minutes before. Then I rolled onto my back, exposing stomach and throat. Submitting. Trusting her as my Alpha to protect me.

Still in human form, Finn knelt next to me. Her hands ran down my sides and flanks. For form, she took my throat between her teeth. We both knew it was symbolic only. But it was necessary. Then she withdrew and rubbed her cheek against mine, accepting me as one of hers.

"You are a beauty, Maggie."

I butted her with my head, relishing in her approval.

"Now shift back. There's a lot to do before Jim gets home."

CHAPTER ELEVEN

"Maggie!"

The front door slammed. Jim's scent filled the air and I smiled slightly. I didn't respond, trusting him to follow his nose. If he didn't scent me, surely he'd come investigate the smells coming from the kitchen. At least he'd better if he knew what was good for him. I hadn't spent the last two hours in here for him not to appreciate it.

A moment later, arms went around my waist and he pulled me against him. He buried his nose in the hair behind my ear. Forgetting the salad I'd been making, I reached up and cupped his cheek. Then I turned, my mouth searching for his.

Only to suddenly be thrust against the counter as he stared at me in surprise.

"Maggie?" One hand reached out to lightly touch the skin near the new inking on my right upper arm and shoulder.

"It seems Finn didn't want to give me a chance to change my mind."

A bemused smile touched my lips at the memory of how she'd bundled me into her car and driven straight to CJ's, the clan's resident tattoo artist and Finn's part-time employer. We'd spent half an hour looking at samples of CJ's work before Finn appeared from the back room with one of her own sketches. Before I could say "boo", CJ had me lying face down on a padded table. There was the hum of her machines and then it felt like a thousand ants were biting me. Six hours later, we left the shop. Now I held my breath, waiting for Jim to say something, anything.

Had I made a mistake?

"For once I'm glad she did." He grinned and gently turned me so he could see all the tattoo. "Her design?"

"Yeah. She wanted to be sure there were elements to honor my family and background, but she also made absolutely sure there'd be no doubting what pride and clan I belong to now." Remembering how she said we'd be returning to CJ's later to add the finishing touches, including my mating with Jim once we were officially a couple, I blushed and ducked my head.

"What?" He reached out and lifted my face so he could look in my eyes.

When I told him, he pulled me close, careful not to put too much pressure on the tender area of the tattoo. "She's right. But we'll go together." He bent to kiss me. "Maggie, I know it's crazy, but this is right. I don't understand it but I'm damned glad you are part of my life now."

"So am I." I nipped at his chin, a promise of things to come. "Now go get changed. Dinner will be ready before long."

Besides, he was a distraction in his uniform. All it took was one look at the silver of his handcuffs where they rested in the black leather holder on his belt to have me remembering the events of the night before. Even as he restrained me, he'd given me complete control. All it would have taken was a word, a look and he'd have released me. He trusted me to tell him if he was going too far just as I'd trusted him not to. Who could ask for more?

I expected him to do as I said. Instead, he leaned against the counter. As he looked at me, I could tell he was unsure about something. I knew the sauce simmering on the stove smelled wonderful. It would taste even better. I had bread baking in the oven. A bottle of red wine was breathing on the counter to my right.

So what was it? Surely, he wasn't upset that I'd cooked. I'd done pretty good cleaning up after myself, at least by my standards. Still, maybe I should have asked first.

And you're babbling, Maggie. Just ask him.

"Jim?" I reached for him, needing to touch him to make sure he wasn't upset.

He drew me close, his lips brushing the top of my head. For a moment, he just held me. Then he led me to the table and sat, pulling me onto his lap.

"I find myself wanting to disobey my Alphas right now."

My brow furrowed, and I looked at him in concern. Fear beat a quick staccato in my veins. What the hell was he talking about?

"You're scaring me, Jim. What's going on?"

"They've called a clan meeting for tonight. In less than an hour, people will start arriving and, damn it, I don't want to share you. I want tonight to be ours."

I held him close and nuzzled his neck. Disappointment filled me. I'd planned the evening very carefully, starting with dinner. By the time we got to dessert, I figured we'd be in bed. As far as I was concerned, it was going to be an early evening, not for sleep but for continuing what we'd started the night before. Now it seemed all my plans were for naught.

"But we have an hour?" My hands worked to pull his shirt out and soon my hands ran across the warm skin of his chest.

"Your dinner?"

"Sauce is always better the longer it simmers." I cast a quick glance at the oven. "The bread has another half hour before it's ready."

He dipped his head, his teeth catching my lower lip. Then he was on his feet, cradling me against his chest. Half an hour wasn't much, but it was better than nothing.

"I want you naked," he rasped as he set me on my feet.

We stood in the middle of his bedroom. His hands worked quickly as they undid the buttons of his shirt just enough that he could pull it over his head. Then he reached for his belt. Carefully he removed his gun and set it on the bedside table. His cuffs and keys followed. As he kicked off his shoes, he looked at me, frowning because I had yet to move.

"Maggie?" Uncertainty filled his voice.

"I like looking at you." I smiled, desire filling me.

"Do you now?" He grinned and slowly unzipped his pants. He hooked his thumbs under the waistband and slowly dropped them. Then he stood, dressed only in his briefs.

"Looks like you like something." I reached out and ran a finger over his hard-on. As I did, he drew a shaky breath. Then I knelt, ignoring the pain in my injured thigh, and slowly eased his briefs down his legs. He stepped out of them, his hands resting on my shoulders. Gently, he drew me to my feet.

"God, Maggie, I need you." He pulled the tank over my head. His mouth followed his hands as they traced a pattern from my shoulders to my breasts and down to my waist. My breath was ragged by the time he finally helped me step out of my jeans. It was probably a good thing we didn't have much time because I wanted him in me and I didn't want to wait.

His teeth scraped my throat. His fingers flicked and rolled my nipples until they felt like they were on fire. I clawed at his back, trying to hold him closer. Then his hands closed around my waist. That was all the prompting I need. I leapt, wrapping my legs around his waist. He gave a short "oomph" and then twisted, falling across the foot of the bed.

"In me," I rasped, tossing my head back and gasping for breath as his fingers played with my clit. Then he pushed one inside me, pumping, getting me ready. But it wasn't what I wanted.

"Now." His fingers withdrew and we moved together for what we both wanted. "Mine," he said as he thrust, his hips bumping against mine. "Mine."

"Yes."

I matched him movement for movement. Every nerve was alive, every sense close to overload. One small part of my mind remembered that we hadn't used protection either last night or now. That was a first. I'd demanded with my other lovers. I hadn't wanted to risk pregnancy or worse. But I trusted Jim. I knew on an instinctive level I didn't have to worry about getting an STD from him and nothing would make me happier than to have his child. At least one day. For now, I just wanted to love him.

"God, woman, I could spend the rest of my life in bed with you." Jim lay on me, and in me. We were both covered in sweat. Exhausted, sated – for the moment at least – I held onto him.

"I say we turn all the lights out and not answer the door when everyone gets here. Maybe they'll take the hint and go away."

"You can say that after this morning?"

I groaned as I remembered how Finn had pounded on the door and leaned on the doorbell until Jim had finally let her in. "Maybe we can run away?"

"I wish." He rolled off me, gently pulling out as he did. "I'll go take the bread out while you start the shower. It would probably be good if we were at least dressed by the time the Alphas get here."

I leaned up on my elbow and watched as he walked across the bedroom. He didn't bother finding his pants or pulling on a robe. He simply sauntered out of the room, giving me a good look at his incredible ass. As he disappeared from sight, I flopped onto my back. Life had certainly gotten fun, not to mention interesting, the last few days.

"You're sure about this, Maggie, right?" he asked ten minutes later as he handed me a towel.

We'd showered together. Unfortunately, because the others would be arriving soon, we'd just showered. Now, hearing the uncertainty in his voice, I knew he was just as worried as I was. Somehow, that reassured me.

"Jim." I moved into his open arms and nestled against him. Passion stirred and I forced it down. "I think you said it best earlier.

Mine. That's how I feel. You're mine. My mate and my partner. You are a part of me. I'd never really believed in it before, but I knew there was something about you, something special, the moment I saw you. If I'd had any doubts, my tiger most certainly did not. She claimed you right away. Even if I wanted to leave, I couldn't. She'd kill me." I smiled up at him.

"Then I guess you're stuck with me." He grinned and then his expression turned serious. "Maggie, I'm not going to ask you not to go after Volk."

"Good."

"But you'd better understand that you aren't alone now. I'm going to be with you every step of the way."

"Jim." I looked at him, pride stung. Did he think I couldn't do the job?

"Listen to me before you get mad." He held me close, preventing me from moving away. "It's not that I don't think you can do it. You proved yourself by killing that feral. If you'd had the training most trackers get, I have a feeling you'd have managed to deal with Volk as well. But you're not alone now. We are in this together and together we will deal with the renegade and any ferals he might have. Once we have, you'll owe nothing else to your former clan and we can focus on our lives. Just understand that I'm not going to let you unnecessarily risk yourself. Not now that I've found you."

A slight smile touched my lips and I leaned up to kiss him. "Possessive a bit?"

"More than a bit."

"Good, then you know how I feel." With that, I tossed my towel to one side and limped out of the bathroom before he could tell me to get my crutches. Unless we wanted to be caught in bed – again – it was time to get dressed.

Half an hour later, I stood inside what I'd thought was a barn until Jim opened the door and I looked inside. The large building had probably once been a mere barn. But there was nothing *mere* about it now. Someone had finished it out, turning it into part meeting center and part training area. I even saw a full kitchen off to one side at the rear of the building. No wonder the clan was meeting here. Between the way the ranch was located well off the road and this, it was perfect.

"My folks did this back when we were kids," Jim said softly from my side.

"It's wonderful." But it was also a little intimidating because it spoke volumes about how involved his family had been with the local pride as well as with the clan over the years. My parents had worked closely with Finn's but after leaving California, they'd been more reticent to get involved with our new clan. I'd come to understand part of it was because they were grieving for their friends. The only problem was it made this sort of involvement more than a bit hard to imagine. "I see Sharon's here." I nodded toward the kitchen where I'd spotted his sister.

"She'll tell you she's our chief cook and bottle washer." He grinned in affection. "When Matt and Finn got together, it was a relief for Shar. She'd basically been acting as the clan's female alpha before then. That's a role she was never comfortable with and not just because she's not an alpha. She might be able to outfight most everyone in the clan and she'd be the first to step up to protect Matt and Finn, but that's not where her heart is. She'd much rather work with our younger members, helping them as they near their first shifts. She's a teacher and a chef at heart."

Remembering how she'd tried interrogating me the first time we met, I nodded. That had been the concern of a sister, not a clan elder. "I assume she's Finn's second now."

"Not officially, but she has been filling that role."

"From what I've seen of her so far, she'd be perfect. Do you think Finn will be able to convince her to formally accept it?"

"No. Shar's been very emphatic that there's nothing any of us can say to make her change her mind."

Surprised, I turned in the direction of Finn's voice. She and Matt had managed to slip in without my noticing. Seeing how Matt's eyes settled on my new markings, I didn't wait. I dropped to hands and knees before him, much as I had earlier in the day with Finn. Before I could roll onto my back, he bent and lifted me to my feet. Approval shone on his expression and, from where he stood behind his brother, Jim smiled in encouragement.

"Thank you, Maggie." Matt glanced around and nodded in satisfaction before turning his attention back to me. "You're home now. Remember that always."

"My arm is yours, clan leader, as is my life. I will protect pride and clan and will have your back. You have my loyalty and I submit to you." I bent my head and waited.

"You are a welcome member of pride and clan. We will protect and honor you as you do us," he responded.

"Thank you."

"Matt, you have my thanks too," Jim said, taking my hand and pulling me close. "She's my mate, my life."

"As if I hadn't already figured that out, big brother." Matt punched his brother in the shoulder, grinning good-naturedly. "I didn't need Sharon telling me that the two of you reminded her of Finn and me when we first met. The sexual tension rising off you the first time Maggie entered the room was enough to tell me you'd finally found your mate."

"Then you understand when I say I hope you don't plan for a long meeting tonight." The look Jim gave me had me blushing from head to toe.

"C'mon. Let's make sure everything is ready."

Matt draped an arm around his brother's shoulders and the two of them walked off. As they did, Finn smiled slightly, affection lighting her expression. Then she turned her attention to me.

"I'd ask if you're all right but I can tell that you are."

"More all right than I've ever been." I couldn't stop the grin that lifted the corners of my mouth.

"I'm glad for you, Maggs. Really." She gave me a hug before stepping back. Almost instantly, her expression turned serious and I knew

I was in trouble. "Care to tell me where they hell your crutches are? I know Stefan hasn't given you the go-ahead to be up without them."

I ducked my head and sighed. I'd hoped to avoid this discussion, at least until after the meeting. Unfortunately, she left me no choice. At least I'd already had this discussion with Jim.

"Finn, this is my first meeting with the clan. Even if you aren't officially announcing I'm now a member, my markings pretty much do it for you. I will not come before them looking weak and unable to defend myself." She continued to look at me as if I'd lost my mind. "Alpha, I don't want any to think you have weakened the clan by bringing me in. I can handle a little pain in order to present a strong face for you and for your mate. I promise to be careful and do nothing foolish, but I will not weaken your stance in the clan by appearing weak myself."

Her eyes narrowed and she shook her head. Then she relented. At least I hoped she did.

"All right. But the first time I see you doing anything that might compromise your recovery, I'm having Jim take you back up to the house and Stefan sedate you." She pinned me with a firm look. Then, when I assured her I understood, she smiled and linked her arm through mine. "Let me tell you a little about what's going to happen tonight."

For the next few minutes, she explained what she and Matt had in mind. After introducing me to the clan as its newest member, Matt would turn the discussion to Volk and the ferals. I was to be ready to answer any questions and fill in any gaps in what Matt said. Once that was done, it would be back to business as usual. Matt would ask if any of the packs or prides comprising the clan had any business that needed to be brought before either he or Finn. Then, once that was taken care of, the official part of the meeting would be over, and Jim and I could slip back to the house.

Before I could say anything, not that I knew what to say, Sharon appeared at my side. She gave Finn a quick hug and then turned to me. I waited, not sure what she might do, as she looked me over. Her gaze started at my black boots and traveled up my black jeans. She nodded in approval as she took in my black tank top and then my new tattoo. Then, with a grin, she enveloped me in a hug.

"Welcome to the family." She stepped back and glanced over her shoulder to where her brothers stood talking about something. "I've never seen Jim happier. He's always been so worried about Matt and me that he's ignored himself. I don't think you'll let him do that anymore."

"Sharon." I smiled as Jim glanced back at us and lifted a hand. "I have a feeling that Jim and I will butt heads pretty often." Finn snorted at that and the look she sent Matt spoke volumes. Unless I missed my guess, they had their fair of head-butting. "But he is a part of me. I plan to do my damnedest to make him happy."

"Good." She nodded emphatically. Then she turned her attention to Finn. "Have you told her?"

Suspicion spiked as I looked from one to the other. "Told me what?"

"That you'll be standing with me today." The look Finn gave her sister-in-law left no doubt that she didn't appreciate Sharon letting the cat, so to speak, out of the bag.

"What?" Now I really was confused. "Jim told me you aren't Finn's official second, but he said you'd been filling that role just as you've helped Matt over the years."

"Yep. But now you're here and the role is yours." Sharon grinned like a kid with a new toy. Or, now that I thought about it, someone who finally was rid of a job they never wanted.

"Finn?"

Panic started tightening my chest. This was not what I'd signed on for. Without thinking, I looked for Jim. For a moment, I couldn't find him. Where had all these people come from? Just a few minutes ago, the room had been almost empty. Now there had to be at least a couple dozen people there. Men, women and children milled about, talking and laughing. But where was Jim?

"Uh oh."

Sharon's soft warning had my head whipping in the direction she'd been looking. At first, relief filled me to see Jim standing across the room. Then I noticed how he stood, arms crossed, his expression closed. When he tried to step aside, someone moved to intercept him. A hand rested against his chest. A very feminine hand with perfectly manicured nails. He said something and shook his head only to have that hand reach up to caress his cheek.

My world narrowed to the sight of my mate and the foolish female trying to home in on what was mine. My lips pulled back, baring my teeth. A growl sounded deep in my throat. If she didn't get her hands off of him now, I'd gladly teach her how impolite it was to touch things that didn't belong to her.

"Told you." Finn's satisfied voice cut through the haze of anger.

"What?" It came out as a hiss and that was enough to warn me I was close to shifting. Damn, no man had ever caused that kind of reaction in me before.

"She said you and Jim really were mated and that it wouldn't take long to prove it." Sharon dug in her pocket and slapped a five dollar bill onto Finn's extended palm. "Now, what the hell are you doing standing here letting that bitch manhandle your mate?"

I looked to Finn. She was my Alpha. Much as I wanted to toss the interloper through the nearest wall, I wouldn't unless Finn approved. I refused to bring trouble to her, especially not on my first day with the clan.

"Go. She's been warned off by Jim, but she didn't listen. Now stake your claim."

That was all it took. I crossed the room, my boots almost silent against the wood floor. My injured thigh protested but I ignored it. I might pay for it later but I wouldn't give in to the pain. Not when that *woman's* hands were on my mate. Not when my tiger wanted release so she could teach the woman a lesson she'd never forget.

As I crossed the barn, I barely noted the people stepping out of my way. As I neared, Jim caught sight of me over the woman's shoulder. The expression on his face as he did was priceless. Or it would be once I'd dealt with this matter. Lust mixed with surprise and approval. I felt his panther responding to my tiger. Then he lifted his face, teeth bared and I could almost hear him thinking "Mine".

"Jim," the woman whined as he brushed her hand away as she once again reached up to caress his cheek. "Don't be like that."

"I suggest you take your hands off my mate," I growled.

The woman turned, surprise reflected on her expression. Then she looked down on me. Yes, down. If anything, she was taller than Finn. But the extra height was the only thing she had on me, especially since a good three inches of it came from the spiked heels she wore. Finely coiffed and dressed in designer clothes, she was a showpiece, not a fighter.

"Mate!" She actually laughed. As she did, Jim took a step back. Wise man. This was about to get ugly.

"Yes, Brittney, mate." I heard the pride and possessiveness in Jim's voice. But this Brittney either didn't recognize it or couldn't believe it. I could almost read her thoughts. How could Jim, the clan leader's brother, want someone like me when he could have her? One part of me knew I should have been prepared for something like this. I just hadn't expected it to happen quite so soon.

Well, there was no time like the present to make sure it never happened again.

"Jimmy." She pointedly turned her back on me. That was mistake number one. Mistake number two was to twine her arms around his neck and try to pull his head down for a kiss.

"Remove your hands before I remove them for you – and from you."

The foolish bitch. No one messed with my mate, not if they wanted to live to see the next day.

"Go away, little kitten. Maybe when you grow up, you'll be able to handle a man like Jim."

Little kitten?

What was it about women like her, especially those who shifted into wolves? They always seemed to think they were so much better than the rest of us. Well, she'd soon learn I was anything but a kitten.

"Alpha?" I growled. I didn't take my eyes off Brittney, but I wanted to make sure everyone understood Finn not only knew but approved of what I was about to do.

"Do it. It's time someone taught her a lesson she won't soon forget."

That was all I needed. If I didn't establish myself as Jim's mate now, I'd spend the rest of my life fighting off females trying to claim him for their own. Worse, I'd be admitting I was the weakest of the clan and there was no way I was going to let this bitch or any others like her have any standing over me.

"Remove your hand before I remove it for you," I said softly.

The room fell silent as all eyes focused were on us.

"Cunt." Brittney spun, her nails lengthening as she lashed out.

Time slowed. As her hand slashed toward my face, I leaned back, avoiding the blow. At the same time, I took a step forward and to the left with my left foot. Using her own momentum, I grabbed her wrist with my right hand. My left hand braced against her shoulder. She cried out in pain as I twisted, forcing her arm up behind her. As that happened, I released my hold on her shoulder, grabbing her wrist in my left hand and a handful of blonde hair with my right. It was all done so quickly, she never had a chance to counter.

"Apologize, bitch." My mouth was close to her ear and I nipped that lobe hard enough to draw blood.

"No!"

She lifted her right leg and I moved again. No way did I want one of those stilettos coming down on the top of my foot. Instead of taking the stomp, I shoved her forward, smiling in satisfaction as she fell into a nearby wooden post with a solid thud. For a moment, I thought that would be the end of it. But no, she wasn't that smart. She turned, swiping at the blood pouring from her nose. Then she kicked out of her shoes. Maybe she wasn't completely foolish after all.

On second thought, she was.

She charged with an outraged yell. Her arms were outstretched as if to wrap me up. God, had no one taught her how to fight? I ducked as she tried to grab me and, as I came up, sent a hard forearm into her ribs. Then I danced back, balancing on my toes.

"Stay down," I rasped when she fell to her knees, gasping for breath.

She knelt there, panting, blood dripping from her broken nose onto the floor. Suddenly, she exploded toward me. My tiger fought for control, recognizing a split second before I did that she was starting to shift. I took a step to the side and pivoted just as she leapt. The steel toe of my boot caught her squarely in the kidney. She dropped like a sack of rocks, the shift not only stopped but reversing.

"You bitch!" I spun in the direction of the man's voice, wondering just what in the hell I'd gotten myself into by agreeing to join the clan. As I did, a short but muscular man with hair as blond as Brittney's shoved his way through the crowd in my direction. "You can't do that to my sister."

"Your sister should learn to keep her hands to herself. I'm not going to let some pansy-assed female maul my mate."

Jim's grin threatened to split his face. He was enjoying this, damn him. Typical male. He obviously loved a cat fight.

"Someone needs to teach you your place." The man continued forward, fists lifting into a defensive position.

"Alec, no!" Jim's voice snapped with command. Now it was my turn to grin proudly. Everyone gathered felt his power, the power I'd sensed in him and knew he'd kept carefully under control. But now he unleashed it and Brittney's brother dropped to his knees, his expression stunned.

As Jim stepped over to the man, grabbing a handful of hair and baring his neck, I moved to where Brittney lay. I planted one knee in the small of her back. My right hand grabbed her hair and I pulled her head back. Come morning I might regret what I was about to do but not right now. Right now, she needed to understand that I would not let her live if she ever put her hands on my mate again.

As one, Jim and I looked to our clan leaders. Matt and Finn had taken their places at the head of the room. Now they walked slowly in our direction. Matt stopped in front of his brother and Finn moved to stand before me. Then she knelt in front of Brittney, her expression hard. At the same time, Matt mirrored her actions.

"The only reason the two of you still live is because we hadn't formally announced Jim's and Maggie's mating," the clan leader said. His voice was cold, and a chill ran through me. I prayed he never spoke to me like that.

"If you ever try to violate their vows to one another, they have our permission to deal with you as they see fit," Finn took up. "Brittney, you've been warned before about trying to poach. Don't try it again." Something in Finn's voice told me the blonde had made at least one play for Matt. If she had, I was more than a little surprised she still lived.

"Let them up," Matt told us.

I leaned down, my lips next to Brittney's ear. "If there is a next time, I promise it will be the last. Now get the hell away from me and mine." I shoved her back down and stood. Jim was waiting for me, hand outstretched. I took it and looked to our alphas.

"Come," Matt said simply and led us back to the front of the room. As he did, I hoped the evening held no more surprises.

CHAPTER TWELVE

J im and I followed our Alphas to the front of the room. Once they sat in two comfortable looking wingback chairs, I took up my position behind and to the right of Finn while Jim stood behind and to the left of his brother. Never before had I taken this position in any of the prides I'd belonged to, much less one of the clans. I could understand Matt having Jim standing as his second, especially after Jim's earlier performance. But for Finn to put me, the newest member of the clan, in that role was almost more than I could take in and I'd be a fool for not worrying about how the others would react.

Matt waited a few moments as everyone found seats or places on the floor. As they did, I kept an eye on Brittney and her brother. When it became clear they weren't going to get any sympathy from those gathered, they shoved their way through the crowd and disappeared outside. A few moments later, the sounds of a car speeding up the drive filled the air. As it receded in the distance, I relaxed some. We wouldn't have to worry about a repeat performance for tonight at least.

Who knew, maybe I'd even be able to sit before long. Otherwise, from the way my injured thigh throbbed, I might just fall flat on my face.

Finally, Matt stood. He extended a hand and Finn's hand slid into it. He helped her to her feet. Together they looked at those gathered, those who had sworn their allegiance to them and who they, in turn, had sworn to protect. Watching them, remembering the girl Finn had been, marvel filled me. Despite everything, she had fulfilled the destiny her parents had wanted for her. She was an Alpha in her own right and had found her life mate. Despite everything Michael Jennings had done, Finn had triumphed and I was glad to be there to see it.

"Before we begin, I want to address what just happened." Matt didn't raise his voice. He didn't need to. The moment he spoke, the room fell silent. Even so, there was no mistaking the bite in it. "Maggie Thrasher is a member of our clan. Finn and I asked her to join us because we both knew she would make the clan stronger. The fact that she is also my brother's mate only increases her value to pride and clan. What happened here tonight was not her fault. If anyone is to blame, it is Finn and myself because we hadn't anticipated trouble. But we all know what Brittney is like. There's not a male of breeding age she hasn't made a move on and there's not a mated female she hasn't pushed. She made the mistake tonight of crossing the path of a female almost as strong and definitely as possessive as my wife." He grinned down at Finn then. "Brittney will be told that this was her last warning. We don't need the trouble she can cause with her flirtation. That is all I will say on this at this time."

As one and then another and yet another of the clan members nodded in approval, I breathed easier. Oh, there were a few of the males who looked like they regretted Matt's edict. But it was clear they were not mated. They stood together in a knot at the back of the room. Before Matt had gotten to his feet, they'd been the ones elbowing one another and posturing for position. Pups and cubs, on the whole, and nothing more. Bodies that had grown without their common sense catching up.

The women, on the other hand, all looked like they approved. Those with daughters bent and whispered in the girls' ears, explaining what the clan leader meant. Others eyed their mates and nodded in satisfaction. Clearly, Brittney had sniffed around more male clan members than just Jim.

Foolish bitch.

"Maggie, come here." Finn turned to look at me as she spoke.

Without hesitating, I did as she said. Once I stood before her, I carefully lowered to my knees. As I did, I swallowed against the knot of nausea in my stomach. Pain ran through me, starting at my injured thigh and radiating outward. Doing my best to ignore it, I silently cursed Brittney. I'd risked reinjury by refusing to use my crutches. But now, after having to deal with Brittney, I wondered if I'd torn out the stitches yet again.

Finn rested her hand on the top of my bowed head. Her fingers stroked my hair much as they would if I'd been shifted. For a moment, she said nothing. I waited, wondering what she was about to do.

"I've known Maggie since we were children. She was one of those who stood up for me when my parents were killed and then when Michael Jennings tried to take advantage of me." Her words were clipped and I heard the undercurrents of remembered pain and anger. "She has been a credit to the Tennessee clan where she and her parents moved after Jennings took over the Northern California clan. When her sister's mate assumed leadership of the Northern California clan, she volunteered to return and help rebuild the clan.

"We will go into how she came to be here later. What is important just now is that it was apparent to both Matt and me the first time we saw Maggie and Jim together that they were mates. They just didn't realize it." She smiled at Matt and he grinned in return. Could it be that they hadn't realized they were meant to be mates when they first met? "When they did finally figure it out, we were more than pleased. As you've seen tonight, they are well suited for one another. We approve of their bond and we are very glad Maggie has agreed to join our clan."

She paused and reached down to help me to my feet. As she turned me to face the rest of the clan, I held my breath. I knew she was up to something. What was another matter.

"You each know that I have been looking for someone to fill the role of my second. Sharon has been kind enough to act in that capacity for the last year but that isn't where her passion lies. She'd rather be working with our youngsters, especially those ready for their first shift. It is my pleasure to tell all of you that she will now be doing just that."

It was instantly clear this was good news. Those gathered applauded and called out their support. A few of the children and younger teens who looked and smelled like they could shift soon ran to where Sharon stood at the kitchen entrance. Her smile could have lit the room as she knelt and drew them in. No one with eyes in his head could doubt that she was anything but happy with the news.

"So that leaves the position of my second open. I'm hoping it doesn't stay that way for long." Now Finn touched my arm and I turned to look at her. Mischief danced in her eyes as I did. "Maggie, we ran together as children. We had our first shifts within days of one another. You were the closest thing I had to a sister growing up. I trusted you with my life then and I trust you with my life now. Will you stand with me and for me? Will you be advisor and confidante, and will you help enforce my word and the word of my mate as clan Alphas?"

If we'd been anywhere except at the front of the clan, I'd probably have shaken her. Was she crazy? There had to be others in the clan who were better trained for what she needed and who were certainly stronger than I was. I might not be as well-versed in clan politics, any clan's politics, as Jim but even I knew the clan alpha was usually seconded by the alpha of one of the prides or packs comprising the clan.

But I was stuck. She'd put both of us in a position where I'd undermine her role as female Alpha if I refused. Damn it, I should have remembered that she had learned how to achieve what she thought was the best for the clan at her mother's knee. There'd be no manipulation for personal gain, unless the gain to the clan outweighed it. Not that that helped me any just then.

Well, I could play my part – for the moment. But as soon as we were alone, I'd be reminding her how much I didn't like surprises, especially ones that could blow up in my face later on.

Once more I dropped to my knees. I took her hands and pressed the backs of them to my forehead. Then I lowered to my belly, my forehead touching the floor in front of her feet. "I will do as my Alphas wish. I have pledged my life and my arm to you and to the clan."

To my surprise, it was Matt who helped me to my feet. When he bent to lightly kiss my cheek, it was as if he was giving me his blessing, not only for accepting the role his mate had basically thrust upon me but for my role as mate to his brother. Feeling the acceptance from most of those present, the last of the knots in my stomach began to unwind.

But that wasn't the end of the surprises, not by a long shot. When Matt started the same basic process with his brother, I almost laughed aloud. Jim looked like he had been struck with a two-by-four as Matt asked him to accept the same position Finn had offered me. As he sank to his knees in front of Matt, Jim shot me a look that was part pleading and part panic. Since he hadn't come riding to my rescue, I simply smiled and assumed my place at Finn's side. It was obvious life wasn't going to be dull in this clan.

I just hoped the day never came when I wanted dull.

Two hours later, Matt signaled the end of the meeting. In that time, he'd briefed everyone on what we knew about Volk and the ferals. Photos of Volk had been handed out and I'd been asked to describe what had happened at that fateful clan meeting when Volk's ferals attacked. There had been questions from some of the pack and pride leaders as well as from Tamara and her people. Matt stressed to all gathered that they needed to get the word out to the few lone shapeshifters in the area, those who refused to join the clan for whatever reason. Most of all, if anyone saw or heard anything out of the ordinary, they were to let their pack or pride leaders know. They, in turn, were to report to Matt and Finn.

Even though Matt had ended the meeting, I knew better than to give into temptation. Much as I wanted to drag Finn, possibly by the hair, into the next room and demand an explanation, I didn't. Until everyone else had left, I had a job to do. I might not have asked for the job, but that didn't matter. I was now her right hand, basically her sounding board and protector. Of course, if any trouble did break out, I had no doubt she was better able to handle than was I.

So, instead of dragging her off, I glanced at Jim. He shook his head and shrugged. It looked like he was having an even harder time accepting our new positions than was I. That, at least, reassured me he hadn't known what his brother and sister-in-law had planned. Maybe it also meant he'd help me get a little satisfaction when the time was right.

"Finn," Stefan began as he appeared at her side. "Maggie's been on her feet all evening and without her crutches." I looked down at my feet, feeling like a kid caught sneaking out after curfew.

"Crap! Maggie, you should have said something." Finn scrambled out of her chair and, before I could protest, pushed me into it. "You didn't tear your stitches out in the fight, did you?" Concern filled her voice and she looked at me closely, worried I'd done just that.

"You call that a fight?" I snorted. "What self-respecting shapeshifter wears stilettos to a clan meeting, especially if she's going to be sniffing around another woman's man?"

"That's my girl." Jim grinned down at me.

"I suggest you remember that I don't share." I arched an eyebrow at him.

"Good, because neither do I."

"Sounds familiar," Stefan chuckled. "Now, how's the leg?"

For one brief moment, I considered hedging. Then I changed my mind. For one thing, I had a feeling he'd know if I wasn't completely honest. For another, if I hedged and Jim realized it later, he'd simply call his uncle back out. "I'm hurting, but I don't think I tore the stitches."

"Can you hang on until the others leave?" Matt asked softly. Stefan looked up at him, clearly not happy.

"I can, as long as I don't have to fight anyone else tonight. But why?" Suspicious again, I looked from him to Finn. "Please tell me you don't have any more surprises in store for me."

"No more surprises – at least not tonight." Finn grinned almost wickedly. "But there's no reason to let word get back to Brittney and her brother that you're injured."

Jim's quick intake of breath came at the same time I realized that throughout his discussion about Volk and the ferals, Matt had been careful to avoid mentioning that I'd been hurt. It hadn't registered at first. I'd been too busy watching everyone else, gauging their reactions. Now that I thought about it, I heaved a sigh of relief. I didn't think Brittney was foolish enough to try to come at me again, but I'd thwarted her attempt to get into Jim's pants. Worse, I'd embarrassed her. What Jim had done to her brother was even worse in a way because he'd stopped the young man with a single word.

Eyes widening in disbelief, I looked up at Jim. Oh my God.

"I think Maggie's figured it out," Finn said softly, humor clear.

"I think you're right, but my big brother's not as smart as she is." Matt's right arm deflected the head slap Jim aimed at him.

"What the hell are you talking about?" He glanced at his brother and sister-in-law before looking at me. As he did, Stefan barked out a short laugh and, after telling me he'd see me at the house in a few minutes, he moved away. Wise man. Maybe he'd take me with him.

When neither of the clan leaders said anything – hell, they didn't even try. They just stood there grinning like loons – I held out a hand and waited until Jim took it. Carefully, I climbed to my feet, shaking my head when he tried to keep me from rising. Then, not wanting to have this conversation in front of Matt and Finn, who were clearly enjoying themselves a bit too much at our expense, I led Jim toward the kitchen.

"Out."

Sharon looked from her brother to me and grinned much like Matt had a few moments before. Then she motioned for Danny to come with her. Before leaving, she lightly patted my arm and wished me good luck. Then they were gone, moving across the main room in the direction from which we'd come from.

"Maggie?" Jim sounded confused and a little worried.

"When this is over, we are definitely killing your brother and sister-in-law. Then we will torment your sister because I have no doubt she was as involved in what happened tonight as were they," I growled.

"Okay, but why? I'll admit being named their seconds tonight was a surprise, but you've got more on your mind than that."

"Darlin', you really don't know, do you?" Smiling, I reached up and took his face in my hands. He bent and touched his forehead to mine. Then, as his hands pressed against my ass, pulling me close, I rested my head against his chest.

"Maggie, what are you talking about?"

"Think back to when Brittney's brother tried to intervene earlier."

He didn't say anything. He didn't have to. His expression said it all. I knew the moment he realized what I'd meant. The color drained from his face and he swallowed audibly. He closed his eyes. I wondered if he was counting to ten or to one thousand. A moment later he looked down at me, a smile playing at the corners of his mouth.

"Damn him," he said softly.

"Who?" Now I was really confused.

"Matt." He cast a look at his brother. From where he stood, Matt grinned and touched a finger to his forehead in a salute. "He's told me for years that I'm an alpha and I needed to stop holding back. I never really believed him. I've always been happy just being there to support him. But seeing that bastard Alec coming at you, I didn't hold back. I couldn't. There was no way I was going to let him lay a hand on you." He bent his head and nuzzled my hair.

"Now you know how I feel." I reached up and kissed him, doing my best to ignore the way Finn whistled in approval. I really was going to have to figure out a good way to get back at her. She was enjoying all this way too much. "Are you okay?" I asked when he didn't say anything.

"Yeah." He smiled and hugged me close. "It's going to take some getting used to. At least there are no pride openings right now. All I want to concentrate on is us."

"Good." I cast a quick look around, pleased to see most everyone had already left. "Let's go home. The sooner we let Matt and Finn explain or apologize or whatever they want to do and let Stefan take a look at my leg, the sooner we can finally be alone."

And that was all I really wanted just then.

"Are you all right?" Jim asked an hour later as he closed the door behind his brother and sister-in-law and leaned against it.

I gave a shrug, not sure how to respond. In the last few days, my life had taken more twists and turns than ever before. I'd been arrested after almost being killed. I'd found my mate, something I most certainly hadn't been looking for. I'd decided not to return to the clan I'd joined less than a year before, despite knowing my sister might never forgive me. I'd taken the markings of a new clan and now found myself named the female alpha's second. None of which mattered nearly as much as the fact I'd wiped the floor with a bitch foolish enough to try to make a move on my man.

What the hell had happened to the calm and detached Maggie Thrasher I'd been the last few years?

Seeing how Jim watched me, concern reflected in his eyes, I held out a hand. He was the one thing I was sure about. We didn't know each other, not really, but that didn't matter. We were meant for one another. Together we were whole. It was something I'd never really understood when my parents and others talked about what it was like to find their mate. For one thing, not everyone did. That made me one of the lucky ones.

"I'm fine. You heard Stefan."

I was pretty sure the entire county heard him as he told me exactly how big of a fool I'd been for being out without my crutches, not to mention fighting Brittney. Then, after confirming I'd managed not to tear the stitches out, he relented a little. Even so, his instructions had been to the point. I wasn't to go anywhere without at least a cane and, if I was going to be up for long, I was to be on the crutches. If I disobeyed, he'd sedate me and tie me to bed until my thigh healed.

"I also heard him saying you hadn't helped your recovery any."

"Jim, I'm all right." I waited until he sat next to me on the sofa and then climbed onto his lap, wrapping my arms around him and nuzzling his neck. "I'd forgotten that Finn has a warped sense of humor and it's obvious Matt has been a bad influence on her." I grinned up at Jim and nipped his jaw.

"Matt!" he snorted. "I'd say Finn's been a bad influence on him except I think it's mutual." His arms tightened around me and he buried his face against my hair. "And I have a feeling that they aren't done with us yet."

I sighed and nodded. "Maybe we can figure a way to deflect their plans?"

The look Jim gave me reminded me of old Mrs. Lawson back in grade school when I'd answered a question with an extremely foolish response. "Hey, a girl can hope!"

"We could go on a very long vacation. Maybe by the time we get back, they'll have found a new target."

Laughing, I reached up and kissed him. "I do like how you think. But, with my luck, they'd decide to come with us. Or worse, they'd wait until we got back and they'd be plotting and planning the whole time we were gone."

His arms tightened around me. My breath caught as desire filled me. God, I wanted him. But there was something else I wanted, something we hadn't done together yet.

"Jim, I want to hunt."

I tilted my head so I could see his expression. The moment the words were out of my mouth, I could see his concern. I knew he was worried about my injured thigh. But I'd fought for him tonight and now I wanted to hunt with him. Surely he could understand.

He touched his brow to mine and then tilted his head so he could rub his cheek against mine. As he did, I relaxed. He wasn't going to say no. Unlike so many men, especially shapeshifter males, he wasn't going to try to over-protect me. At least I didn't think so. Well, if he did, he'd learn pretty quickly that wasn't the way to deal with me.

"I'd like that." He nuzzled me again before leaning back, a slight smile on his lips. "You've seen the security setup here. We'll be safe hunting."

Grinning, I brushed my lips over his and climbed off his lap. His laughter rang out as I reached down and stripped off my tank top. A moment later, he stood and stripped. With a grin, he dropped to his hands and knees. Muscles tensed and his back arched. A growl escaped his lips as he tossed back his head. I knelt before him, watching as he began his shift.

Never before had watching another person shift been so personal, so sensual. It was almost like a dance of seduction and my snow tiger pressed for release. Soon, very soon, but I wanted to see this through. That part of me that still hadn't quite accepted the fact Jim and I were mated needed this. There was always a moment of disorientation after a shift. If you were smart, you never put yourself within striking range until the shifted animal had a chance to get its bearings. But, if we truly were mated, his panther would recognize me even if disorientated. I had to know.

All questions and doubts disappeared as the sleek black head butted against me. He opened his mouth and his canines flashed in the light. Then he licked my cheek before nuzzling my hair. When his lifted his left front paw and pulled at my bra, I laughed gaily. He was just as impatient in feline form as he was in human.

Thankfully.

I grabbed his head and rubbed his ears. Then I lightly nipped his nose. He ducked his head and pushed, shoving me onto my butt. Laughing, I removed my bra and let it drop to the floor. A few moments later, I'd shed the rest of my clothes. Forgotten was the fight with Brittney. Forgotten was the throbbing in my thigh. Nothing mattered beyond shifting and hunting with my mate. Everything else could wait until morning.

CHAPTER THIRTEEN

The soft strains of *I Shot the Sheriff* penetrated the layers of sleep. Not ready to be up, I ground my face deeper into the pillow, except it wasn't a pillow. It was too warm and too hard. A smile touched my lips as my sleep-fogged mind identified Jim. Still smiling, I pressed my lips to his chest before settling back to sleep some more. As I did, the arm tossed over my waist tightened slightly. Then his other hand ran down the leg I'd thrown over him as he muttered that it was too early to be up.

Since I happened to agree, I didn't argue. Unfortunately, *I Shot the Sheriff* started up again. Just a couple of cords, enough to be recognizable and then silence. When it sounded seconds later, my brain grudgingly identified it. Someone was calling Jim. That had to be it. For one thing, I was pretty sure I killed my cell phone when I tossed it against the wall a couple days ago. I'd been so angry at Declan that I hadn't tried it since then and, with everything that had happened since then, I hadn't even thought about it until now.

"Jim, answer your phone."

I rolled off him and smiled as he grunted in ill-temper when the phone sounded yet again. There was a slight breeze as he tossed back the sheet. The bed shifted as he sat up. His hand patted my bare ass and I turned to him, opening one eye, only to groan to realize it was still dark outside.

Dear God, what time was it?

He stood and stumbled across the room, mumbling something about killing whoever had the audacity to call so early. Doing my best not to laugh, I reached over to switch on the lamp. New aches and pains registered, ones that had nothing to do with my encounter with Volk or the fight with Brittney. These kind of aches and pains I'd gladly suffer for the rest of my life as long as Jim was the cause.

"Where the hell are my pants?" Jim demanded, squinting as the light came on.

"Over the back of the chair."

He nodded and grabbed for them, his hands searching the pockets. A moment later he produced the phone. He answered the call and listened closely to whoever was on the other end. Watching him pace the confines of the room, shadows playing off the long lines of his legs and back, desire returned. He couldn't return to bed soon enough to suit me.

"Say that again."

Desire fled to hear the concern in his voice. Without a word, I tossed back the sheet and sat up. As much as I didn't want him having to go anywhere but back to bed with me, I hoped this was a call out to an accident scene or routine drunk and disorderly. I couldn't hear what the caller said but I heard enough to know I didn't recognize the voice. Maybe that meant whatever the call was about, it didn't involve Volk. But I had a sinking feeling in the pit of my stomach that it did.

Damn it, why couldn't I have killed that bastard when I had the chance?

A few moments later, Jim tossed the phone onto the bed and moved to the closet. When he turned, I knew he was worried. Without a word, I moved to him and slid my arms around him, holding him close. I wanted him to know I was here for him, no matter what.

"Tell me," I said as I stepped back.

"A couple of local fishermen found a body near the river. They told Dispatch it looked like maybe coyotes or wolves attacked."

My stomach did a lurch and I dropped onto the edge of the mattress. Coyotes don't attack humans and wolves don't except in very rare circumstances. It had to be Volk or his ferals. From the look on Jim's face, he felt so as well.

"I need to shower and get out to the scene." He turned to me and rubbed his hands over his face as if he could scrub away the last of the exhaustion he felt. "Will you make some coffee and then call Matt and let him know? Tell him I'll call as soon as I've had a chance to check the scene."

"Of course." I'd do whatever he needed. But he had to do something for me as well and I had a pretty good feeling he wasn't going to like it. Well, that was too bad. We'd already discussed how I needed to finish what first brought me here. Maybe now I had the chance to do just that. "Answer one question first. Do you think Volk had anything to do with it?"

He sighed and the look he gave me spoke volumes. Unless I missed my guess, I'd asked the one question he'd been hoping I wouldn't. For a moment, I wondered if he'd try to deny it. Then he sighed and moved to sit next to me on the edge of the mattress. His left arm went around my shoulders, pulling me close. I let him hold me, both comforting and drawing comfort.

"I'm trying to convince myself that he can't be involved but part of me is worried this is his opening salvo." He pressed his lips to the top of my head and then stood. "So I don't have any time to waste. I'd really appreciate it if you'd call Matt and tell him what you can and let him know I'll report in as soon as I know anything." Now he smiled slightly, his hand cupping my cheek. "And I'll love you forever if you fix me some coffee."

"Jim." That's all I said. He looked down at me and blew out a breath. His mouth firmed, and I knew he was trying to figure out what to say to convince me to stay behind. Well, good luck with that. "I need to go with you."

"Maggie, you can't." He moved back to my side and reached for my hand, his fingers linking with mine. "We don't know that this is Volk's work and, if it's not, I can't have you there. I know you'd do nothing to compromise the scene, but your presence would compromise the case. A good defense attorney would want to know why I brought a civilian to a crime scene and then use that to undermine my status with the judge and jury."

I understood his concerns, but he had to realize that I was right too. Somehow there had to be a way we could do this. Damn it, for once in my life I wished I shifted into something a bit more common than a white tiger. As a coyote or wolf, I'd be able to shift and then just wander up to the scene and take a look around. Of course, I'd have to be careful to make sure one of the cops didn't take a shot at me, but it would be worth it.

Well, it was night. Maybe I could go in shifted and just stay in the shadows. There had to be an answer.

"You're thinking awfully hard." He tilted my face up and looked into my eyes. "What's going through that brain of yours?"

"Jim, I don't want to do anything to compromise your investigation if this doesn't have anything to do with Volk. But I know his scent and I know what to look for if his ferals were involved. You'd know if another of our kind had been in the area at the time of the killing but not if it was Volk. I have to go."

He shook his head and stared at the ceiling. I could almost hear his mind working as he weighed what I said against the realities of his job. Frankly, if I knew the area, I'd simply find out where the scene was and go on my own. I could sneak in close enough to catch the scent if Volk or a feral had been there. But I didn't so I needed Jim to work with me on this. I just hoped he realized how important this was. Otherwise, he'd learn firsthand just how stubborn I can be.

"Damn it, you're right. Not that I like it or that it makes my job any easier." He shook his head, frustration clear. "I probably should have asked you this before, but what do you do? Your job, I mean. Is it something we can use as a reason for your presence at the scene?"

For a moment, I didn't say anything. I was too surprised to. Between everything that had happened and realizing that we were mates, there hadn't been a lot of discussion about our lives. It simply hadn't dawned on me to talk about things like where we went to college and what our favorite colors were because we felt so right together. But at least now I could, hopefully, ease at least some of his concerns.

"Believe it or not, I'm an attorney. I handled a lot of the clan's legal business when I was still in Tennessee. I wasn't licensed in California because they don't have reciprocity with other jurisdictions and before I could take the modified Bar Exam they offer lawyers licensed elsewhere, Volk attacked the clan. That sort of put everything else on hold. But my license in Tennessee is still valid."

"Then that's our out. Your client sent you here as part of your investigation into some case – we can flesh that out later if we need to – and when the call came in, it was close enough to something you'd run into before I decided you might be of help." He gave a decisive nod. "You get the coffee started and I'll call Matt. Then we'll shower and dress and get on our way."

Now that had been settled, he had a duty to do and nothing was going to stop him. Not that I wanted to. If Volk was involved, the sooner we got there, the sooner we had a chance of getting on his trail. If not, well, hopefully the fishermen had been wrong and this was nothing more than a false alarm.

"When we get there, I want you to stay in the SUV until I send for you," Jim said fifteen minutes later as we sped away from the ranch. "At least one of my men should already be there, but I want to make sure the scene is secured."

"I understand. You don't have to worry."

"I know, sweetheart." He glanced over and smiled. Then he hit the lights and siren and floored the accelerator. "Snyder is on duty tonight. So it's possible he'll have responded. If he is, I'll handle him."

"Jim, I'll follow your lead. I promise." I lightly touched his arm, not wanting to distract him but wanting him to know I meant what I said. "Just so you know, this won't be my first crime scene. I interned with the Nashville District Attorney's Office. I know what I should and shouldn't do."

"I knew you were pretty close to perfect." He shot me a grin and I fought the urge to suggest he pull over for a few minutes so I could show him just how perfect I was, at least for him. I probably ought to ask Finn if the desire ever eased up any. I wasn't going to guarantee I could keep it in check all the time and throwing him down on the table during Christmas dinner could be a bit embarrassing. "Now, if you'd been a defense attorney, we might have had a problem."

"Well," I drawled and then laughed. "The only time I played defense attorney was when I had to get one of our people out of jail after losing control and fighting. It didn't happen often and, fortunately, never went past misdemeanor charges."

"That's not criminal law. That's just housekeeping." He slowed and turned onto a side road I hadn't realized was there. The flashing of lights against the dark sky pinpointed where we were going. Jim reached for the radio and let Dispatch know he was on-scene. Half a mile or so later, he pulled in behind a patrol car and parked. "Let me see what's going on. When I give the nod, come join us. I'm hoping I don't need your eyes and nose, but I'm afraid I might."

So was I, unfortunately.

"I'll be right here."

He gave my hand a quick squeeze and then stepped out of the SUV. I watched as he crossed to where Officer Snyder stood with two men I assumed were the fishermen who'd made the initial report. Jim shook hands with his officer and then listened as Snyder quickly reported. Then he turned to the two men, motioning for them to lead him somewhere. My guess was they were going to the body.

And that was my cue to get out. I waited until the men were

almost out of sight. Then I carefully eased open the passenger door and stepped out. There was just a hint of dawn starting to touch the eastern horizon. The night air was filled with the sounds of crickets and frogs and all the sounds that made me feel at home. But ruining the peace of the night were the agitated voices of the fishermen as they recounted their tale for Jim and the sharp smell of blood and other things I didn't want to think about that hung in the air.

Leaning heavily on the cane Stefan insisted I use if I was too stubborn to use my crutches, I stepped around to the front of the SUV. Then I tilted my head back and closed my eyes. As I did, I eased my control, letting my tiger come closer to the surface. I didn't dare shift, not with so many normals around. But I needed the enhanced senses of my cat to tell me if others of our kind had been around. Even as I did, I prayed my suspicions were wrong.

God, how I wanted them to be wrong.

I breathed deeply once, twice and then a third time. There! It was just a hint, almost hidden by the stench from the kill. But beneath that stench was the same foul, carrion-like odor I knew meant Volk had been there. Recognizing it, I ground my teeth in frustration. I didn't know whether to be relieved or furious as the stench dissipated. He'd been here but it had been hours ago. He was gone now, but where?

Just as important, had he been alone?

I sniffed again. Nothing. Before I could do anything else, the sound of a step on the road had my eyes flying open. Jim stood a few feet away, looking as grim as I felt. At his unasked question, I simply nodded, trusting him to understand. The way his hand fisted at his side was all the confirmation I needed. Then he moved to my side. After a quick glance down the road to where Officer Snyder stood with the fishermen, he reached for my hand and gave it a quick squeeze.

"I need you to look at the scene, see if you think Volk's responsible. Just because he was in the area doesn't mean he did the kill."

As he spoke, I nodded, not quite sure I agreed. But Jim was a cop and he had to do his duty, especially if it meant he could actually tie the murder to a normal and not one of our kind. Not that he'd ever let an innocent man go to jail. No, like me, he hoped there was a mundane explanation for what had happened. That would make his job a whole lot easier.

"All right."

Part of me wanted to ask him to tell me what he could about the scene and the victim. But another part knew why he hadn't volunteered any information yet. He wanted me to come to my own decisions without anything he said – or didn't say – influencing me. I'd probably be doing the same if our roles were reversed.

Not that I wanted to see the body. Unlike the Hollywood movies, we don't go around hunting normals and killing them. At least not if we want to keep living. There are few laws we enforce on our own kind but the hunting of normals is a capital offense, especially these days when forensic science can all too easily reveal our existence. The fact that our animal selves hunt and kill animals isn't enough to prepare for the sight of a dead body, especially not one who met their end through violence. That's something I'd learned during my internship. Hopefully tonight I wouldn't toss my dinner the way I had that time.

Knowing there was no sense in putting off the inevitable, I shoved away from the SUV. As I did, Jim nodded in approval. Then he matched his pace to mine as I moved toward Snyder and the fishermen. As we neared, I reminded myself that I was here not as Jim's mate but as a professional. We didn't need Snyder questioning my presence, at least not in front of the civilians. Most of all, we needed the normals to leave me alone long enough for me to have a chance to examine the body.

God, don't let me throw up or do anything equally embarrassing.

"Chief?" Snyder's surprised question was enough to let me know he recognized me. So much for hoping he wouldn't.

"I believe you remember Ms. Thrasher, Officer."

Damn him, I could hear the smile in his voice even if Snyder didn't.

"Sir, what's she doing here?"

I had to give it to the kid, at least he hadn't reached for his gun – yet. Even so, it was obvious he was more than a bit suspicious. I guess I couldn't blame him. The last time he'd seen me, he'd been convinced I'd just killed someone and he'd arrested me. His last sight of me was after Jim had secured me in the rear of the SUV and we left, purportedly for county jail.

"Stand down, Snyder." Jim placed a reassuring hand on his rookie's shoulder. "Ms. Thrasher is one of the good guys. She's an attorney who's here on a case, one that might just have something to do with our DB. After Dispatch called me, I sent for her, asking if she'd like to take a look around and share information."

For a moment, Snyder said nothing. Then he nodded. The way his suspicion seemed to flow away from him told me a lot. He trusted Jim implicitly. Good. Not only did it mean Jim was one of those cops who took their duty seriously but that he was also a cop others looked up to. It also meant Snyder wasn't going to ask questions I'd just as soon not have to answer.

"Ma'am, wish I'd known that earlier." He touched a finger to the brim of his cap and I smiled slightly. I wasn't sure it would have changed anything, but it was good of him to say it.

"Don't worry about it, Officer. You were just doing your job." I smiled, hoping I didn't blush as Jim nodded in approval. "Chief, shall we?"

"Snyder, finish taking these two gentlemen's statements and then wait for the coroner. We'll be back in a few minutes."

Jim took my arm, like any Texas gentleman would do, and escorted me off the pavement and down a slight embankment. As he did, he clicked on his flashlight. Seeing the tall grass and hearing the sounds of the river nearby, I was glad I'd worn my boots. I might be a big, strong white tiger when shifted, but in this form there was one thing sure to scare me – snakes. I had no doubt those slithery little devils loved this tall grass and were just looking for a piece of tasty flesh to snack on. I'd just as soon it not be mine.

I didn't need Jim's soft directions to lead me to the body, not when the stench of death got stronger with each step we took. But, in case Snyder or the others were watching, I kept up the pretense. We had enough to worry about without having them wondering how I knew where to go.

"Shit!"

It was out before I could stop it. Near the edge of the water, looking more like a pile of rags than anything else, lay the body. Jim's light played over it and then over the ground around it. The ground was wet, and I could see the signs of struggle. But what I didn't see were paw prints. Of course, I could be missing them so I moved closer to the body, careful of where I stepped.

Three feet from the body I stopped and crouched, sitting back on my heels. Without a word, I held out my hand. A moment later, Jim placed the flashlight in my palm. Then he knelt at my side, looking on as I shone the light over the ground. I was stalling because I really didn't want to see the body. But what I'd seen so far had me doubting my initial conclusion. Volk had been in the area but now I wasn't as sure that he'd been involved in what happened here.

"Maggie?" Jim prompted softly when I finally shone the light on the body.

The man, at least I think he'd been a man, lay on his side. His legs had been drawn up and his arms covered his head. He wore jeans and what had been a white tee shirt. Blood and dirt covered him. I could see a number of slashing wounds in his arms and side and my nose told me his abdomen had been opened. But there was one thing my nose didn't scent. I didn't smell a shapeshifter on him and I would if he'd been attacked by one of our kind.

"Volk was here, at least nearby, but he didn't do this." I stood and moved away from the body before handing the flashlight back to Jim. "But you knew that."

"No, I suspected it. I needed you to confirm it." He looked back at the road, making sure no one could see us. Then he reached for my hands and pulled me so we stood toe to toe. "You know what one of his kill zones looks and smells like. I don't. I needed you to confirm my suspicion that Volk hadn't done this while in human form." He paused and I knew he was waiting to see if I believed him.

"I know. Sorry. I don't do dead bodies well." I smiled slightly, glad for the way he still held my hands. I needed the contact just then. "The only ones I scented down here are those two up there and your rookie. I'd suggest taking a closer look at your so-called witnesses."

"I plan on it." He blew out a breath. "I can say this to you and know you'll understand. I'm relieved the victim isn't one of us and that this wasn't Volk's doing. But what I want to know is why Volk was here and where has he gone?"

Those were questions I'd like answered as well. But, for now, all I could do was shrug. "I need to come back after it's light and have a look around. How long do you think your people will be here?"

"I don't know. Depends on what those two jokers up there tell us." He released my hands and took a step back as the lights of a large vehicle coming down the road hit us. "Coroner," he said softly.

"Go do your job, Chief. I'll wait at the SUV until you're through."

"No." He dug into his pocket and pulled out his keys. "Go on home. Call Matt and let him know what we've found here. The good news is that this wasn't one of Volk's kills. The bad news – and the good – is that we know Volk is still in the area. Matt will get in touch with Tamara and she will get a team out here. We've clan members who shift into coyote and wolf forms. That will let them sniff around without raising any red flags until my people are done here."

I didn't like it. I wanted to be part of the search. But I also knew he was right. We'd risked a lot by me just being there now. So, instead of arguing, I nodded and took the keys. Then he took my arm and escorted me back to the SUV, telling Snyder as we passed that he'd be right back.

"If you aren't sure about how to get back, use the GPS. Just say *home,*" he said as he helped me in behind the steering wheel. "I may need you to come get me later. I won't know for a while. Since you pretty much killed your cell phone–" Now he grinned and I rolled my eyes. –"when you talk to Matt, ask him to have Finn bring you a new one. Then call me so I have the number."

"All right." I reached up and lightly caressed his cheek. "Be careful."

"Always."

His hand closed over mine and it was very, very hard not to lean in and kiss him. Before I could give into temptation, he stepped back and closed the door. Then, with a quick wave, he turned and moved back toward Snyder and the others. I watched for a few moments and then slid the key into the ignition. I couldn't do anything else here but maybe I could at home or, better yet, at Tamara's. But first things first. I needed to get back to the ranch and call Matt. Maybe by then, Jim would have called with a bit more information.

As I pulled up the drive, a smile touched my lips and I shook my head. I should have known. Parked out front was a Mustang I'd already come to know. Finn sat on the front steps, her head thrown back, her expression relaxed. Then, as if just realizing I was there, she stood and stretched. I didn't have to ask why she'd come. It wouldn't surprise me to know she'd driven over as soon as Jim had called Matt. Not that I minded.

"You could have gone inside," I said as I climbed out of the SUV. In fact, I wished she had. Then I wouldn't have to try to remember the security code. The last thing Jim needed right now was to have me set the thing off and the security company send the local cops out to check on a possible break-in.

"I will now that you're here." Finn unlocked the front door and quickly entered the disarm code. Then she flipped on the lights, looking me up and down. "Well?"

"It wasn't him." I tossed Jim's keys into the basket on the half-wall separating the entry hall from the family room. "But don't relax yet. He had been in the area and recently. I scented him. But the killing was done by a normal. My bet is on the fishermen who claimed to have found the victim."

"I don't know whether to be glad or not." She frowned and dug out her cell phone. "Let me call Matt and fill him in. Then you can tell me everything."

I nodded and started toward the kitchen. Before going more than a couple of steps, I remembered what Jim had said. "Finn, my cell phone is trashed." When she grinned, reminding me that she'd been there when I'd basically thrown it against the wall, I rolled my eyes. Well, at least it hadn't really been mine. It was one Declan had gotten for me before sending me and the others after Volk.

"And Jim figured I could set you up with another one."

I nodded.

"I'll take care of it. Why don't you put on a fresh pot of coffee? I'll call Matt while you do."

Since coffee sounded very good just then, I nodded and went to do as she said. Besides, it gave me a few minutes to duck into the bedroom and make the bed before she saw Jim and I had been together before he'd been called out. It was foolish, I know. If anyone understood what it meant to be mated, especially when you hadn't been looking for it and really hadn't even believed in life mates before having it smack you in the face, it was Finn. But what I had with Jim was still so new, I wasn't sure I believed it yet. I sure didn't want to face any teasing about it, at least not until I knew Volk was dealt with. Maybe then, with that stressor done, I'd relax about my relationship with Jim.

"Matt said to tell you thanks. He's going to contact the heads of the neighboring clans and ask them to meet with us day after tomorrow. That should give everyone time to get here. It's time we let everyone know what's going on. The more eyes on the lookout for Volk the better."

All I could do was nod. That was exactly what I'd told Declan he needed to do after Volk's attack at that fateful clan meeting a lifetime ago. He'd refused, not wanting to appear weak before any of his peers. The fact that Matt was doing so now simply confirmed that I'd done the right thing in agreeing to join the clan. Of course, I still needed to talk to my sister. By now she knew I'd left the Northern California clan. Matt or Finn would have informed Declan and he would have told Eileen. Frankly, it worried me that she hadn't called. Well, it was something I could do later, while waiting to hear from Jim to get home.

"Finn, do you have any idea how good it is to hear that?"

"Yeah, I do." She slid an arm around my waist and led me into the kitchen. "Maggie, you don't have to worry about betraying Declan. I really do understand why he kept this to himself. But I also know what sort of culture shock you're going through. I'd been on my own since leaving California. I made the choice not to associate with any of our kind until I knew it was safe. In other words, until I knew Jennings was frying in Hell.

"I'd been in Fort Worth for a while, longer than I'd been anywhere in years, when Jennings' trackers cornered me in a parking garage. God was looking out for me that day because Matt scented us and realized there was trouble. He came speeding around the corner and stopped next to me just as the trackers hit me with a Taser. One of them had already knifed me." She paused and I gave her the time she needed.

"Matt took me to his place, assuring me they'd never find us. I didn't realize until later he was an alpha, much less the clan leader. But, by then, I knew he was the sort of alpha our kind needed, someone who realized how times are changing and how we have to figure out a way to be prepared for the day when our existence is finally revealed. He doesn't put up with bullshit, but he also doesn't hide behind tradition or worry about his ego."

"That sounds a lot like your dad." I reached across the table for her hand. "And I have a pretty good idea that you're a lot like your mom, which means I need to remember never to cross you."

She grinned and gave my hand a squeeze. "You knew that much when we were kids."

"True." And it was. She'd been the protector back then even if she had also been the one to lead us into trouble. "Now, why don't you see what's in the fridge for breakfast while I put the coffee on? Jim said he'd call as soon as he knew something more."

A few moments later, we worked side by side, laughing and talking almost as if all those years apart had never happened.

CHAPTER FOURTEEN

"You were right. Those so-called witnesses finally admitted that the vic had been one of their fishing buddies. Seems they went down to the river last night after spending some time in a club near the college. Of course, they'd also stopped and picked up a case of beer to keep them company overnight. One thing led to another and, as best as I can tell, the vic insulted the wife of one of his buddies. The wife also happens to be the other buddy's sister. They came to blows and, well, you saw the result."

"What's going to happen to them?" I cradled the phone between my shoulder and ear and limped into the den.

"That will be up to the DA and then a jury." He paused and even though he must have put his hand over the receiver to muffle what he was saying, I knew he was talking to someone else. "Sorry, Maggie. I need to finish up here on the scene and then go in and deal with the paperwork."

"I know. How long will you be?"

"It's almost noon now. I doubt I'll be able to get away before at least six."

I sighed and sank onto the sofa. "You do what you need to. Don't worry about me."

"I'll always worry about you." His voice was soft, as if he was trying to keep from being overheard. I grinned. He really was sweet.

"Then you'd better understand that it goes both ways, Chief." And he'd better. Our lives were dangerous enough because of our shapeshifter nature. The fact that he was a cop, well, that meant even more danger. "So you'd better take care of my cop."

"I will." I could hear his grin. "You stay at the ranch unless you're with Finn."

I shook my head. We'd known each other less than a week and he already knew me too well. Or at least it seemed that way. I had planned to go back to the scene and have a look around. It had been all I could do to stay at the ranch until he called. Of course, his insight could be because of Finn. She'd been with me since I returned to the ranch and she did know me well enough to guess what I wanted to do.

If I agreed to do as he said, there was no way I'd be returning to the scene, at least not today. Finn had already told me she wasn't letting me go back there. She'd reminded me that I was not back to one hundred percent. Nor was I in any way associated with the official investigation. Besides, Tamara and several others were already out there, sniffing around.

And I do mean sniffing. They were there in their animal forms. That way no one would take a second look at them. Well, not unless they realized there were more coyotes and wolves and wild cats of various shapes and forms around than usual. But the chance of that happening was slim. Tamara's people were experts at moving around undetected.

So that left me to sit here and wait. Unless Finn agreed to take me to Tamara's office. At least there I could work on tracking Volk through more mundane methods.

"Don't worry, Jim. Finn's already read me the riot act." I grinned at my old friend as she appeared from the kitchen. "Just promise me that you'll be careful."

"I will. Now let me talk to Finn for a second."

Rolling my eyes, I held the phone out to Finn. Since I had a pretty good idea what my mate was going to tell her, I stood and returned to the kitchen. Maybe another cup of coffee would help. It had been early, much too early, when Jim and I left the ranch this morning. As a result, I felt like I was dragging. That wasn't good. Not with confirmation Volk was still in the area.

A few minutes later, a mug of fresh coffee in hand, I stepped onto the back porch. From there, I could watch the horses in the pasture behind the house. Overhead, a couple of hawks circled lazily. Several people worked in the fields, schooling the horses and doing other every day activities I'd probably have to learn in order to help out.

"Are you all right?" Finn asked when she joined me.

"Just tired." And I was.

"Maggie." She reached out and turned me so I looked at her. "Well, at least you aren't pissed."

My brow furrowed, and I cocked my head. Why would I be pissed? Then the answer dawned on me I shook my head. "No, I'm not pissed." I sipped and turned my attention back to the horses. "But I'll admit it's a little disconcerting to know that Jim understands me well enough already to realize I planned on returning to the scene this morning."

"Maggs, he knows because it's what he'd want to do if your roles were reversed. Besides, he knows that's exactly what I'd want to do, and he told me just now that he has a feeling that you and I are an awful lot alike. I, of course, told him he was a very lucky man." She grinned mischievously and I laughed. I could almost hear her saying just that. "He's also worried about you. Yes, you've almost fully recovered but you aren't there yet. He doesn't want you risking yourself against Volk until you're completely healed. Nor does he want you going after Volk on your own. On both of those, I can agree.

"But I also know you. I know you're going to go crazy if we just sit around the house waiting for Jim to get home." She waited until I nodded in confirmation. "So, how about we go to Tamara's and see what we can do from there? Jim's going to call when he's on his way home. I promise you'll be here to meet him."

I tried not to smile. That had been my second choice of things to do. Not that Finn needed to know. It was bad enough that Jim knew me well enough to anticipate my moves. No need to tell Finn she did as well.

"All right." I drained my mug.

"When do you want to leave?"

"After we clean the kitchen. I hate coming home to a mess."

Finn rolled her eyes. Then she nodded. This time I did smile. When we'd started talking about what to do for breakfast, she reminded me in no uncertain terms that she didn't cook. Well, that wasn't exactly true. She could cook. She just didn't like to. That was all right, since I did. Cooking was something I did not only for enjoyment but when I needed to think, to work things out. So, I'd made a spinach frittata with bacon and cheddar. Then I'd sliced some fresh fruit. By the time everything was done, there'd been a sink full of dishes. No way did I want to come home to that sort of a mess later.

"You cooked, so I'll clean." She held the door and waited as I limped back inside. I poured myself another mug of coffee and took my place at the kitchen table, watching as she moved to the sink. "Tell me, Maggs, what are you going to do about a job?"

"As soon as we've dealt with Volk, I'll apply to take the Bar Exam."

Finn turned to look at me, a smile on her lips. "You did become a lawyer. I'd wondered. I know your dad always wanted you to."

"Not quite. He wanted me to become a lawyer and join his firm. I only did the first." Now I grinned a little ruefully.

"What sort of law?" She abandoned the dishes and joined me at the table.

"I interned with the Nashville DA's Office. After passing the Bar, I had a general practice, so I did a little bit of everything but I mostly practiced corporate law. A lot of my work was for the clan, but I had a large number of normals as clients as well."

She nodded, her expression thoughtful. "Danny works for the DA's Office. I'm sure he'd be glad to show you around and make introductions if you'd like."

"I would like that – after we deal with Volk. I can't worry about anything else until then."

"I know, Maggs." She cocked her head to one side, studying me. "Tamara and I were talking yesterday–"

"Of course, you were." I grinned. I had no doubts Finn had been talking to any number of people about me and what needed to be done.

She grinned and shook her head before continuing. "We were talking, and she asked if I thought you'd like to work at the security firm until you decided what to do on a more permanent basis. You impressed her the other day. You know the systems we use, and you know the legal system."

"All right."

I almost laughed to see the stunned look on Finn's face. She'd obviously thought she'd have to try to convince me. Damn but it was as much fun to surprise her now as it had been when we were teenagers.

Shaking her head, Finn reached over and gave my hand a pat. Then she stood and moved back to the sink. "Nicely played, Maggs. I'll call Tamara when we get to the shop and let her know. I promise she'll head back in to brief you on what she's found at the scene and then she'll get you set up in an office. I think you'll agree that she's a good boss."

"You sound like you work for her." Which surprised me. I knew about her work with CJ. That made sense considering her interest – and talent – in art. But this?

"I do part-time. I fill in when she needs an extra body or when she needs some work done on the computers." Plates clattered as she filled the dishwasher. "I am good, really good, at two things, Maggs – drawing and computers."

"Oh, I have a feeling you're short-changing yourself, Finn. You always did." I handed her my now empty mug and watched as she put it into the dishwasher. "Let me grab my purse and I'll be ready."

"Take your time, Maggie. We're in no rush."

L eaning back, I stretched my arms over my head, reaching toward the ceiling until my back popped. Then I checked my watch. No wonder I was stiff. I'd been sitting there, doing computer searches for the last three hours, looking for anything that might help pinpoint where Volk was staying. So far, I'd located three possibilities. All were out of the way motels that anyone in their right mind would avoid like the plague. But they were exactly the sort of places I could see Volk choosing. They presented easy hunting grounds for him because those staying there were often transients and undocumented aliens.

I made note of the locations and sent them to both Finn and Tamara. Almost instantly, my computer pinged, signaling a new email. Pulling it up, I shook my head. Tamara was back and wanted to talk. Give her five minutes and she'd find me. Somehow, I had a feeling she wouldn't be alone. It wouldn't surprise me at all for Finn to join us.

When Tamara rapped her knuckles against the doorframe exactly five minutes later, I realized I had been wrong. The clan's resident security specialist and lead tracker was alone. At my nod, she stepped inside and closed the door behind her. As she did, concern knotted in my stomach. The only thing keeping it from blossoming into full-blown panic was the fact that she was alone. If something was really wrong, or if something had happened to Jim, Finn would have been there.

"Relax, Maggie," she said with a smile as she dropped onto the chair before my desk. She leaned back, crossing her long legs at the ankles. "I closed the door simply so no one will come looking for me for a few minutes. I've been up almost as long as you have today. A few minutes of peace and quiet are needed right now."

Since I understood, I nodded.

"To catch you up, I still have two of our people out at the scene. But I doubt they will discover anything you don't already know. Volk was there but he didn't make the kill. In fact, we didn't find any evidence of any sort of kill in the area that he could have been responsible for, including wildlife. But, since I don't believe in coincidence, I have Mitch and Alyx searching to be sure.

"I also ran by the motel where you stayed just to check there. Nothing. That means he hasn't tracked you back there. Which is good since the clerk can place you with Jim."

Good. I really didn't like the thought of becoming the hunted.

"What about the ranch?"

That was my real worry. Even with thy security system Jim had installed, there were too many places someone could sneak in, especially if they were in animal form. The thought of Volk getting that close, not to me but to Jim, made my blood run cold. I'd die if anything happened to Jim because of me.

"I'll be going out there later today to check to see what we need to do to tighten security. But don't worry, I've had people checking the perimeter for the last two days. So far, they've picked up nothing to be concerned about."

Good news, yes, but I knew better than to underestimate Volk. Just because he hadn't been scented near the ranch, it didn't mean he might not have someone else checking it for him. But who and how in hell do you defend against something like that?

"Unfortunately, that doesn't exactly reassure me." I leaned back and rubbed my hands over my face. "Tamara, he uses people and he's had more than enough time to find someone to replace the feral I killed. Even if he hasn't turned someone yet, he's a charmer and a blackmailer. As long as he's still in the area, he's a danger to all of us."

"I know, Maggie, and I understand your concern. Just remember that you aren't alone now." She spoke with such confidence that I did feel better. "Any way, your email said you'd found something?"

"Well, I found some possibilities," I corrected and quickly briefed her on the three locations I thought Volk might be using.

She listened closely, occasionally asking a question. Then she nodded, a look of approval on her face. Before I could say anything else, she produced her cell phone from the pocket of her slacks and signaled for me to hold on. A few minutes later, she put the cell phone away and grinned. As she did, I realized why she would always be a better tracker than I ever would be. She enjoyed the game. I didn't.

"I've got people going to each location. If he's there, or if he's been there, we'll know." With that, she pushed out of the chair and moved around the desk to my side. I leaned to one side, watching as her fingers flew across the keyboard in front of me. A series of documents opened on the screen. She made sure they were what she wanted and then stepped back. "Read those over. If they're okay, digitally sign them. If you have any corrections or changes you want made, note them. Then send them back to me. I want to get you on the books as soon as possible."

"You're sure?" Much as I wanted to work here, at least until I passed the Bar, I wanted to have earned the job and not be offered it just because I'd been Finn's best friend growing up.

"Maggie, you found something in a matter of hours that my people hadn't, and they've been working on this since Declan contacted Matt. So, yes, I'm sure." She glanced at her watch. "And I've got a meeting downtown in an hour, so I've got to run. You look over those documents and get them back to me. Also, keep up the good work. Finn's going to be tied up for another hour or so. She said to tell you she'll drive you home then."

"Sounds good." I watched as she walked to the door. "Tamara, thanks."

She turned and smiled. "Don't thank me yet, Maggie. Once you sign those papers, you're going to really get to work. That includes getting the training you should have received before your former clan leader sent you out as a tracker."

With that, she opened the door and walked out. I watched as she disappeared down the corridor. Then I turned back to the computer monitor. There was still a lot to do before I left.

"Are you about ready?"

Finn stood in the doorway to my office and leaned against the doorframe. As she did, I smiled and shook my head. If Tamara hadn't told me Finn had been working on the computers, I'd have sworn she'd been working on a car or three. Strands of hair had escaped her braid. The knuckles of her right hand were scraped. There was a streak of what looked suspiciously like grease marking her left cheek. But she looked satisfied. So whatever technological demon she'd been fighting, she'd managed to defeat it.

"Just about." I reached for the stylus and scrawled my digital signature across the bottom of the last page of the contract Tamara called up for me earlier. I saved the document and then attached it to an email to send back to my new employer. "Five minutes."

She nodded and a moment later sank onto the chair Tamara sat in earlier. Unlike our mutual employer, she draped herself over it. It should have been inelegant, but it wasn't. Finn had a grace I'd never had and that I'd envied when we were younger. Now, I was simply glad I no longer tripped over my own two feet when I was chewing gum. Well, at least I didn't do it too often.

"What are you working on?"

"Just finishing up some paperwork for Tamara. I located a couple of sites where Volk might be holed up. She also had some contracts she wanted me to look over."

Finn nodded. At first, it seemed like she wasn't paying that much attention. Then she sat up, her booted feet hitting the floor with a thud. Expectation lit her expression as she leaned forward. She waited for me to explain but it was too much fun to look back at the computer monitor and act like I was working.

"Contracts?" she prompted.

"Yeah. Nothing major. She just wanted to know if there were any changes I'd recommend being made."

"Maggie." She drawled out my name, frustration clear.

"What?" I looked at her with what I hoped was an innocent expression.

"Did you sign on with us or not?"

"Oh, that?" Now I grinned and waved a hand dismissively. "I did. She made me an offer I'd be a fool to refuse. Besides, she promised to give me the training I should have had before Declan sent me out."

Finn was out of her chair and around the desk in a flash. My laughter rang out as she pulled me to my feet. A moment later, she was dragging me across the office, saying we needed a drink to celebrate. I pulled free, laughing,

"Damn. I forgot something." Finn snapped her fingers and moved quickly toward the door. "I'll be right back."

Shaking my head, I sat back down and reached for the keyboard. I entered a few notes in the file I'd opened on Volk, just enough to remind me where to pick up my search come morning – as if I'd need the reminder. But there was no sense in taking any chances. I was just turning off the computer when Finn returned, grinning broadly.

"Here. Tamara said to be sure to give these to you." She placed a top of the line tablet in a protective case with a blue tooth keyboard and a cell phone on the desk. "The tablet is synced to your computer here."

"Finn." I looked at her, wondering if she'd pulled some strings.

"What?"

"Did you–" "

"If you're about to ask if I asked her to do this, the answer's no. She furnishes all her employees with these, including me." She patted the leather-covered tablet tucked under her left arm. "One thing about our boss, Maggs, she gives us the best toys. In return, she expects us to give her our best work, even if we're only part-time."

"I've got no problem with that, Finn." And I didn't. I'd been brought up to do just that. Of course, so had Finn. "Now, since I have a phone, I'm going to call Jim. Then we can be on our way."

"All right. I'll be in the control room. Come get me when you're ready."

I nodded and reached for the cell phone. I turned it over, looking at the various buttons and ports. Then I turned it on. After it booted up, I slid my finger across the screen, unlocking it, and tapped the icon for the address book. Just as I'd suspected, someone – probably Finn – had transferred the address book from my old phone onto this one. Better yet, they'd added numbers for Finn, Matt, Sharon, Danny, Stefan, Tamara and, best of all, Jim. I tapped on Jim's name and then tapped the "call" icon. Leaning back, I lifted my heels onto the edge of the desk and waited.

"Kincade." He sounded tired but professional.

"Thrasher," I replied.

"Maggie." Gone was the weariness. Replacing it was an affection I felt as much as heard. "You got a phone."

"Finn says it's one of the benefits of working for Tamara."

"She likes her toys almost as much as Finn does. So, I take it you accepted her offer."

"I did. Hope you don't mind."

"Maggie, the only thing I'd mind is if you decided to go back to California without telling me."

"Sorry. It's going to take some time to get used to not being on my own." And it would. I hadn't been *with* anyone since law school and even then we hadn't lived together.

"Tell me about it," Jim laughed and I relaxed. For some reason, it was reassuring to know this sudden finding your mate thing was as disconcerting to him as it was to me. "Look, I need to get back to work. I should be able to get away in about an hour."

"Sounds good. Finn and I are on our way out. I'll see you at home."

"See you then." He paused, and I could almost see him looking around to make sure he couldn't be overheard. "Be careful, sweetheart, and tell Finn that I expect to see her tail lights as I pull in. I want you to myself tonight."

"That sounds like a plan. See you soon."

I ended the call and reached for my purse. I'd tell Finn the drink would have to wait for another day. I was tired and I wanted to spend some alone time with Jim. Now that we knew for sure Volk was still in the area, Jim and I needed to talk. We needed to plan what our next step would be and he needed to know that I didn't want him taking any unnecessary risks just because he wanted to protect me.

An hour later Finn stood next to me as I punched in the security code for the house. As I stepped inside, I tossed my keys into the basket near the door. Telling Finn to grab a beer if she wanted one, I continued through the house to the bedroom. I placed the tablet on the bedside table. Then I dropped onto the mattress to take off my boots. That's when I realized my injured thigh hadn't bothered me nearly as much the last few hours as it had been. Hopefully that meant it was finally healing.

"Jim just texted to let me know he's just a few minutes out," Finn said as I entered the kitchen. "According to him, I'd better not be here when he arrives or he won't be responsible for the consequences." She grinned, and I felt myself blushing.

"Well, you could stay if you want, but I warn you that I don't share."

Now Finn blushed and ducked her head. "I think I'll be on my way. Maybe Matt will be home by the time I get there." At the front door, she turned back to me. "Are you going in tomorrow morning?"

"I am. Until we find Volk, I'll be going in every day I'm not in the field."

Finn surprised me by not arguing. Instead she nodded in understanding. "I'll call later tonight to find out when you want me to pick you up. In the meantime, enjoy your man. I plan to go home and do the same thing."

I walked outside with her and watched as she climbed in the Mustang. With a wave as she drove off, I turned and back inside.

Hopefully I had time to change clothes before Jim got home. I wanted out of what I'd worn since he and I had left the house so long ago. But first, I'd grab a beer.

I'd just tossed the cap off the beer bottle onto the counter top when the doorbell rang. Assuming Finn must have forgotten something, I hurried toward the front of the house. The sooner I found out what she wanted, the sooner she'd be on her way.

"What did you forget?" I asked as I opened the door.

"Hello, Maggie."

I took a step back. The beer bottle slipped from my grasp and shattering on the tile at my feet. The stench of carrion filled my nose and I fought the urge to gag. In my mind, my tiger roared a challenge, telling me to slam the door and throw the lock into place. Jim would be here soon and together we could deal with Volk. But another part of me, the part that remember what he'd caused his ferals to do at the clan meeting, had me standing firm. I wouldn't run. Not at all. It would be him or me and I had no intention of it being me.

"All alone, Volk? Where are your ferals?"

"Silly little cat. When have I ever been alone?"

A soft step behind me and I whirled. My lips pulled back and I snarled to see Brittney and her brother standing behind me. Then I realized my mistake. I'd turned my back on the real danger. I spun around just in time to see Volk's fist flashing forward. There was pain and the sensation of falling. Then nothing else.

CHAPTER FIFTEEN

G od, I hurt. Every muscle, every nerve seemed to scream in agony. My head pounded. No, it felt like someone was pounding on it. And I was hungry. Starving. My stomach ached with it and my white tiger demanded release. We needed to hunt, to feed. The need to shift was almost overpowering. But not yet. Not until I knew what had happened.

I didn't want to move. I didn't want to, afraid of how much it would hurt when I did. Instead, I tried to think. But it was hard, so hard. My mind seemed to focus only on the pain and the hunger. Everything else was a dark morass not to be passed, at least not easily. But I had to.

I swallowed hard, noticing for the first time the taste of blood. Carefully, I ran my tongue over my teeth and the inside of my mouth. My teeth, not my tiger's at least, were intact but I could feel where the inside of my right cheek had been badly cut. It had started healing, so whatever had happened had been at least several hours earlier.

But, damn it, what had happened?

Why couldn't I remember?

I couldn't put it off any longer. No matter how badly I hurt, I needed to figure out where I was. Maybe then I'd have an idea about what happened. More importantly maybe I could find something to eat. Never before had I been this hungry. If I didn't find food soon, I'd lose control and shift and that would be bad. I wasn't sure why, but I knew it would be.

I drew another deep breath and tried to focus on my surroundings. I lay on something cold and hard. Concrete? I was, for the most part, on my stomach, arms above my head but bent slightly at the elbows. My legs were slightly bent at the knees, Okay, so far so good. At least I had all my limbs.

Gritting my teeth, I gathered my strength and tried to rise to my hands and knees. The metallic sound of chains dragging across the concrete broke the silence. Suddenly, I couldn't move any further. Not that I'd managed to move much, maybe six inches per limb. What the hell!

My eyes flew open and my tiger once again fought for release. How dare they! Someone had chained us! No one chained us! We'd kill them.

I released my breath and closed my eyes again, counting to ten. As I did, I forced my cat back. I needed to think and not as a predator. Something had happened, something bad. My stomach pitched as the probable explanations dawned on me. Being captured by a normal who'd figured out about our existence was bad enough, especially if he was going to try to force a shift on me in order to reveal our existence to the world-at-large. But another explanation sent chills of fear through me.

Volk.

Oh, God, please don't let it be Volk.

How long I lay there fighting down the panic threatening to overtake me, I don't know. Between fear and hunger, I wanted – no, I needed – to shift. If I shifted, I could slip my bonds and escape. That thought had my eyes snapping open again and a slight flicker of hope formed. Surely if Volk had captured me, he'd make sure I couldn't shift. He wouldn't make a mistake like this.

Focusing on the leather cuffs locked around my wrists, I slowed my breathing. I couldn't do anything about the hunger – how long had I been unconscious? – But I could keep control. I needed to know more about where I was before shifting. Once I did, I'd shift, slip the chains and get the hell out of there.

I changed positions slightly and pain washed over me again. With it came a new wave of hunger. My stomach hurt so badly. It felt like it was on fire and would soon consume me if I didn't find something to ease it. No, not something. Meat. Red meat from a fresh kill. I needed meat and I needed it now.

Just the thought of it was enough to start the shift. Teeth elongated and muscles tensed. I pulled against the chains, fighting them much as I'd fought against the shift just moments before. Why had I been denying my tiger her release? I no longer remembered and didn't care. She was the one best able to get us out of here. Then we could hunt.

Nothing else mattered.

"Maggie, don't!"

Caught in the middle of a shift, time suddenly seemed to stop. For one very long moment, I fought my tiger for control. Never had it been so hard to stay human. Never before had I wanted to shift so badly. But one small part of my mind told me I couldn't. He told me not to. My mate wouldn't do anything to hurt me. So he had to have a reason to keep me human. He'd tell me what was going on. I had to trust him.

I turned my head in the direction of his voice. A gasp was torn from my lips the moment I saw him. He lay against the far wall. His face was bruised and swollen. From the twist of his body and the way his arms disappeared behind his back, I knew he was bound. But why secure him so he couldn't shift but not me? Could it be that whoever had taken us didn't know what we were?

"J-Jim."

I tried to focus on him. He was my link to sanity.

He twisted and tried to sit up, wincing in pain. As he did, I gritted my teeth. Moving like that he looked so helpless, so much like – prey.

Food.

No! God, what was wrong with me?

Terrified and appalled at the thought, instinct took over and I tried to move as far from Jim as the chains would allow. Soft whimpers escaped my lips and my fists pounded against the concrete. I welcomed the pain. It was a distraction from the hunger. Maybe if I kept hitting the concrete, sanity would return. Something had happened to drive me mad. That was the only explanation for the need to feed that almost consumed me.

A soft chuckle sounded from behind me and a moment later a hand stroked down my back. My bare back. Until then, I hadn't realized anyone else was in the room with us. Nor had I realized I was naked. Chill bumps broke out and a new fear filled me as I finally caught the scent I'd hoped never to come across again. Gagging against the stench of carrion, I'd have dug a hole to hide in if I could. But I couldn't. I couldn't do anything to escape the hand running across my bare skin any more than I could shut out the image of Jim struggling to free himself.

Fingers twined in my hair and my head was painfully pulled back. Volk's face was suddenly next to mine, his breath warm against my cheek. I fought against his hold as his tongue ran up my neck and across my cheek, the pain in my scalp a welcome relief to the hunger and fear. This was my worst nightmare come true.

"Shh, little Maggie." His voice was soft and seductive. Listening to Volk was like listening to a dream lover. That had always been one of his best weapons. Now he was using it against me. I wouldn't give in. I couldn't. "Such a little tigress. A hungry little tigress."

Oh, God, so hungry. As if his words were a catalyst, my stomach started hurting again and that need to feed filled me. What had he done to me?

"Quit fighting it, little one. All you have to do is shift and then you can feed. Once you do, everything will be all right. Trust me. That's all you have to do."

He made it sound so simple and he was right. That's all I had to do. Shifted, I'd be free of my bonds. Then I could hunt. But that wasn't what he meant. Nothing was ever that simple or that clean where Volk was concerned. I had to remember that. But it was so hard when hunger drove me.

"Maggie, don't listen to him."

Jim's voice had been no louder than Volk's, but there was something in it that drew my attention even more than Volk's had. I canted my eyes toward him, unable to move my head. I had to focus on him, remember what we were together.

With a growl, Volk slammed my face against the floor. I tasted blood and fought to maintain consciousness. Without a word, he was across the room. His booted foot caught Jim in the ribs once, twice. Then his fists pummeled Jim. The scent of blood teased me, taunted me, and I beat my head against the floor. I didn't care if I lost consciousness now. I couldn't give into the instinct brought on by whatever Volk had done to me and the smell of Jim's blood to shift and feed. No. I'd die first.

Then Volk was back at my side.

"Look at him, little tiger. He isn't worthy of you. Of us."

His voice washed over me. I closed my eyes. It shut out the image of a battered and bleeding Jim but it didn't keep me from hearing his whimper of pain as he struggled to sit up once again. Nor did it block the feel of Volk's hands as they caressed my back and ass.

God, this was my worst nightmare come to life. Helpless and at the mercy of a monster, a real monster.

"Look at him, Maggie," he commanded as one hand wandered over my ass and down to my injured thigh. "Look at him!"

"N-no." I closed my eyes even tighter and tucked my chin into my shoulder in an attempt to keep from doing as Volk ordered.

"You will look at him," he growled.

Fingers dug into my injured thigh. Pain blossomed and my

stomach pitched. A scream was torn from my throat as Volk tore at my wounds. I twisted against my bonds, fighting for release. But somehow, some vestige of sanity remained. I not only kept my eyes tightly shut but I refused to shift. I held onto what Jim told me. I needed to stay human. I couldn't give in to Volk.

I couldn't.

"Look at him!" Volk ordered.

His fingers once again twisted in my hair and he pulled my head back. Fury seemed to rise off of him. Maybe he'd go ahead and kill me. Part of me hoped so. I didn't want to be at his mercy one more moment. I didn't want to know what else he had planned for me or for Jim.

"You aren't going to win, little tiger," he growled.

There was a sharp prick in my neck and something like liquid fire flowed into me. I screamed, pulling against my bonds and not caring if my struggles against his hold pulled the hair from my scalp. Never before had I hurt so badly.

"Fight it all you want, bitch. You won't win. I give you a couple of days before you give in. Everyone gives in sooner or later." He nipped my neck at the injection site and then laughed.

"Even now your tiger is trying to take over. She is so strong and you're weak, too weak. You know it and so does she. So why postpone the inevitable? Let her loose. Let her take the role she so rightly deserves as the strongest of the pairing. Then you can hunt and feed." He twisted my head around so I could see Jim lying there, bleeding from a number of new cuts. "Look at him, little tiger. He isn't worthy to be one of us. Prove your superiority by killing him. He's barely worthy to be food for you."

Volk's voice purred seductively in my ear. Whatever he'd injected into me made it hard to deny him. But I had to. I wouldn't, couldn't give in to him.

"Feel that burning, Maggie?" Now he twisted my head so I looked into his eyes. God, how had so many of our kind missed the true evil that existed in him? "That's a nice little drug I invented. It's breaking down your inhibitions, all of them. In another day, maybe two, you'll do exactly what I say. You'll beg to let you please me in whatever way I want. Then you'll be my own little feral and we'll have so much fun together. It's only fair, after all. You killed one of mine, so you will take his place."

There was another prick and the liquid fire returned. Another scream and all went dark.

Consciousness returned slowly and with it the hunger. God, the hunger. At least the burning pain from whatever Volk injected me with had faded. But I still felt its effects as my tiger fought for control. It wanted out and it wanted out now. It wasn't right that I refused her release. Volk was right. I was weak. She was the only way we'd survive.

I pulled against the chains holding me and pounded my forehead against the floor. The pain helped me focus. I didn't care if I injured myself. Hell, it would be better if I managed to knock myself out again. At least then the scent of blood and flesh wouldn't be driving me out of my mind.

"Maggie." Jim's voice was soft, worried.

A growl formed on my lips and I fought harder against my bonds. Looking at him, seeing how Volk had beaten him, smelling the sharp tang of his blood as well as my own, I felt like I was being torn in two. Part of me struggled to maintain control, knowing it was the only thing keeping him alive. But another part, the animal demanding release, only saw food.

Just the thought of food started the shift. Crying out, praying like I never had before, I struggled for control. There was enough slack in the chains to allow me some movement but not enough to get to hands and knees. Definitely not enough to get a purchase so I could pull the chains from their anchors in the concrete. Not that I didn't try. I cursed and pulled and writhed, exhausting myself until I could do nothing but lie there, panting and crying in frustration.

"Shh, Maggie." Jim's voice found me in my despair. "I want you to listen to me. Nod if you understand."

Gone was the worry I'd heard earlier. Now he sounded calm, almost confident. Was this one of Volk's tricks?

I moved slightly and opened my eyes again. Jim had somehow managed to push himself up into a sitting position. His face was bruised. Blood from various cuts as well as his broken nose covered the front of his shirt. But his eyes were clear and they were focused on me. This wasn't a trick. It was Jim. So why did he sound so calm? Didn't he understand what was happening, how much danger we were both in??

"Maggie, I need you to nod if you understand me," he repeated, keeping his voice soft. It was almost as if he was trying to reassure me even as he watched for my response.

I nodded and he smiled slightly. "Good girl." He cast a look to my right but when I started to follow his gaze, he shook his head. "No, baby. I want you to keep your eyes on me. Listen to me. Do you understand?"

"Y-yes."

"That's my girl." He smiled again. "Sweetheart, we've got a couple of hours before Volk comes back."

"No!"

Panic filled me. I knew what would happen if Volk gave me another of those damned injections. I couldn't let that happen. Better to beat my brains out than to risk that.

"Maggie, stop that!"

Jim's voice cut through the fear. As it did, I realized I'd been pounding my head against the concrete again. Blood stained the hard surface and, as I lifted my head to look at my mate, it ran down my brow and into my eyes. But it wasn't enough, it would never be enough to make me forget the hunger driving me to shift.

"Maggie, look at me."

For the first time, his power rolled over me. My tiger, fueled by the artificial hunger brought on by the drugs, rebelled. But even she wasn't strong enough to ignore Jim in alpha mode. So she sulked in my head, waiting for the moment when she'd be free and able to deal with him. No one treated her that way.

"I-I'm scared."

"I know, baby." With a groan, he pushed himself up until his back rested against the wall. "Do you trust me?"

"Yes."

"Then I want you to shift. You need to shift to get out of those cuffs. Then you can free me and we can get out of here before Volk returns."

"No." I shook my head, panic returning. "I can't."

"Yes, you can." He sounded so sure. Had the beating he'd taken damaged his thought process?

"Jim, I can't shift. I won't be able to control it." Even now I could feel the push of the shift and fought against it.

"Maggie, look at me."

Reluctantly, I did as he said.

"Maggie, you're my mate. Right?"

I nodded.

"And I'm yours. You have to remember that. You have to trust that. Trust yourself. Volk hasn't won. He won't win. You can control your shift. You know you can."

"No." I shook my head, tears filling my eyes. "How can you be sure he hasn't turned me already?"

There. I'd said it. This hunger, the almost uncontrollable need to shift and feed could only mean one thing.

"Because you haven't shifted already. If he'd turned you, you would have shifted before you could stop it. But you haven't. You are still in control. You're still my mate and my life. Now you need to trust me to help you through this so we can both get out of here."

"Jim, what if you're wrong?" Somehow I had to make him understand. "I'm hurt and the hunger's so strong." I pounded one fist against the floor as hard as I could, once and then again. "Whatever he gave me, it's stripping me of my control. I'm barely human now. I won't be able to stop myself once shifted." The pain in my fist wasn't enough to keep me focused. Cursing, I raised up as high as I could and then slammed my head back to the ground. Pain radiated through me and my vision blurred. I didn't pass out but it was enough to let me focus for a few more moments. "I'm so close to turning feral now, I don't know if I can stop it once shifted."

"Sweetheart, you have to trust me. I'll keep you anchored." Again, his power rolled over me, this time like a comforting blanket. "You have to believe in me. In us."

He continued to talk, doing his best to soothe, to remind me who and what I am. I was stronger than this. I'd beaten Volk once and I would do so again. All I had to do was hold control for a few moments, just long enough to shift and then shift back. He'd help me. He was my mate. He'd protect me.

"Maggie, you have to do this. If you don't we're both dead." Now his voice turned serious and my heart broke. "I'd rather die by your hand than by his. But I know you. You won't hurt me. So please, trust yourself like I trust you and let's get the hell out of here."

God, I wanted to believe him. I had to believe him. I'd managed to hold control this long. Surely I could a little longer with his help.

Pain coursed through me as I released my hold on my white tiger. Muscles tensed and twisted. Bones broke and reformed. I threw back my head. My scream turned into a roar as the shift progressed. As my vision shifted, becoming truer, sharper, I watched my arms transform. Paws slid through the leather cuffs with little real effort. Twisting, I pulled my hind legs free. Growling, hunger and anger at war with one another, I leapt away from the chains that had held me, only to whimper in pain as I put weight on my injured leg.

Damn Volk. He'd reinjured my thigh.

"That's my girl."

He spoke. I swung my head and bared my teeth. His blood called to me. Food. I needed to feed.

"Easy, Maggie. Easy."

There was no fear in this one. Didn't he know I could rip him apart with the swipe of a paw? Why didn't he fear?

"Now shift back."

Growling, I slowly padded nearer. Why should I shift back after being held in that weak human form for so long?

"Maggie, you're my mate. You aren't going to hurt me. Just listen to my voice and shift back. I need you to shift back so you can free me and we can get out of here."

Mate.

I threw my head back and roared again.

Mate, not food.

Listen to his voice. I had to listen to his voice.

"That's it, baby. That's it. Remember that I need you and love you and I'll always protect you. Just as you will me. All you need to do is shift back and we can get out of here."

A moment or an eternity later, I knelt on the floor, on my hands and knees instead of on four paws. I panted, straining for air even as I fought to maintain control. If possible, the hunger was worse. If I didn't get food soon, I'd start eating my own arm or leg or anything else I could get hold of.

"That's it, Maggie. I'm so proud of you, baby."

I followed Jim's voice, putting one hand in front of the other and crawling toward him. He leaned forward so I could get at his bound hands. But my fingers were numb and fumbled over the knots. Cursing, I tried again. I had to get him free before just being this close to him forced me into another shift. I knew if that happened again, all would be lost. I wouldn't be able to stop myself until I'd fed.

"There's a knife in my boot," he said.

I pulled up his pants leg and reached for the knife. It seemed to take forever to cut through the ropes. When the knife slipped, he flinched and blood pooled where the blade cut him. My breath came out in a ragged rush and I swallowed hard. I couldn't think about that. No, I needed to get him free. Then he'd get us out of here.

Finally, the rope fell away. He pulled his arms around and rubbed his wrists. I tried not to look at the raw skin at his wrists. Instead, when he took the knife from my hand, I backed away. I needed to put some distance between us. I didn't know how much longer I could hold on and we were so close to getting out. So close.

"Here." He stood and whipped off his shirt. Before I could react, he'd moved to my side and slid the shirt over my shoulders. "Put that on while I get this door open."

Glad to have something to do, and even more glad that he'd moved away from me, I slid my arms into the sleeves. But that just made it worse. His blood was all over the shirt, reminding me of the hunger fighting for control. I couldn't stay in the shirt. I had to get it off. I had to get it off now.

"Maggie?" He took a step in my direction as I tossed the shirt aside. When I shook my head and stepped back, he stopped.

"Need to hunt, feed." My voice was barely more than a whisper, my control less tangible.

"Don't worry, baby. I'll take care of you."

Before I could react, he'd closed the distance between us. The look of apology on his face was the only warning I had before his fist flashed forward. There was pain as my head snapped back and then all went mercifully dark.

CHAPTER SIXTEEN

My next conscious thought, if you could call it that, was that I was moving. Not that I was walking or running, but that I was in something moving very fast. The hunger was just as bad as it had been and the need to shift hadn't changed. But something told me not to. It would be dangerous to shift. But this time it would be dangerous to me, not to anyone else.

I was sitting up and whatever I was on was at least somewhat comfortable. But my hands were secured behind my back and my ankles tightly bound. My legs had been drawn up on the seat and something ran between ankles and wrists, connecting them. It wasn't a hogtie, but it was close. Part of me was relieved because, tied like this, I couldn't shift without seriously injuring myself. Fortunately, my cat realized it as well, despite the drugs in our system.

I glanced down and growled softly. Once again, I wore Jim's bloody shirt. The human part of me understood. He couldn't drive around town with a bound, nude woman in the vehicle with him. But the blood called to me, making it even more difficult to maintain my tenuous hold on my human side.

Then I turned my head and saw Jim. He sat behind the steering wheel. But this wasn't his truck or his official SUV. This was a battered pickup. Where he'd gotten it, I didn't know and frankly I didn't care as long as he was taking us far away from Volk.

"Easy, sweetheart," he soothed, glancing quickly at me before turning his attention back to the road. "I'm sorry I hit you and I promise I'll never do it again. But I didn't know what else to do."

My lips pulled back and I bared my teeth. My heart told me he was safe but my brain, influenced by the drugs simply saw food. And that was all it took. I lunged toward him, held in place by the shoulder harness and seatbelt. Snarls escaped my lips and leaned as close to him as I could, snapping like a wild animal. Part of me knew it wasn't right but it was just a small voice and I was so hungry.

"Stop!" His voice rang in the small confines of the truck. If there had ever been any doubt he was an alpha, there couldn't be now. Snarling and growling, my cat cowered in the back of my mind, giving me a chance to reassert control. "Maggie, you need to calm down."

"C-can't."

"Yes, you can." He glanced at me and I could see the worry. Hell, I was worried. "You either sit there and try to relax and quit fighting or I'll have to secure you better. I can't risk wrecking out until we're safe."

Safe? Didn't he understand that we'd never be safe? Not with Volk on the loose and not as long as I lived. That bastard had turned me. God, he'd made me into one of his monsters.

Tears ran down my cheeks and burned my eyes. I'd become what I once hunted. Why hadn't Jim just killed me? It wouldn't have been as cruel as keeping me alive like this, where I knew what would happen the moment I lost control.

"No," Jim's voice broke through my misery. Huddling against the door, I looked across the cab at him. He held a cell phone in his left hand. His expression was tense, his tone terse. "I'm not risking my place. We're heading to Stefan's. She needs his help more than she needs any of the rest of us right now . . . You and Finn meet us there .

. . No, I can't go into it now. But it's bad . . . I'll explain when I see you."

He ended the call and tossed the cell phone onto the dash. His hands gripped the steering wheel so tightly his knuckles turned white. Then, looking at me, he tried to smile in reassurance. For the first time, I saw the doubt in his eyes and my fear ratcheted up. Whimpering, I closed my eyes and swallowed hard. If he'd lost faith, what hope did I have?

"Maggie, it's going to be all right." He might have looked concerned but I didn't hear it in his voice. "Stefan will know what to do."

"God, Jim, it hurts."

"I know, baby. Just hang on. Please."

I nodded even though I knew it was hopeless. Even now I could feel the hunger taking over again. It felt like I was burning up. My level of aggression was off the board. The only reason I hadn't already shifted – and attacked Jim – was the way he'd tied me. But soon even that wouldn't matter.

A lifetime later, at least it seemed that way, Jim turned the truck up a tree lined drive. Some distant part of my brain realized we were headed somewhere even further off the beaten track than his ranch. Good. When they had to put me down, there'd be no witnesses.

No! I wouldn't let them put me down. They were weak. They didn't understand what it was like to give in to the animal. The strength that filled me was almost as heady as the hunger was painful. I'd bide my time and wait until I could escape. Then I'd show them. They'd realize just how foolish they were to underestimate me.

By the time Jim parked the truck and hurried around to the passenger side, I was in full attack mode. Or maybe it was panic. No clearer than I was thinking, it could have been both. As the door opened, I lunged, sensing freedom. The seatbelt and shoulder harness held me in place. Part of me was glad they had. Otherwise, tied as I was, I'd simply have fallen to the ground. I hurt badly enough as it was. But what were a few more aches and pains if it meant freedom and the chance to finally feed?

Jim moved with the ease of much practice as he braced his left forearm across my chest and shoulders, holding me in place. With is right hand, he reached over and released the buckle for the seatbelt. Then he pulled me to the edge of the seat. He looked at me, probably trying to figure out the best way to get me out of the truck without suffering any further damage. Too bad. I was tired of being tied up. It was time to reverse our roles.

"Damn it, Maggie, I don't want to hit you again," he growled as I twisted my head in an attempt to bite him.

"Let me go," I snarled.

"Stop it!" His power rolled over me. If I'd been shifted, my ears would have flattened against my head and I'd have dropped to my belly. Instead, I dropped my head, growling softly.

"Get her inside."

Stefan stood to one side and watched as Jim carefully pulled me out of the truck. Before I could react, Jim had me slung over his shoulder. The indignity of it was more than I could take. I tried writhing out of his grasp but his arms only held my legs tighter. I twisted at the waist, ignoring the pull of the ropes on my arms and legs. Lips pulled back and my mouth opened. Jim let out a curse of pain as I sank my teeth into his side. Blood pooled where my teeth broke the skin. The hunger flared and I bit down harder.

Before I could tear the flesh, a heavy fist cuffed me hard. Stunned, I released my bite. A hand twisted in my hair and pulled my head back. Stefan. Keeping pace with his nephew, he held my head so I couldn't use my teeth on Jim again. Bastard. They were all bastards. I needed food. I needed to hunt. Why wouldn't they let me hunt?

"Where?" Jim asked simply as we entered the house.

"The basement."

Without a word, Jim moved quickly through the house. Between them, they kept me under control as we climbed down the stairs at the rear of the house. Then we were in the basement and Jim was carefully lowering me onto a narrow bed. The moment my back hit the mattress, he place one hand across my forehead, holding my head in place. The other arm went across my chest holding me down. Damn it, he was too good at this.

"Hold her still while I get her legs secured," Stefan said. He didn't even sound ruffled. But I could smell his worry. Well, he'd know fear if I ever got loose. Then he quickly freed my ankles from the rope binding them. Before I could kick out, he'd pulled the right ankle down and toward the edge of the bed. A cuff of some sort was fitted around it. Then he did the same to my left.

Pissed, I renewed my struggles. But it was useless. With my arms still bound behind me and my legs secured, I couldn't throw off Jim. All I was doing was exhausting myself and that, in turn, increased the hunger.

"Maggie, look at me." Jim's voice was firm but there was something else there. Something that had me doing as he said. "Maggie, you need to trust us. Volk messed you up but you haven't turned. We're not going to hurt you. But we have to make sure you don't hurt yourself or us. Do you understand?"

"Let me go."

"I can't, baby." He looked down at me and shook his head, regret and something else reflected in his eyes. "Focus on my voice, Maggie. Remember what we are to one another. You're my mate and I'm yours. You know I won't hurt you. But you have to let me help you. I don't want to lose you and I'm going to fight for you, even if that means having to fight you to do it."

"I-I can't control it, Jim." Tears trailed down my cheeks.

"Yes, you can. You've controlled it this long. You can do it a little longer." He gave me a reassuring, loving smile. "Sweetheart, we have to secure you until the drugs are out of your system. Please don't fight us."

"I'll try." That was all I could do.

He eased his hold on my forehead. As he did, I closed my eyes and focused on the sound of his voice as he spoke. I had to keep the hunger under control just a few more moments. Then he'd have me secured and I wouldn't be able to hurt him or anyone else. I didn't want to hurt him. But I couldn't keep the animal at bay much longer.

"All right, sweetheart. Relax." Jim's hand stroked my cheek.

I tried to sit up. I couldn't. Lifting my head, I didn't know whether to growl or cry in relief to see the straps crossing my shoulders and waist, holding me against the mattress. My wrists were secured to a wide leather belt that was fastened around my waist. I wasn't going anywhere.

"Hungry."

"Not yet, sweetheart. Stefan needs to check you first."

"Hungry!" I repeated and struggled against the straps holding me down. Damn it, I'd behaved. Why couldn't I eat now?

"Oh my God!"

Finn's shocked exclamation came just moments before I realized she was standing next to the bed, one hand reaching out to grab Jim's arm. My cat railed against my fragile control. How dare another female come near me! How dare she touch my mate!

God, I was going insane. Whatever Volk had given me had finally torn away the last of my sanity. Why else would I react this way to my oldest friend, to my Alpha?

"What did that bastard do to her?" Matt demanded as he moved to stand next to Finn.

"He drugged her. Something he injected into her neck. He did it at least four times. Twice that I know of while she was still unconscious and twice after she woke. That last time, he told her that he gave her just a few days before she broke and became one of his ferals. Told her all she had to do was shift and eat. Then she'd be his." Now, for the first time since I'd regained consciousness, his voice broke. "Whatever he gave her, it hurt her. She screamed in agony and writhed against the chains he'd put on her. Then she passed out."

"Did she eat?" Stefan asked.

Why were they talking like I wasn't there?

"No." Jim shook his head, his hand once again stroking my cheek. "If she had, I wouldn't be here. Somehow she managed to keep control, even when Volk beat the shit out of me so she'd smell my blood."

"Couldn't," I rasped between clenched teeth. "Mate."

"That's right, baby. We're mates." He smiled down at me.

"Please. I need to eat something, anything."

"Stefan?"

"Not until we know what he gave her."

As he spoke, I felt a slight prick near my left ankle. Memory of Volk and that last injection returned. "NO!"

I bucked against the straps holding me down. The bed creaked and I thrashed, doing everything I could to break free. My nails dug into the palms of my hands, drawing blood. Cries of fear mixed with angry snarls. I wouldn't return to that hell. I wouldn't.

"What happened?" Male but not mate. Alpha. Clan Alpha.

"The needle." Mate. Angry. With me? No. With himself. "Damn it, I should have thought."

"It couldn't be helped, Jim. I have to have a blood sample to find out what he gave her." Stefan. Calm, reassuring but angry too.

"Maggs, listen to me. You don't have to be afraid." Female. Alpha. Friend. Her hand stroked my face, my hair. "You're safe. We aren't going to let anything else happen to you. I promise. We're going to protect you. Then, when you're better, we're going to get Volk and make him pay for what he's done. I promise." More reassurance but could I believe her? "Maggie, I never broke a promise to you when we were kids. I won't start now."

"Scared. So scared."

"I know, Maggs." Her palm cupped my cheek and I pressed my face into it. "We've been worried too. When we realized you and then Jim were missing–" Now her voice broke.

"Maggie, please trust us. Trust me." Jim brushed his lips against my forehead.

"Do. You're my mate." I looked up at him, praying he understood that the bitch who'd been fighting him wasn't me. "Sorry."

"Shh. No. You don't have anything to apologize for." His hand closed over mine where it was secured at my waist. "Rest now. You're safe and I'm not going to leave you."

"None of us are going to leave you, Maggs." Finn took my other hand. "Rest now."

She and Jim soothed with hands and voices. As they did, the hunger receded. My eyes grew heavy. I was safe. I had to believe that. I did believe that. Safe and loved. They'd take care of me. All I had to do was rest.

CHAPTER SEVENTEEN

I woke, hungry and wondering why I'd been sleeping on my back. I never sleep on my back. Irritated, I tried to roll over and couldn't. My body barely moved. Something held me down. If that wasn't bad enough, my head hurt. No, it felt like it was ready to explode. Every muscle in my body screamed in agony and my thigh hurt more than it had after fighting Volk's feral. I felt as if I'd fought every member of the clan – or several clans – and lost. At least I lay on something soft.

Soft.

My eyes flew open as memory of the nightmare returned. Please let it be a nightmare. But if it was, why was I tied down and why were there so many people watching me, their expressions worried, even wary?

Then Jim was there, sitting on the mattress at my side. He looked like he'd aged a decade in – how long? God, how long had it been since I was last conscious? More importantly, what had happened to Volk? Had they found him?

"Shh, Maggie. You're safe." Jim's voice soothed as his hand stroked my hair.

Scared, I tilted my head, just about the only part of my body I could move just then. His hand moved to my cheek and I rubbed against it. As I did, tears blinded me and fear almost choked me. What happened? Had Volk managed to turn me after all?

"No, Maggie. No." Finn moved to sit on the mattress opposite Jim. Her voice was soft, reassuring. Her touch was gentle as she reached out to brush a lock of hair from my brow.

"Finn's right, child," Stefan said from the foot of the bed. His confidence reassured me. "I won't lie. It was close. If that bastard had given you another injection or if you'd given in and shifted and killed, you would have turned. That would have broken you and Volk knew it. But you beat him."

"No. Jim did." I turned my head to look at him. He'd believed in me, in us, and I'd turned on him. "I hurt you."

"No, baby. You didn't do anything. Volk did." He leaned down and kissed my cheek. Then he rubbed his nose against mine.

"How did you stop it?" I knew that, despite everything Stefan said, I'd been on the verge or turning. The prick of the needle had been that last shove I'd needed to go over the edge.

"You and Jim did that, Maggie," Matt said from his uncle's side. "Your bond did it."

"They helped, baby. They've been here with us, making sure you knew you were safe. None of us were about to let Volk win. We weren't going to lose you."

"Love you." I rubbed against his hand again, the only thing I could do to show him what I felt. "What about V-volk?" Just saying his name brought the nightmare back.

"Tamara and her people are searching for him," Matt said. He sat at the end of the bed and his hand rested reassuringly on my foot.

"And I contacted my grandmother. She's sent my uncle and their clan's trackers to help," Finn took up. "Believe me, we'll find him."

"Much as I hate what he did to you, sweetheart, it did tell us one thing. He hasn't had a chance to replace the feral you killed."

"Good." I never wanted anyone else to have to go through what I had. What I was still going through. But there was something wrong with what they said. Something important and yet missing. God, if only my mind would work.

I looked around, not recognizing the room I lay in. It looked like a treatment room but it was big, too big. Then there was the sound-proofing on the walls and ceiling. My memory of the time after waking in the truck was spotty at best, which was probably a good thing. But it also meant I needed the holes filled and quickly, before the fear set back in.

"Where?"

"You're at my place, Maggie," Stefan answered. "Jim decided it was safer to bring you here."

"Why?" Brow furrowed, I tried to figure it out. The answer was there, just out of reach. Was this trouble thinking because of the drugs or simply because I'd been out of it for however long?

"First, I knew Stefan could treat you better here than at the ranch. As you can see, he has a full clinic set up here for those times when it's not safe for one of our kind to go to the hospital. But I also didn't want to risk Volk going back to the ranch. I wasn't in the best of shape and you certainly weren't able to protect yourself if he managed to track us. So I wanted somewhere I knew we could bunker down."

"Good." I rubbed my cheek against his hand again, aching to be able to hold him. "But you? Are you all right?" As if the beating Volk had given him wasn't bad enough, I remembered trying to take a bite out of his side. What else had I done?

"He's fine, Maggie," Finn assured me. "I promise. As soon as he had you stabilized, Stefan checked him. Volk beat the crap out of him, but he was already healing. Frankly, he's been so worried about you, he forgot to whine about his injuries." Now she grinned and I felt myself smiling weakly in return.

"How bad?"

"You?" Jim asked.

I shook my head. "You."

"Sweetheart, I'm fine. He broke my nose. Not the first time it's happened and it sure as hell won't be the last. A couple of ribs were broken but they barely hurt now. And, before you ask, you barely marked me. It really was nothing more than a love bite."

I remembered how I'd locked onto him, the taste of his blood. It had definitely been more than a "love bite".

"Maggie, I'm fine." He waited until I nodded. Then he turned to look at Stefan. "Can't we let her up?"

"Not quite yet." The older man moved to my side, his expression reassuring. "Maggie, I got the preliminary blood reports back. So I know at least part of what that bastard was injecting you with. Another twelve hours or so and it should be out of your system. Until then, we need to keep you secured."

"Stefan–"

"No, Jim. He's right." All I had to do was close my eyes and the hunger was still there, lurking below the surface until my control slipped. It wasn't as bad, but that didn't mean I wouldn't try to shift and hunt the moment I was freed. "You can't risk it."

"Maggie." His voice roughened and he bent so his forehead rested against mine.

"Jim." Finn's voice was soft, reassuring. "Matt, take him upstairs and get some food into him. Stefan and I will stay with Maggie."

"No. I'm not leaving her."

"It's all right." I really wasn't sure I believed it but I knew Finn wanted to talk to me and didn't want Jim there when she did. Heart pounding, I did my best to look reassuring, not easy when you're strapped down and can't move. "It's not like I'm going anywhere." A slight smile lifted the corners of my mouth.

For a moment, he looked like he was going to protest. Then he squeezed my hand and stood. "Are you sure?"

"I am." Not really, but I wasn't going to let him know that.

"Jim, you know I'm not going to let anything else happen to her." Finn stood and walked with him to the door. "You need to eat and at least shower and change clothes. Then you can come back."

I wasn't sure he'd agree. Hell, I wasn't sure I wanted him to agree.

He'd kept me from turning. I knew it just as I knew I wasn't out of danger yet. But I could see the exhaustion etched in his features and the worry reflected in his eyes. He needed to take care of himself now and I had to trust in my childhood friend, my Alpha, to do what needed to be done.

"Tell me," I said simply once the door closed behind Matt and Jim. I waited, convinced Finn, or maybe Stefan, was about to tell me that I'd never recover from what Volk had done to me. If that was the case, they might as well go ahead and kill me. I didn't want to live knowing I could turn at any moment and kill Jim or someone else I cared for. "Or let me tell you." I fisted my hands, focusing hard on anything but what I was about to say. "You can't guarantee I'll ever be free of what Volk did. If that's the case, I want you to get Jim out of here, Finn, and I trust you to do what's necessary, Stefan."

For a moment, they simply looked at me like I'd grown another head. Then Finn was across the room and sitting at my side. One hand rested on my shoulder and the other stroked my hair, my cheek. Tears gathered in her eyes and she shook her head, looking at Stefan for help.

"That's not what we wanted to talk to you about, child," he said gently as he sat opposite Finn. "I didn't lie when I said we'd identified at least some of the drugs he'd given you. You should be free of their effects by tomorrow. But you need to tell us what you can about what happened. You need to start believing that you didn't break. That you never turned. That is as important as you knowing the drugs are working their way through your system."

"I don't know what I can tell you. I woke up in that room, chained, naked and starving. My tiger was pushing for release. She's never fought me like that before. But I managed to hold her back. I had to, especially after realizing Jim was in the room with me. I couldn't risk hurting him.

"Then Volk was there. He kept telling me that I'd give in, sooner or later. When Jim tried to interrupt, Volk beat him. He hurt him and the smell of his blood called to me. It was all I could do to keep from shifting. If I had, I'd have gone after Jim without a second thought. That's what Volk wanted. When I didn't shift, he injected me again. I don't know how many times he'd done so before.

"When he did, it felt like fire was running through my veins. I'd never hurt like that before. I screamed. I think I screamed. Then I passed out. When I came to, Jim told me I needed to shift long enough to slip the chains and then shift back. He said he trusted me and he'd help me. I didn't want to, but I trusted him. But, when I shifted back, the hunger was worse and if he hadn't knocked me cold and tied me up, I'd have shifted again and I would have gone after him."

Tears rolled down my cheeks and Finn gently wiped them away. Her voice was soft as she soothed me, doing her best to reassure me that everything was going to be all right, that I'd proven I was stronger than Volk. But it was Stefan I was watching. I'd just asked him to put me down if I'd turned or if there was a risk of me turning later.

"Maggie," he began as he freed my left hand. I left it laying where it was, not wanting to risk him thinking I was trying to attack. He smiled, understanding reflected in his eyes, and took my hand in his. He lifted it from where it lay. A moment later, he wrapped my fingers around a glass. Then he helped me lift my head so I could drink. Never had water tasted as good as it did in that moment. "You didn't break and you won't break. Not now. But, until the drugs are out of your system, you can, as the kids used to say, trip out. The cocktail of drugs that bastard gave you included, among other things, LSD."

"God." I closed my eyes and, as he took the glass from me, placed my hand back at my waist where he could secure the leather cuff around it again. "You're sure I won't turn?"

"Positive." There was so much confidence in his voice that I wanted to believe him. Hell, I almost did. "And no more talk about doing *what's necessary*. The only thing that's necessary is finding that bastard and killing him."

"On that we all agree." Finn's voice was cold.

Thank God they believed in me. Maybe I could start to do so as well. But, before I could, I had some questions for them to answer.

"Other than the drugs, what did he do to me?" I hated asking and I wasn't sure I really wanted to know. But I couldn't not know either. He'd stripped me and chained me but he hadn't stripped Jim. There was only one explanation I could think of and my stomach churned at the thought.

Finn's quick intake of breath was all I needed to know she understood exactly what I was asking. Scared, I looked at Stefan, praying for – well, I don't know what I was praying for. Maybe that this was all just a really bad nightmare from which I'd soon awaken.

"Maggie, he didn't rape you. That's the first thing I asked Jim and I also did a full exam to be sure."

I exhaled and closed my eyes. At least one nightmare had been avoided. But I had to make sure he wasn't holding anything back. "What else?"

"He beat the hell out of you, child, and he did he best to do even more damage to your thigh."

I shivered at the hatred in Stefan's voice and reflected on his expression.

"It's going to be a while before you are walking on your own again."

"That's all?"

"Maggs, there is nothing else. At least nothing you don't already know." Finn's fingers brushed lightly against my cheek. "Like Stefan said, that bastard beat you and he drugged you. That's bad enough. But one thing he didn't do: he didn't break you and he didn't turn you."

"Maybe I'll believe that when the drugs are out of my system and I'm back on my feet." Or when I could touch Jim and not want to tear him to pieces. But there was one more thing I needed to say before Jim got back. "Finn, there's only way we're going to get Volk."

For a moment, she looked like she didn't know what I meant.

Then, as understanding dawned on her, she shook her head, her expression darkening. "No. Oh hell no."

"Yes. You know I'm right. It's the only way." And maybe it would be a way for me to get a little of my own back. Damn it, that bastard owed me.

"I've beaten him twice now. Well, once. Jim beat him the second time by getting us out of there before I could give into the drugs. Don't you think he's going to want to get his hands on me again? He wants to make me pay for killing his feral and he's going to want to hurt me by killing Jim when I can do nothing to stop him. So let's use that. Use me to trap that son of a bitch."

"No way in hell, Maggie. Absolutely no way in hell." Finn shook her head, her expression firm.

"Finn, please."

Stefan's hand tightened slightly on my arm, silencing me. "Finn, much as I hate to say it, she's right. It fits with what I know of Volk's psychology. More than that, she needs this to prove to herself that he hasn't won." Now he looked down at me. "But not before you are back on your feet. It will take that long to convince Jim not to take our heads for suggesting it." He smiled and I couldn't help it. I grinned in return.

"You're both out of your minds." Finn threw her hands up and stood, crossing the room. "And, damn it, you're both right. I'll discuss it with Matt. Until I do, neither of you say anything about this crazy idea to anyone else."

"Now, I want you to get some more rest, Maggie. We'll sit with you until Jim returns." Stefan carefully adjusted the sheet over me. Then, much to my surprise, he bent and kissed my forehead. "You're a strong young woman. Trust in yourself as much as we do."

There was nothing I could say to that. Until the hunger was gone, I'd not be able to believe I hadn't been turned. But I'd trust them to take care of me – one way or another.

CHAPTER EIGHTEEN

A hand stroked down my side to my leg. A voice murmured that everything was all right. I was safe. It was nothing more than a nightmare. Lips brushed against my forehead, my cheek, my lips. My hands found bare flesh and I breathed in the scent of him. My snow tiger preened and purred, *Mine*.

"Shh, sweetheart. It's fine. You're safe." Jim's voice was a balm and I clung to it.

Jim?

My eyes flew open. He lay on the bed next to me. I lay on my side, one arm and leg thrown over him. For a brief moment, I exulted in the knowledge he shared my bed. Then memory returned and with it fear of what Volk had done to me.

"No!"

Terrified the drugs might still have hold of me, that I might do something horrible, I shoved away from Jim. I rolled off the bed, landing with a thud on my butt that jarred every injury, bringing tears to my eyes. So much for cats always landing on their feet. Heart pounding, breath coming in ragged gasps, I crab-walked away from the bed until my back was against the wall.

"Maggie, it's okay." Jim slid off the bed and slowly moved toward me. "Baby, you've got to believe me. Everything's all right."

"T-the drugs?" My teeth chattered as reaction set in. It had been so wonderful to wake in his arms and to feel his lips on mine. What if it was all a mistake or a dream?

Damn Volk for bringing me to this!

"Are out of your system."

Jim knelt before me and slowly reached out. He waited, giving me time to avoid his touch if I wanted. For a moment, I focused on his eyes, looking for any hint of doubt or fear. But all I saw was love and reassurance. He was telling the truth. Or at least he thought he was. That was enough for me. It had to be.

Swallowing hard, I reached out, taking his hands in mine. As our fingers touched, there was that tingle I always felt when we touched. Better yet, there was no hunger. At least not like before. My stomach growled, but it was the sort of hunger you feel after being sick for awhile and unable to eat anything solid. There was no urge to shift and definitely no urge to attack and feed.

"Oh God."

It came out, soft and shaky, and I threw myself forward. Jim's arms went around me and he cradled me against his chest. He spoke softly. I'm not sure what he said. It didn't matter. Nothing mattered beyond the feel of his touch and the beating of his heart beneath my cheek.

Carefully, he eased me to my feet. The moment I stood, my knees almost buckled. Whether it was from weakness or relief, or maybe a combination of both, I don't know. What I do know is that Jim's arms tightened around me and a moment later he was settling me back in bed. Then he slid in next to me and pulled the sheet over us.

Relieved to finally be free of the restraints, I reached up to touch his cheek. The stubble of his beard tickled my palm. How long had it been since that talk with Finn and Stefan? Hell, how long had it been since I'd awakened and realized we were in Volk's hands?

God, if it hadn't been for Jim, I'd have turned. I'd never be able to make it up to him. All I could do was make sure he knew I'd be the best mate and partner possible for however long we had together.

"Maggie, don't." His lips brushed the top of my head and his arms tightened around me.

"Don't what?"

"Don't keep beating yourself up." When I looked up at him, he smiled and cupped my cheek with his right hand. "Sweetheart, you have to start accepting the fact you aren't responsible for what happened. Volk is and we're going to make that bastard pay. I promise you."

"Tell me what's been going on. How long has it been?" I sat up, bunching a pillow behind my back. I might feel weak as a kitten – and that worried me – but I'd had more than enough of lying flat for awhile.

"It's been a week since I got home and realized Volk had you and five days since we got free."

A week? No wonder I felt so weak.

"How did he get you?"

Jim snorted and shook his head. One corner of his mouth turned down in a slight frown. "I screwed up big time. When I arrived home and saw the front door standing open, I didn't think twice about it. I figured you'd heard me coming and opened it. So I walked in and found you out cold on the floor. Before I could react, he hit me with pepper spray and then I was tased. I was cuffed, gagged and in tossed in the back of a van that had been parked at the rear of the house before I could recover. A few minutes later, he returned with you. " He swallowed hard and sat up, drawing me close. "I'm sorry, baby. I almost got both of us killed."

Now I shook my head. He couldn't think that way. It was wrong. He was no more to blame than was I. One man, one very sick man, was responsible and now it was up to us to rid the world of him and his evil.

"No." I nuzzled his neck. My tongue ran along the line of his jaw. I nipped his chin before pressing my mouth to his. He needed to know I didn't blame him. "You tried to save me. You *did* save me. The only one who did anything wrong was Volk."

No, that wasn't right. Someone else had been there with him. My memory of those last few minutes before I'd lost consciousness were hazy, but I did remember that. I'd opened the door and found Volk standing there. Then I'd heard someone behind me. I'd turned. So who was it?

I closed my eyes and tried to bring those few minutes into focus. Jim must have figured out what I was doing because his hands gently stroked me, more to let me know he was there than anything else. His voice was soft and reassuring as he spoke. He trusted me. He knew I could do this.

"God damn it!" I sat bolt upright as memory returned. Fury filled me and my cat roared in response. But there was no fear as she stirred. Not when I shared her fury.

"What?" Jim's concern was clear in his voice.

"That son of a bitch had help." If I hadn't felt weak as a kitten, I'd have been out of bed and dressing. Much as I wanted to hunt Volk, I wanted the bitch who helped him more. "Jim, was he alone when you got home?"

I needed to know. Maybe I was wrong. Maybe the drugs Volk had given me had made me imagine what happened.

For a moment, he didn't say anything. I knew from his expression that he was doing what I had been just a few moments before. He was revisiting those moments after he entered the house and found me unconscious in the entry hall. The muscles of his jaw tightened and a growl, soft and deadly, escaped his lips. That was all the answer I needed.

"I hadn't realized it until now. But Volk pepper sprayed me from the front and the Taser hit me from behind." His hand reached up to massage his neck and I wondered if that's where he'd been hit. "No way that bastard could have done both." Now he sat up and pulled me onto his lap. "Did you see who it was?"

I nodded, anger at how they'd betrayed him building.

"Who?"

"The two from the clan meeting."

Without a word, he reached across to the bedside table. I watched as he grabbed his cell phone and tapped out a quick text message. Then he returned the phone to where it had been and settled back, easing me down at his side.

"God, Maggie, I'm sorry. I should have realized they'd be trouble."

"Jim, don't. From what I gathered, that blonde bitch has been trouble for a long time, but only in that she wanted males she couldn't have. I can't imagine your brother, or Finn for that matter, letting her or her brother stay in the clan if they even remotely suspected the two would turn on one of their own. If our Alphas didn't realize they were trouble, why should you?"

His arms tightened around me. "You mean I should trust myself just as I've been telling you to trust yourself?"

"Yep." I grinned up at him, relaxing some to see the tension ease around his eyes. "What's happened since you got us out?"

"Matt and Finn have been busy." Now he grinned and it was easy to see the predator in him. "Do you remember Finn telling you that her grandmother had sent her uncle and their clan's trackers to help look for Volk?"

I nodded.

"Well, what Finn didn't tell you was that Irene came with them. She's been working with Matt, contacting the neighboring clans. Day after tomorrow, their Alphas will be here for a meeting. Seems my baby brother and his wife have declared war and they will do whatever it takes to find and deal with Volk once and for all."

Something Declan should have done months ago. Yet another reminder of the differences between this, my new clan, and the Southern California clan.

"Stefan has been riding the lab, making sure they don't miss anything in your blood work." Now he tipped my face up so I could see his expression. "Sweetheart, he said your last blood test came back clear. The drugs are out of your system. You aren't to worry about them nor are you to worry about going feral. You won't – ever. You beat Volk. You beat that bastard. Remember that.

"And now we know what he's been doing to turn our kind into his ferals. Stefan thinks we might be able to reverse the process, if we catch it soon enough after they turn. From what we can tell, Volk's using a drug cocktail that tears down your will and self-control and increases paranoia and aggression. Because he's already figured out what his victim's weaknesses are, he uses those to break them mentally. Then he shows what the turned victim did and, if they don't kill themselves, they are his. Broken and feral."

I licked my lips, remembering how close to breaking I'd come. Thank God for Jim. He kept me focused and never gave up on me.

"Stefan's sure I'll be okay?"

"He's sure you *are* okay." He smiled and then dipped his head to kiss me. "And I'll prove it. How about something to eat?"

I grinned as my stomach growled. I was starving, but not for red meat of any kind. No, a nice cup of soup or something bland would be just fine. "Soup?" I asked hopefully. "I'm afraid to put anything heavy in my stomach yet."

"Soup it is. Then we'll get you showered and back to bed. When you're feeling stronger, I want CJ to finish your markings as well as add to mine. After what happened, I don't want to waste another moment before we show all our kind that we belong together."

"I'd like that." And I needed it. Fortunately, so did he it seemed. "And I need you. I'm just afraid I'd fall asleep on you right now." My fingers traced random patterns across his chest and down his abdomen.

"Not to mention that there are too many people in the house right now." He grinned wickedly. "But, when you're a bit stronger, we can always take a shower. Running water covers a lot sounds."

With a laugh, I reached up to kiss the line of his jaw. "I do like how you think."

He nuzzled my neck and then stood. "I'll be right back. Do you want anything besides soup?"

"Just soup and maybe some juice."

"Got it." He paused at the door. "Maggie, you are all right."

"I know."

I wasn't quite ready to accept it yet, but I was getting there. The fact he wasn't securing me before leaving went a long way to convince me.

CHAPTER NINETEEN

H ot water beat down on me, easing the stiffness from my muscles. Steam filled the small bathroom. The scent of soap teased my nostrils. I'd spent the last ten minutes scrubbing my body, with the exception of my injured thigh that was carefully wrapped in plastic to keep the stitches dry, until there was no possible trace of the last week on me. Unfortunately, it wasn't as easy to scrub away the memories. But that's all they were – memories. Volk had lost again and soon we'd move against him.

Assuming he hadn't left the area.

It was possible that he'd done just that. But I didn't believe and neither did Jim. We knew Volk would come for us. In his mind, he had to. We'd beaten him and he didn't accept failure. The only way he'd ever quit coming after us was if he managed to turn us or we finally managed to kill him.

But I was safe here. I had to remember that. Volk couldn't get anywhere near me. Not until we were ready to spring our own trap.

I just hoped that day came soon, before anyone else fell victim to him.

As much as I wanted that, I wanted the chance to deal with Brittney and her brother even more. God, so much pain and fear could have been prevented if I'd simply killed the bitch when she'd dared put her hands on Jim. But I hadn't – and that had been the right decision at the time – but by helping Volk capture me and then Jim, she and her brother betrayed the clan and all our kind. They also signed their own death warrants.

I'd never be able to forget the moment Jim and I told Matt and Finn what we'd remembered. Matt's anger was cold and hard, but he'd kept it under control as he called Tamara and filled her in. Finn, on the other hand, exploded. Guilt for not giving us permission to kill the two combined with fury over the betrayal of clan and so much more. The only thing that kept her from going hunting for them herself was Matt's reminder that I needed her. She got her temper under control and had barely left my side since then.

An hour ago, the call came that we'd been waiting for. Tamara and her people had located Alec. He'd returned to his apartment and they moved in. Before they could contain him, he jumped from his second story balcony. Then he'd shifted and fled.

Fortunately or the rest of us, his freedom had been short lived.

I couldn't help feeling a touch of satisfaction to know how Tamara's people, most of whom shifted into some form of jungle cat, had quickly caught the grey wolf shifter. As foolish in shifted form as he was in human, he'd tried to fight. He hadn't had a chance. When Tamara reported back, it was to tell Matt that they'd transported the wolf's carcass to be cremated. Since it was clear Alec had been about to leave in a hurry, they really didn't have to worry. She'd make sure nothing pointed back to the clan if anyone should investigate to see what happened to him.

That left Brittney and, as far as I was concerned, she was mine. But we had to find her first. I had a feeling that when we found Volk, we'd find her. The only question was if she'd still be sane or if he'd have turned her—or worse. My bet was that he'd have grown tired of her and would have killed her. Still, I hoped I was wrong because she owed me and I wanted to make her pay.

Shaking my head, I forced the thoughts of vengeance from my mind. Sooner or later, I'd have my chance with Volk and, hopefully, with Brittney. Until then, I needed to concentrate on getting my strength back and accepting the fact I had beaten Volk again. It might have been close, but he hadn't turned me. I had to remember that and draw strength from it.

A smile touched my lips a short time later as the bathroom door opened. I didn't need to hear it opening over the sound of the water. The sudden change in air pressure and the short burst of cool air that billowed the shower curtain inward would have been enough. But it was his scent, that wonderful smell of grasslands, that brought a smile to my lips. I ducked my head under the water and waited, hoping he'd join me.

A moment later, a hand pushed back the shower curtain. Grinning, I waited. The curtain dropped back into place and he was standing behind me. As I lifted my face so the water flowed over it, his hands moved up my back to my shoulders. His fingers found all the muscles tight with nerves and remembered fear and anger. As they worked to ease the tension, his lips found my neck, the line of my jaw.

My breath shuddered as his hands moved from my shoulders to my breasts. I leaned back, needing to feel more of him. I reached up, pulling his head down so my mouth could find his. When I tried to turn, he held me firm. His right hand massaged my breast, his fingers playing with my nipple. His left arm wrapped around my waist, holding me close.

Pleasure rippled through me as his left hand cupped me. His teeth scraped my neck. His tongue then laved the line of my shoulder. When first one finger and then another thrust inside me, my knees went weak. My right arm reached up and I twisted my fingers in his hair, holding his head down and relishing the feel of his lips on my neck and then the line of my jaw.

"Jim." It was barely more than a whisper.

"Hush, just enjoy it."

His breath tickled my ear. Pleasure and need filled me as he played with my nipple and my clit. I rode his fingers, relishing the sensations that finally convinced me I was alive. The need for Jim I felt now turned the need to feed I'd experienced at Volk's hands into nothing but a fading memory. It would come back, but then I'd remember this and know Jim had helped me beat that bastard.

Panting, pulse pounding, my world centered on the emotions filling me and the sensations centered between my legs. But it wasn't enough. I wanted to ride more than his fingers. God, I wanted him.

Just as I was on the brink, Jim withdrew his fingers. He turned me and his mouth crushed down on mine. Moaning, I slid my arms around him, pressing him close. Skin to skin, if we could have been one, I'd have done it. Since that wasn't possible, I ran my hands down his back to his waist and over that fantastic ass of his. Then I grinned. His erection left no doubt he wanted me just as much as I wanted him. I braced my hands on his shoulders and jumped. His hands closed around my waist and I wrapped my legs around his waist. As I buried my face his the crook of his neck, he buried his cock in me. He braced his legs against the sides of the tub. One of my hands braced against the ceiling and the other against the wall to my right. We might fall and break our necks before we were done but, damn, it would be worth it.

We moved as one, slowly at first and then with an urgency neither of us could deny. Nothing else mattered. I was here with the man who I knew was the only man I wanted to share my life with. We were meant for one another. Thank God that, unlike our animal counterparts, our kind mated for life. At least if you were lucky enough to find your mate. If having to deal with Volk was the price I had to pay to have Jim in my life, it was worth it.

"Maggie, when this is over, let's go away for a while." He kissed the line of my jaw and shifted slightly. I'm not sure when it happened, but we were now lying in the tub, arms and legs twined, his back against the end of the tub. I rested against his chest, the fingers of my right hand teasing his nipple. "Where do you want to go?"

"Somewhere with a beach." I lifted my face and pressed my lips to his jaw. "But I have something else I want you to take care of right now."

"Really? And what would that be?" His hand cupped my breast as he looked down at me.

"Well, if you have to ask."

I grinned wickedly and carefully shifted positions. The tub was cramped and certainly not as comfortable as the bed would have been. But the running water, even if it had long ago turned cold, covered the sounds of our lovemaking. At least I hoped it did. There were others in the house – there were always others in the house – and I didn't want them listening in.

Jim's soft growl of protest brought a laugh to my lips, my first since before falling into Volk's hands. Keeping my eyes on his, I pushed back my wet hair and placed my knees on either side of his legs. He drew a quick breath as my right hand closed around his penis, stroking, teasing.

"Damn it!" he cursed as someone pounded on the bathroom door. "What?" he bellowed.

He shuddered as I took him in my mouth, my tongue swirling around the head of his cock. His eyes almost crossed as I took him deeper. It was both embarrassing and strangely erotic to know someone stood on the other side of the door as I deep throated my mate. From the look on Jim's face, he was having a hard time main-taining control. When he tried to withdraw, I only took him deeper, sucking, teasing with my tongue. It was time for us, even if it was stolen time in a bathtub with cold water beating down on us.

"I'm sorry to interrupt." Finn. I rolled my eyes and cupped Jim's balls in my hand. His hands fisted on my shoulders and a growl rumbled deep in his chest. "But everyone's here, including CJ, and there's food."

"All right." He looked down at me and I realized that his frustration at the interruption matched my own. "Now go away. We'll be out in a few minutes."

As his penis grew thicker and stiffened under my teasing, I slowly eased him out of my mouth. His hands closed around my waist and his mouth fastened on my breast as I shifted and then lowered myself over him. Now, as we both neared release, I could finally start believing that Volk really hadn't won. He hadn't turned me and, somehow, I would find a way to beat him once and for all.

But, damn it, couldn't Finn have waited ten more minutes before coming to tell us everyone had arrived? Well, an hour would have been even better.

"I don't care if every clan leader in the country is here," he growled. "I need you."

"Thank God." I bent down to kiss him. "Show me."

We took more than ten minutes but not the hour I'd have preferred. By the time we turned off the water and climbed out of the tub, the last of the steam had dissipated. If we tried to stifle giggles like a couple of teenagers sneaking in after curfew, I didn't care. For the first time opening the front door and finding Volk standing there, I felt clean and relaxed. More importantly, I felt loved. Jim still wanted me, as he'd proven several times.

There really are benefits to being a shapeshifter.

When we entered Stefan's den a few minutes later, I took two steps. Then I came to an abrupt halt and blushed deeply. At least I assumed it was deep because my face suddenly felt like it was on fire. If Jim hadn't been standing directly behind me, I'd probably have turned and fled. It was bad enough that Finn sat on the arm of Matt's chair, grinning at us like a loon. Matt simply smiled and winked. But they were almost a side note just then. There were six others sitting or standing around the room, seven if you counted CJ. The only way I'd not have realized all of them, save CJ, were Alphas would be if I happened to be unconscious. Since I wasn't, instinct had me trying to drop to my knees even as my tiger stirred and told me to face them as equals.

Well, that was new and I wasn't sure I liked it.

Swallowing hard, I reached back, relieved when Jim's hand closed around mine. Then he moved to my side and escorted me further into the room. We moved as one to stand before Matt and Finn. Without a word, we sank to hands and knees, showing submission to our Alphas. Let everyone there see that Matt and Finn commanded respect even from those closest to them.

"No formalities tonight, Maggie, Jim," Matt said as he motioned for us to stand. "In fact, while we discuss what happened these last two weeks and what our next steps should be to deal with Volk, CJ here is going to finish your markings."

"We haven't figured out a design yet," Jim began as he helped me to my feet.

"I made some sketches I hope will meet with your approval."

Finn grinned and I shook my head. Of course she had. Not that I minded. The design she'd done for my initial clan tattoo was a work of art.

"Thanks." What else was there to say?

"Then let's get down to business."

Matt quickly made the introductions. Jim and I greeted the clan leaders from New Mexico, Louisiana and Oklahoma. Finally putting a face with the name of Finn's grandmother, much less the power, it was easy to see who my dear friend took after. Irene Walkinghorse didn't look like she could defeat any or all of us, much less do so without breaking a sweat. Even so, I had no doubt she could do just that. It seemed only right, and somehow natural, to move to stand before her and then sink to my hands and knees. For once, my tiger didn't object. Funny, in that moment, I realized the only female she'd willingly submitted to before then had been Finn. I probably ought to think about that later, but this wasn't the time.

"When we were kids, Finn used to tell me about visiting you in Tulsa. I'm honored to finally meet you," I said, head bowed. "She once told me if I ever needed anything and she wasn't there to help, I was to go to you. Even though she is here to help now, the problem before us affects all our kind. I've learned that the hard way. I hope you, and the others, will help."

I felt Jim's approval as he stood a step behind me. But I was almost undone as I felt Finn's approval and support. Then Irene Walkinghorse reached out, her hand tilting my head up so I'd look her in the eye.

"I remember the stories she used to tell me about some of the *adventures* you two got into together."

Amusement colored her voice and I had a feeling Finn had been much more open with her grandmother about what the two of us had done over the years than she had ever been with her parents. Not that I could say anything. I still hadn't told my parents everything we'd done. Hell, I hadn't told them most of it.

God, my parents! I hadn't told them I'd joined the Texas clan. Of course, I had a feeling Eileen had already bent their ears more than once over it. How in the world was I going to explain to them why I'd done it . . . and what had happened since then?

"And I'm glad you two have found one another again. You'll keep the rest of us, those of us who don't always want to be dragged into the modern age, in line." Irene's smile, full of mischief and approval, made me forget my worry about how my parents would react, at least for a little while.

"Thank you." I bowed my head and accepted Jim's help in standing. "Clan leader?" I looked to Matt, knowing I needed to take my next cue from him.

"Why don't you let CJ finish your markings, Maggie? She's set up her table in here. So you can listen in and add anything you think we need to know."

"All right." I'm not ashamed to admit I was a little confused. I thought he'd want me to tell the others what I could about Volk and what had happened.

"Maggie, Matt and Finn have already told us what you and your former clan leader had to say about Volk's activities in California. They've also filled us in on what happened to you and Jim last week.

Stefan showed us the lab reports from your blood tests and explained exactly what he thinks Volk has been doing to create his ferals," Irene said. "I don't know about the others, but I believe we need to figure out if he's been working in our territories and if he's managed to take any of our people, especially any of the loners. Then we can decide what our next move should be."

One thing did bother me about this gathering – Declan's absence. Sure, his clan didn't come close to bordering on the Texas clan's territory. But the trouble had started with the Northern California clan. I had no doubts there was still information about Volk and what he'd done, both before Declan took over the clan and after, Declan hadn't told Matt or me. That information might be the final piece we needed to find and defeat Volk once and for all.

"Maggie." Finn's voice was soft and understanding reflected in her eyes. "We asked Declan to join us and he turned us down. He said he needed to deal with the situation at home and that you'd understand."

Chewing my lower lip, I shook my head. What in the world could be more important than finally dealing with Volk?

God, I was a fool. Declan hadn't said he needed to deal with clan business. No, he'd said "the situation at home". That could mean only one thing: Eileen. Maybe instead of being mad at me for leaving the clan, she was mad at Declan for putting me in danger and in a position where I'd want to move on. God, in a way that was even worse. The clan needed them to be united and strong. The last thing a new clan, and that was what the Northern California clan was, needed was their Alpha and his mate fighting. I made a mental note to call my sister just as soon as possible. I'd almost rather her be angry with me than with Declan.

Almost.

"I'll do whatever I can to fill in any blanks. Believe me, the sooner Volk is dealt with, the better I'll feel."

"Let's get you and CJ settled and then we'll all get down to work." Finn got to her feet and moved to my side. "Jim, there's food in the kitchen. Hannah and Stefan made sure we have everything we could want before heading upstairs. Why don't you fix Finn a plate and then grab something for yourself?"

He gave my hand a quick squeeze before moving off. Feeling a bit overwhelmed, I let Finn lead me across the room to where CJ had set up her table. As the others started discussing strange occurrences in their territories over the last few months, Finn handed CJ several sheets of paper. The tattooist studied them, nodding slightly. Then she handed them back to Finn, tapping one finger against the top drawing.

"That one. Do you have a stencil made?" CJ motioned for me to remove my tank top. Once I sat on the edge of the table, clad only in jeans and a sports bra, she checked my earlier tattooing. Her fingers were light as they ran over the tattoo. "It looks good, Maggie. I was worried that bastard might have done something to it."

In a way, it surprised me Volk hadn't tried to ruin the tattoo. "Do I get at least see what the two of you have planned for me?"

"Nope," Finn replied with a grin as she produced the stencil from a folder. She watched as CJ prepared my upper lef arm and shoulder for the new ink. Then she nodded as CJ applied the stencil. When I craned my neck in an attempt to see, Finn simply cocked an eyebrow and shook her head. With a sigh, I lifted my legs onto the padded table and flopped onto my stomach. "No looking, Maggs."

I resisted the urge to stick my tongue out at her. "Let's get this over with, CJ."

"Don't worry, Maggie. She's outdone herself with this design."

"Why doesn't that reassure me?"

CJ laughed and told me to relax. Easy for her to say. She was a walking canvas. Me? All this inking was new to me.

Doing my best to ignore the pain, which really wasn't much, more like a million little bee stings, I listened as the clan leaders spoke. None of them had heard of any disappearances of our kind in their territories over the last few months. There had been a couple of deaths that had raised some concern but those deaths could also have been the accidents they seemed to be. Hearing about one in Oklahoma near Lake Texhoma, my stomach knotted. It sounded too much like what Volk had been doing before Declan took over the clan to be coincidence.

"Hang on a second, CJ." I waited until I was sure I wouldn't ruin the tattoo by moving. Then I sat up. No way could I address the clan leaders lying on my belly when I wasn't dying or at least showing submission. "Pardon me, clan leaders, but before Declan took over the Northern California clan, Volk would hunt normals on the trails and in the woods. He always made sure the kills looked like animal attacks, whether he actually killed the person involved or they died by falling over a cliff or running into traffic or whatever. I know of at least two more instances after Declan arrived at the clan and before Volk tried to take over. That's why Declan wanted to try him by our laws. It wouldn't surprise me to know that's what happened in Oklahoma."

"It makes sense," Adam Walkinghorse, Finn's uncle, said from where he stood behind his mother's chair. "Volk has proven that he's no fool. Sadistic and a threat to all of us, yes, but not a fool. He'd enjoy knowing he killed innocents right under our noses but he wouldn't do so in such a way that would call attention to him. At least not before he was ready to make a move. You threw him off, Maggie. First, by actually locating him and then by killing his feral. That made you a target. He won't leave the area until he's killed you."

"He can try, but he's never laying a hand on her again." Jim's voice was low, harsh, and my heart warmed to hear it. He'd fight for me just as I would him. I just hoped he understood what I knew was coming.

"Adam's right." I caught my lower lip between my teeth and thought hard. "Volk has had a week to fume. His ego won't let him just walk away. If he hasn't been trying to locate Jim and me, he soon will be. My bet is that he's been watching Jim's ranch, waiting for us to finally return home."

"I have to agree," Finn said. Even as she did, she motioned for me to lie down so CJ could get back to work. Sighing, I complied. With a chuckle, CJ told me to relax.

"So what do we do?" Jerrod Young, New Mexico's clan leader, asked.

"We set our own trap," Matt said. "Adam?"

Finn's uncle stepped forward. A moment later he sank to the floor at his mother's feet. Even as he did, there could be no mistaking his power or the respect with which the others held him. He looked across the room to where I lay and smiled. It wasn't much of a smile but there was no mistaking his approval and support.

"I've been scouting Jim's ranch along with Tamara and several of your trackers as well as our own. We picked up the scent of the renegade and his partner earlier today. It was strong enough to convince us that they've been going there for several days now. But Volk's not as smart as he thinks he is. They're using the same path and staying in the same basic area each time."

"Where?" Jim moved to stand next to the padded table. His hand rested on the small of my back. That one simple action spoke volumes and I doubted anyone in the room didn't realize we were mated and that we'd do whatever it took to deal with Volk once and for all.

"Near the cattle guard on the eastern side of the property. It looks like they're parking about a mile up the road near the creek and shifting there. Then they're coming in at the cattle guard."

"Then we have video of it." Jim grinned at his brother. "I told you I wasn't being paranoid when I put in the surveillance system."

"Can you access it from here?" Irene asked.

"I can."

"Then I believe we need to see what that can tell us," she said and Finn was the first to agree.

"What do you need to set it up, Jim?" Matt asked.

"A laptop or computer and internet connection."

"Let's get on it then." Matt got to his feet. "Adam, will you help?"

"Of course." He rose with an effortless grace I admired and wished I possessed.

"We'll take a break while they work," Finn said. "Well, most of us will. CJ and Maggie will keep at it." Now she grinned and moved in our direction. As she squatted next to the table so we were basically eye-to-eye, everyone but her grandmother drifted toward the kitchen. Irene joined us, nodding in approval as she looked at CJ's work.

Why did everyone but me get to see the tattoo? Shouldn't I have been the first to see it?

"Your design, child?" Irene asked Finn, her fingers lightly tracing my clan markings.

"Both of them are. I wanted something special for Maggie."

"They're both beautiful." Now she knelt at her granddaughter's side. "Maggie, I want you to listen to me."

"A-all right." I swallowed hard, not sure I wanted to hear what Irene had to say.

"I know you're still worried about what Volk did to you. That's normal. But I've talked with Stefan and I have seen the results of all the blood tests. The drugs are out of your system. You didn't break when he had you, when you were the most vulnerable. You trusted in the bond you have with your mate. Now you need to trust in your own self, in the strength you have. If you don't, that bastard will have won even though he failed to turn you."

I closed my eyes and breathed deeply. Intellectually, I knew she was right. But I remembered all too clearly how close I'd come to breaking. It would have been so easy to give in. I couldn't deny how I worried that just seeing Volk would return me to that hell. That's why I needed to be there when he was finally dealt with. I'd like it to be by my hand, but that was secondary to simply making sure he never did to anyone else what he'd tried to do to me. Besides, I had a feeling that I'd be busy dealing with Brittney, something that brought a warm feeling to my heart.

"Maggie." Finn lightly touched my cheek and I opened my eyes. Her grandmother no longer knelt next to her. Looking past Finn, I saw Irene standing at the far end of the room, watching as Jim, Matt and Adam set up a laptop and a series of monitors so everyone could review the security video from the ranch. "My grandmother's right. Here's what I want you to think about. Grandma is the strongest Alpha I've ever been around. Everyone here respects her and we'd all defer to her if she'd let us. The most important thing in her life is making sure our kind is safe. The next important thing is making sure I am safe. She'd not hesitate one moment to kill you if she thought you were a danger to either our kind as a whole or to me individually. Instead, she's entrusting you with my safety as my second."

The buzzing of CJ's machine stopped and shed wiped down my shoulder. "Finn's right," she said. "So figure out how to wipe that bastard from existence. He's caused more than enough trouble as is. By the way, I want to be there when you wipe the ground with that bitch Brittney's ass."

"All right." I grinned as Finn winked in approval. "How much longer?"

"Until this is done?" CJ asked and I nodded. "Another couple of hours or so. You up to it?"

"Finn?" All they were supposed to be doing was finishing up the clan markings and adding my mating to Matt. I'd assumed the mating marks were what CJ had been working on at my left shoulder. But now that I thought about it, maybe I shouldn't have assumed anything where Finn was concerned.

"Shh. This is necessary and I'm hoping you'll like it."

"All right. But tell Jim I want to be able to see the video feed."

With a nod, Finn got to her feet. As she crossed the room to where Jim and the others stood, CJ got back to work. I closed my eyes and concentrated on the sound of Jim's voice as he worked with Adam and Matt to set up the monitors. As long as I could hear him and sense him nearby, I knew everything was going to be all right.

"There!" Finn's voice was hard and I opened my eyes. As I did, I realized that I'd somehow managed to fall asleep. If CJ hadn't reached down and held me in place, I'd have rolled over and then I'd really have been in trouble. She'd have killed me if I did anything something to ruin the tattoo she'd been working so hard on.

"What?" God, I wanted to sit up. I couldn't see what they were looking at from where I lay.

Jim moved quickly to my side. In one hand he held a tablet. As he pulled a chair up next to the table where I lay, he ran his finger over the tablet screen. A moment later, the same video feed the others were watching appeared. The moment it did, my lips drew back and I bared my teeth. I'd know that black wolf anywhere. I'd watched it standing back from the melee as the ferals attacked the clan meeting that night almost a year ago. The smaller grey wolf I'd never seen before but I had no doubt who it was.

"The black wolf's Volk," I confirmed and watched as he jumped the cattle guard before trotting down the dirt road like it owned the place, the smaller wolf trailing behind. That overconfidence would doom him.

"They've shown up at almost the exact same time every day for the last three days. They wait several hours and then leave. I've no doubt they're waiting for the two of you to return home," Adam said from across the room.

"Then let's oblige them."

CJ somehow understood I wasn't going to lie still. She gave my tattoo a quick wipe. Before she could smear ointment on it, I was on my feet. It didn't matter I wore only jeans and a sports bra. All that mattered was the end of the hunt was in sight and I wanted it over, one way or another.

"What do you have in mind?" Irene asked. She leaned back in her chair and crossed her legs at the ankles. There was something in her expression that might have been approval. Not that it mattered. I'd come here to find and deal with Volk. Now, with a little help, I'd be able to finish that mission and get on with my life.

"We know the renegade's habits now. That's the one thing we didn't have before. So we use it to our advantage. We put others onto the ranch before he and that bitch with him get there, preferably not long after they leave the day before. I don't want to run the risk of Volk catching on to our plan." Several of those gathered nodded in agreement. "Our people will keep out of sight and downwind so Volk doesn't get scent of them when he and Brittney return. Before that happens, some should shift. The others will remain in their human forms, armed and documenting what happens next."

"And what would that be?" Finn asked, a hint of disapproval in her voice. She knew what I planned and still didn't fully agree.

"Jim and me returning home. Matt, Finn, you'll come with us. It's what he'd expect, especially now that Brittney is with him and feeding him what she saw at that last clan meeting. Once you've been there long enough to be sure we're okay and settled, you guys will leave. Let him see you drive off. But then you circle back. It won't be long before Volk makes his move and that's when we have him and his little friend."

"And what then?" Jean-Paul Boudreaux, the Louisiana clan leader, asked.

"That won't be up to us. They will be given the chance to surrender and answer for their crimes." I reached for Jim's hand as he joined me. "But I know Volk. He won't surrender. He will do what-ever it takes to kill Jim and me. If I'm right, know this. I will not let him hurt my mate again."

"Nor will he get near what's mine," Jim growled.

"So unless he completely surprises me, he'll fight. If he dies in the fight, so be it. He would have made his choice. What we have to accept here and now is simple. We can't let Volk's form of evil continue to exist."

"And the female?" Irene asked.

"Clan leaders?"

I turned to Matt and Finn. Left to my own devices, she'd be dead for what she'd done. Not because she helped Volk take me, although that was reason enough. No, she'd be dead because she helped that bastard get his hands on Jim. For that she had to pay.

"If she doesn't fight, she faces clan justice. If she fights, do what needs to be done, Maggie," Finn said, her voice hard.

I bowed my head, glad she understood.

"Are you sure this is what you want, Matthew? Volk has violated our laws, but is the tracker voicing your will or that of her former clan leader?" Young asked.

Before either Jim or I could respond, Matt turned to Young, his anger clear. "You're out of order!" he snapped. "Yes, she is fulfilling the mission that first brought her here. But this is what I want and what I know to be true. I've seen what that bastard did to her and to my brother. I've talked with her former clan leader and know what sort of cancer Volk is. If you don't want to be part of this, that's your decision. My clan will do whatever it takes to make sure Volk doesn't harm anyone else, normal or shapeshifter."

"As will mine," Irene said as she stood and moved to Matt's side.

"And mine," Boudreaux added, his Cajun accent thicker than before.

Young ran a hand over his face and then looked at me. Much to my surprise, he bowed his head before speaking. "My apologies, Maggie. I know we need to deal with Volk. You have my support and the support of my clan." Now he lifted his face and looked at Matt. "My apologies to you as well, my friend. Put my stupidity down to lack of sleep and worry about what will happen if we screw this up and the normals find out about us."

"When do we make our move?" Boudreaux asked.

"Next weekend," Finn said and pinned me with a firm look, instantly stopping me from objecting. "We need time to set everything up. Part of that will be letting 'leak' news that Maggie was much more seriously injured than we first thought as was Jim. Let Volk think he broke her and we are still trying to put her back together. Let him believe he managed to, at the least, damage their mating bond. It will make him more confident—and careless."

"Plus it gives Maggie more time to heal," Irene added, clearly approving of her granddaughter's plan.

I knew better to object when each of the clan leaders voiced their approval. Not that I liked it. The longer we delayed, the more likely the chance Volk would flee the area—or kill an innocent.

"It seems we have a plan to set into motion then." Matt motioned for everyone to return to their seats.

CJ crooked a finger at Jim, signaling that it was his turn. If that wasn't my cue to find the nearest mirror and see what Finn had designed, I didn't know what was.

CHAPTER TWENTY

"Are you sure about this?"

Five days had passed since the clan meeting. Finn and I stood in Jim's—our—kitchen, cleaning up after dinner. Hearing the concern in her voice, I put the last plate in the dishwasher and straightened. Then I turned to face her. Her expression was troubled and worry was reflected in her eyes. I wished I could reassure her but I knew it was useless. She'd seen what Volk tried to do to me. Now I was willingly acting as bait for the trap to finally ensnare him and, if we were lucky, Brittney as well.

"No." I'd be honest with her even if I wouldn't admit my concerns to anyone else, not even Jim. "But I have to do this. Please understand. I have to, not only to finish what I started but to prove to Volk that he hasn't beaten me."

Okay, I also needed to prove it to myself. That, however, was one thing I couldn't admit to her.

"You just be careful and don't do anything foolish." The look she gave me spoke volumes. If I managed to get myself killed, she'd find a way to resurrect me just so she could kill me again.

"I won't. I promise. Jim and I are going to play this by the book.

Once you guys are gone, we're going to wait and see if he takes the bait. If not, then we'll try again tomorrow."

"Are you armed?"

Was I armed? She had to be kidding. Before leaving Stefan's, Jim had watched with a critical eye as I slid a knife into my boot and a matched pair into arm sheaths. Then he'd handed me my Glock. He'd nodded in approval as I checked the clip and then chambered a round. The Glock now rested in a pancake holster at my right side. Not that I wanted to use any of those mundane weapons. Given the chance, I wanted to shift and teach the renegade what a fatal mistake it had been to try to subvert my white tiger.

Instead of answering, I simply nodded. Finn would worry if she knew how well armed I was. Hopefully she wouldn't ask me to prove it.

"You know what you and Matt are to do?"

"Yeah. When we leave, we'll drive out the front gate and turn like we're heading home. But understand this. As soon as we're out of sight, we're pulling over and getting back here on the double. We're not about to let you face that bastard on your own."

"I'm not going to argue." Even if we wouldn't be alone. Tamara's trackers, not to mention those who'd come from Oklahoma, were already in place around the ranch, ready, waiting. "You just be as careful as you've been telling me to be."

She nodded and looked over her shoulder as Matt and Jim joined us. Neither said anything. They didn't need to. It was now dark outside. Time to put our plan into action. Then Finn was holding me close, her mouth near my ear.

"You will take care of yourself and not do anything foolish, Maggs. Promise me."

"I promise to do whatever I have to in order to bring that bastard down. He's not hurting me or mine again."

She nodded and then stepped back, her hand reaching for Matt's. "We'd best be on our way then."

Despite the butterflies in my stomach, or maybe because of them,

I reached for Jim's hand. The four of us moved through the house, talking and laughing. To anyone watching, nothing would seem out of the ordinary. Jim and I were a couple glad to finally be home and Matt and Finn were relieved to see us well and safe.

As we stepped outside, I lifted my head and inhaled. My stomach churned and my mouth went dry as that foul carrion stench I associated with Volk filled my nostrils. Part of me wanted to turn and run inside, locking the doors behind me. But I didn't. Instead I drew Jim's arm across my shoulders and leaned into him, laughing at something Finn said. I knew from the way Jim gave my shoulders a quick squeeze that he'd scented Volk as well.

"You two be careful going home," I called a few moments later as Matt started the engine.

Finn leaned across him so she could respond through his open window. "You get some rest, Maggie. You still aren't fully recovered."

Oh, that was a good one. Let the renegade think I was still weak and probably damaged. Finn always could think on her feet.

"I'm fine. Call when you get home."

I could think on my feet too. If Volk thought Finn would be calling, he'd move sooner rather than later and that suited me just fine.

"I will."

Finn gave a wave and sat back, nodding to Matt she was ready to leave. Matt nodded in response and put the car into gear. A few moments later the car disappeared into the darkness.

Step one complete.

"Glad to be home?" Jim asked as climbed back up the steps to the porch.

I slid my arms around him, relieved to feel his own weapons. "Very. It's good to be alone with just you. I love your brother and Finn, but we need some alone time."

A slight breeze, one that would normally be cool and refreshing, blew through the trees. It carried Volk's scent. He was closer. That meant he was on the move. It was all I could do not to tense. I wouldn't let him know I'd realized he was near. No, we needed – I needed – him to come closer so we could spring the trap.

At least I didn't scent any ferals with him. Like Volk, ferals had their own particular scent. It didn't matter what their animal form. They all smelled sick, like they were ill. After what I'd been through at Volk's hands, I understood why. They were sick and broken. The fact he didn't have any with him would make things much easier.

For maybe five minutes, we stood there, arms around one another, talking softly about nothing in particular. Then Jim suggested it was time to go inside. I nodded and turned. This was all according to the plan we'd mapped out with the clan leaders. Still, I'd feel better once inside. We'd be able to watch Volk's approach through the surveillance feed but he wouldn't be able to see our preparations.

The moment the door closed behind us, Jim reached for the tablet PC he'd left on the hall table. A few seconds later, we were looking at the security video of the front of the house. He then gave me a nod. We had our individual assignments. While he watched the feed, making sure Volk didn't get too close to the house, I needed to make it look like we were getting ready for bed.

I moved through the house, turning off lights and then turning one on in the bedroom. I moved around the room, much as I would any normal evening. Anyone watching the house would see my shadow against the blinds as I turned down the bed. Once I had, I switched off the light and moved to the bathroom. I flicked on the light and turned on the shower. Then, to add one finishing touch to the illusion I'd been creating, I called for Jim to come join me. He called back that he was on his way.

I moved silently through the now dark house back to where I'd left Jim. The glow from the tablet illuminated his face as he watched the video feed. His hand found mine and together we waited in silence, our eyes glued to the screen. Five minutes, then ten passed and I wondered if I'd been wrong. Maybe I hadn't scented Volk. Then I saw a change in the shadows on the other side of the drive, almost directly across from the front door. Before I could say anything, Jim reached out and enlarged the image.

"There!" I whispered, lips close to his ears.

We watched, both of us hardly breathing, as a dark shape slowly moved forward. A dark wolf with green eyes. Volk. A few feet behind him, a smaller grey wolf slinked, stomach low to the ground. Good, he'd brought his *friend* with him. They were almost in our trap. Just a little bit further. That's all. A few more yards and we'd have them.

A low growl pulled my attention away from the tablet screen. For one brief moment, I stared at Jim, not quite sure what he was doing. His hands worked to pull his shirt over his head even as he toed off his shoes. As he fumbled with his belt, he bared his teeth and arched his back. He was going to shift. No, he was shifting.

Well, two could play that way.

"No," he hissed as he kicked his jeans to the side.

"Yes," I countered softly. I needed to do this just as much as he did.

Then his panther stood next to me, its large head rubbing against my leg. Damn it. By shifting first, he forced me to wait. Otherwise, we'd be stuck inside. Paws and claws are great for fighting but not for turning door knobs. Well, we'd be having a discussion about that later.

Besides, it wouldn't delay my shift by much. With one eye on the video displayed on the tablet and the other on my mate, I began undressing. I carefully put aside my weapons before stripping out of my clothes. Pain coursed through me as the shift began. I let it go only so far and then held it. I might still look human – well, mostly human – but my tiger waited just below the surface. Once I released control, she'd take over and the shift would finish in moments.

All I had to do was hold on a few seconds longer.

There! The video image showed what I'd been waiting for. A dark shape slowly separated from the shadows from across the drive. It paced forward and then stopped. I watched as it raised its head and sniffed. In a very human move, it nodded its head once, as if in satisfaction. Then it lowered until its belly almost touched the pavement and crept nearer to the house.

"Go!"

I threw open the door and watched as the panther launched himself through it. The black wolf now stood at the top step of the porch. It paused, confused. Then, as it was thrown off the porch under the panther's weight, it snarled and growled and the fight was on.

And I was damned if I was going to be left out of it.

I dropped to hands and knees and released the last of my control. There was a moment of almost overwhelming pain as the shift settled on me. I cursed the slowness of the transformation even though one part of me knew it was happening quicker than ever. But not quickly enough. Not when I could see that damned wolf biting and tearing at my mate.

"Maggie, no!"

The order sounded the moment I leapt through the door. I slid to a stop and turned my head toward the speaker. Frustration filled me. That was my mate. He was fighting for me, for us. I smelled his blood. He was hurt but not as badly as he'd hurt the wolf.

I growled and paced forward. Before I could leave the porch, her hand reached down. Her fingers caressed my ears, soothing and reassuring. Then she knelt, putting her arms around my neck.

"Let him do this, Maggie. He needs to do this," Finn said. "If the renegade gets past him, then you'll have your chance."

I wanted to argue but the Alpha was right. Still, seeing how the wolf's jaws clamped down at the curve of the panther's neck just above his powerful shoulder, I roared. When others of the clan, as well as our allies, answered my roar, the wolf startled and loosened his grip. A large black paw, claws fully extended, slashed forward. Blood sprayed into the air and the wolf yelped in agony as long gashes opened down his side and flank.

But now the wolf was focused exactly where I wanted – on me. Good. Let him see that he hadn't broken me. Let him realize what a mistake he'd made by not killing me when he had the chance. Instead of making a feral devoted to him, he'd created the device of his demise.

Volk slowly circled back and forth in front of the porch, growling, frothing from the mouth. My lips pulled back, baring my teeth. Another roar and I gave myself a huge shake. Finn's arms loosened from around my neck as she fell back with a startled cry. She could punish me later, but now it was my turn.

At the top of the steps, I roared again, challenging Volk. He'd endangered all of us, including my sister and her family. He'd tried to turn me. Worse, he'd tried to make me kill my mate. For that, he'd die.

Teeth bared, the wolf danced back and forth on stiff legs. Blood poured from the wounds in his side and down his flank but he acted as if he didn't feel them. His jaws snapped as he dashed up the steps. One paw slashed forward, claws unsheathed. A high whine of pain filled the air as I lay open several long wounds across the wolf's snout. I roared in satisfaction and started down the steps. It was time to finish this before he managed to find some way to slip out of our grasp.

Another roar sounded and a black blur streaked forward. Before the wolf could change his line of attack, Jim's panther hit him full body and they went rolling across the drive. Pride in my mate filled me. Not only an alpha but a warrior as well.

Jaws snapped, teeth tore and claws slashed. Blood filled the air as did the cries of pain from the wolf.

Even better was his fear. It was like a perfume that filled the night air. Good. Let him know what his victims had felt.

Suddenly, a howl from the right sounded. I swung my head in its direction in time to see the smaller grey wolf sprinting toward the fight. Roaring, I charged. She was mine. She'd tried to lay hands on my mate in human form. Then she betrayed both of us to Volk. But that had not been enough. Now she dared try to harm Jim. Foolish wolf.

When I slammed into her, she rolled head over tail across the drive and into the grass. Slowly, she regained her feet. Ears flat, growling, I crept toward her. I could smell her fear. What I couldn't smell was the taint of her being turned. As we circled one another, I watched and waited.

She was no more a fighter as a wolf than she had been as a human. Like a boxer telegraphing his next punch, I watched the muscles of her shoulders bunch as she prepared to launch herself at me. Good. It was time to end this.

My right front paw, claws fully extended, caught her in mid-air. Blood sprayed over me from the deep gashes left in her side. My roar was a direct contrast to her pain filled yelp. She landed in a heap near me. But the fight wasn't out of her yet. She tried to drag herself to her feet, her jaws snapping as I neared. The same paw that had opened her side, swiped at her head. She gave another yelp as more blood spilled from new wounds. Coldly, confidently, I moved closer. She was suffering and I wasn't Volk. I'd give her a quick death unless the Alphas stopped me.

"End her suffering, Maggie," Finn ordered from where she stood a few feet away.

I bent my head and closed my mouth around the grey wolf's throat. The human part of me gagged as I increased the pressure, biting through skin and muscle. With my right front paw resting on the wolf's body, I twisted my head, tearing out her throat. Blood gushed. I turned away, spitting out what was in my mouth. One down. One to go.

I looked to where my mate and the renegade fought. Another roar, triumphant and proud, filled the air as my mate's beautiful black paw sliced through the air and catch the renegade in an unprotected moment.

"Finish him, Jim," Matt ordered as Jim opened the wolf's belly.

Instead of doing what the Alpha ordered, the panther turned its head in my direction. We didn't need to speak. He knew I needed to be there, to see up close and personal that my own private nightmare was dead. I padded to his side and rubbed my head against his neck.

As I did, the wolf feebly tried to get to its feet. Before it could, I butted him with my head, knocking him back. Then I placed a heavy paw on his side. It was time to finish it.

The panther ducked his head, his mouth closing around the wolf's throat. The sound of muscle and tissue tearing filled the air. The wolf gave a shudder beneath my paw and then went limp. Satisfied, I nuzzled my mate. Then I returned to where the lifeless form of the grey wolf lay. I grabbed it by the scruff of the neck and dragged the corpse to the steps, dropping it there for the clan leaders to see. A moment later, Jim dropped the black wolf's body next to it.

"Adam, Tamara, take them down to the stable and clean them up," Finn said as she moved to our sides. Kneeling, she hugged us both. "You two are not to shift until you are back here where we can treat your injuries." There was no mistaking the command in her voice.

"Danny, I'll leave it to you to take care of the carcasses," Matt said. Then he turned his attention back to us. "We'll wait for you two to return. Then Maggie can call Declan and let him know this is done."

"You did good, both of you," Adam said we started down the drive toward the barn.

We had. Maybe now we could spend some time just getting to know one another instead of worrying what a madman might do next. Of course, there was still one bit of unfinished business I had to deal with. But it could wait a little while longer.

CHAPTER TWENTY-ONE

"They're up to something."

Two weeks had passed since that final confrontation with Volk. After making sure Jim hadn't been too badly injured, I'd called Declan and told him it was over. Volk would never bother any of our kind again. Then I'd spent half an hour reassuring my sister that I was all right and happy. She'd promised to fly out to visit as soon as she could. Her parting comment had been to remind me that I'd better get in touch with our parents and let them know what was happening.

That conversation waited until the next day. Which was probably for the best since both Mom and Dad had wanted to speak with Jim. I still don't know what they said to one another but by the time Jim came looking for me to give me the phone back, my parents had been reassured. They made me promise to come for a visit, and to bring Jim, before too much more time passed.

In the time since, Jim and I had been getting to know one another despite more than a few very long days he'd had to put in at work. After being off-duty the better part of three weeks, he had a great deal to catch up on. But that had given me time to start the process of getting licensed to practice law in Texas. It would take time and, heaven help me, I'd have to take at least part of the Bar Exam, but it beat the alternative of having to go back to law school. Until then, I'd study, do some work for Tamara and learn the lay of the land.

Now, with the weekend finally here, I'd been looking forward to a couple of days alone with Jim. Unfortunately, Matt and Finn had something else in mind. That morning, Finn called to say there was a clan meeting scheduled for tonight.

Now, with the sun beginning to set, everyone was starting to arrive. When I tried asking Finn what was going on, she simply told me not to worry, that everything was all right. It was just that some business had come up and Matt wanted to deal with it right away.

Not that I believed her then or now, ten minutes later.

"I have to agree with you, but I can't figure out what it is." Jim pressed the back of my hand to his lips and then nodded when Matt signaled him. "Maybe now he'll let me know what's going on."

"Somehow I doubt it."

"Me too." He brushed his lips against mine and then hurried to where his brother stood across the room. As he did, Finn appeared and linked arms with me.

"Ready?"

"It would be nice to know what I'm supposed to be ready for," I groused.

"Nothing bad, I promise, Maggs. Just some business and then a party. Matt and I figured the clan – and especially you and Jim – needs it after all that's happened."

"What I need is a weekend away with my mate," I growled.

"Let him get caught up at work and then you guys can run away for a long weekend. I assume that works for you."

"Yeah, except then I'll be up to my neck studying for the Bar."

Okay, I'll admit it. I was pissy. But this was going to be the first night in almost a week Jim had been home before ten. He wasn't on duty the next two days. I'd planned on spending most of it in bed.

Now I wasn't sure what was going to happen because there was definitely something going on. Finn was up to something. But what?

Five minutes later, I took my place to the right and slightly behind Finn's chair at the front of the great room. To my left, in his role as Matt's second, stood Jim. We'd had just enough time to confirm that our Alphas were definitely up to something and most definitely pleased about it. Unfortunately for my peace of mind, Jim had no more clue about what that might be than did I.

It still amazed me how even the children grew silent when Matt called for order. Oh, not complete silence. But not the mid-level buzz that seemed to accent clan meetings under Declan. It was yet another indication of the respect the clan members had for Matt and Finn.

For the next few minutes, Matt brought everyone up to date on what had happened with Volk. There was a real sense of relief that went through the room when he told how the renegade would never bother any of us again. Jim found some very interesting point on the ceiling to study when a few of those gathered cheered to learn he'd been the one to dispatch Volk. Pride filled me to hear their approval and support for my mate. He deserved it and so much more.

"Before we adjourn for a well-deserved party, there's one more piece of business we need to deal with," Matt said.

Something in his voice warned me this "one more piece of business" was behind his and Finn's attitudes. Not that he was giving anything away – yet. Damn, I really did need to remember to never, ever play poker with him.

"Alton, will you join us?"

Jim's quick intake of breath, so soft I barely heard it, had me looking at him in concern. The muscles of his jaw jumped, and he reached for my hand. Then he did something I'd never have expected. He broke protocol and stepped toward me, leaving his position as Matt's second.

"Are you all right?" I didn't try to keep the concern from my voice.

"That's Alton Royal," he said softly, his mouth close to my ear. "He took over the pride when Matt became clan leader."

Jim quickly told me how Alton had been married to a normal. About a year before Finn joined the pride, his wife had been killed when her car was struck by a drunk driver. Her death had almost killed Alton and he'd never really recovered. He'd tried stepping down as pride leader when Jenny had died. Matt had asked him to stay on, knowing the man would need something to keep him anchored as he grieved. That Alton was coming before the clan leaders now could mean only one thing: he was going to renew his request to step down.

As Alton approached Matt and Finn, the clan waited in silence. You could feel the support and apprehension that hung in the air. Even those who belonged to one of the other prides or packs cared for this man. They hurt for him and his loss. All I could do was wait and wonder what was about to happen.

Three feet from where Matt and Finn sat, Alton stopped and slowly dropped to his knees. Before he could speak, Finn was out of her chair. The clan's approval as she knelt, taking his hands in hers, was clear. Then she stood and helped him to his feet.

"Matt, Finn, I'm tired and I want to have time to play with my grandkids and take my boat out and fish," he began. "When my Jenny died, I asked to step down as pride leader. Matt, you were right to ask me to stay on. I needed the anchor you and the pride gave me as I grieved. I'll always miss Jenny, but now I know I can live without her.

"I've known that for some time now, but I've waited to ask to step down. I wanted to make sure there was someone at least as strong as I once was to lead the pride. I found that person at the last clan meeting. With your approval, I'd like to step down in his favor. He's not only younger than me and stronger, but I know he will always have the best interest of the pride and clan at heart. More than that, he has a strong mate to stand with him. She will be the omega to his alpha and together they will be strong arms to the two of you, our clan leaders."

As if that had been a cue, the front door opened. I didn't need to look to know one of the newcomers was Finn's grandmother, not when I sensed her power. Before I could wonder why she happened to be there, much less Adam, my eyes went wide and my breath caught. Irene Walkinghorse grinned and winked as she led my parents and sister toward the front of the room. Adam peeled off and moved to take up a place near the door next to Danny and Sharon.

What is going on? I mouthed silently, looking at Jim and trying not to panic.

He looked as stunned as I felt as he shrugged in response.

Before I could demand an explanation, Finn moved to greet her grandmother. Then she stood before my parents and pulled them into a tight hug. As she did, my heart skipped a beat. What must she be feeling to greet my parents, people who had been close friends with her parents? After releasing them, she grinned at Eileen and gave her a quick hug before returning to Matt's side. Of course, she very carefully avoided looking at me.

We were so going to have a long talk when this was over.

"Who would you name as successor, Alton?" Matt asked as if nothing had happened.

"Jim Kincade and his mate, Maggie Thrasher."

My mouth went dry. Jim's quick intake of breath as Alton named us was almost lost in the thundering of my pulse. At least now I knew why my parents and sister were here. It was just like Finn to let them know about this but not me. Boy were we going to have a talk after this was over. But right now I needed to try to just get through the next few minutes without bolting out the door, dragging Jim with me.

I vaguely heard Matt telling us to come to stand before them. But it was the humor reflected in Finn's eyes as Jim and I complied that snapped me out of my shock. She might see the humor in the situation but I sure as hell didn't. In just a few short weeks, I'd gone from a lone tracker to joining a new clan and finding my mate and now this? Surely I'd wake up soon and life would be back to normal.

No, I'd wake up and Jim and I would be on a beach somewhere

and we'd laugh about how I shouldn't have had that last mojito. Please let me wake up and find this was all just some weird dream.

But no, this appeared to be the new normal and it was a scary one. At least Jim seemed as stunned as I felt. His fingers tightened around mine and I felt his pulse racing. That reassured me some. Then I realized Matt was speaking and I struggled to concentrate on what he was saying.

"Alton, there are not enough words to describe how important you are to the pride, the clan or to Finn and me." He moved to where the older man stood and looked down at him. Then he drew the man close. He held him for a moment, letting everyone present see how much he cared for the man. Then he released Alton and returned to his chair. "I know how badly you grieved after Jenny's death. She was a special woman and we all loved her. She'd be very proud of how you carried on, doing everything you could to be the man she knew you could be. You've been a strong, caring pride leader.

"If we accept your request to step down, it is with one proviso. That you understand and accept that you are a valued member of the clan and will be respected as an elder. That means Finn and I will still come to you for counsel."

"I think I can live with that." Alton smiled, tears glistening in his eyes.

"Then we will accept your request and we will accept your recommendation for your successors, providing the pride approves of them." Matt leaned back and crossed his legs, a satisfied smile touching his lips.

A knot of worry twisted in my stomach. The pride knew Jim and I had no doubts they'd accept him as their new leader. But they didn't know me. They had no reason to accept me. But I was damned if I'd let them see how worried – or scared – this whole thing made me. I wouldn't do that to Jim.

"Matt, I call for a vote now, while everyone is here." Now Alton grinned. "I stressed to the pride the importance of being here. Only two members couldn't attend and they have already told me they would gladly accept Jim and Maggie as their leaders."

"Then what says the pride?"

The great room shook as the pride members loudly shouted their acceptance.

"I think that's a yes."

Finn chuckled and placed her hand in Matt's. Together they rose and moved to stand before us. As they did, Jim gave my hand a squeeze. A moment later, we dropped to our knees. Jim then released my hand so we could go down on all fours.

"Well, big brother, are you ready to admit what most of us have known for some time now and take your place as Alpha for the Denton pride?" Matt asked, his affection and pride clear.

I cut my gaze to the right and saw how Jim's jaw clinched. He didn't reply right away. Instead, he looked at me and waited. I knew without asking that he wouldn't accept if I had any doubts. Closing my eyes, I counted to ten. I knew this was right. He'd make a wonderful pride leader and, as such, he'd be an even stronger ally and advocate for his brother.

My role, on the other hand. . . .

Opening my eyes, I reached over and smiled as our hands met. Then I nodded. He was my mate. I'd support him now and forever, just as he'd support me.

"I am." Jim's voice was strong and firm. I doubted anyone, except maybe his brother, heard the faint note of apprehension in it.

Finn reached down and lifted my face so I looked at her. I might be ready to skin her just then, but I couldn't doubt her pride and affection as our eyes met. She smiled slightly and nodded.

"Maggie, are you ready to stand at your mate's side and support him as Alpha of the Denton pride?" she asked.

I licked my lips. I knew what I needed to say but I seemed to have lost the ability to speak. Then Jim squeezed my hand. In the back of my mind, my tiger purred in satisfaction. This was right. She knew it and now it was time for me to accept it.

"I am."

Well, I might not be, but my tiger and my mate were, so who was I to argue?

The next few hours were a blur. Jim and I pledged our oaths to the pride and to Matt and Finn as the new pride leaders. When Finn's grandmother stepped forward, we promised to do all we could to help protect all of our kind. We recognized Irene Walkinghorse as a welcomed ally and confidante. Then Matt and Finn drew us to our feet and presented us to the gathering.

After that, we found ourselves the center of the celebration. It was after midnight before the last of the clan left. My parents and sister promised to be back for breakfast come morning. Irene and Adam said they'd drive them to their hotel. As the front door closed behind them, I didn't know whether to run and hide or what. The only thing that kept me from rounding on Jim was the way he turned to Matt. Eyes flashing, he closed the distance between them. Before Matt could react, Jim grabbed him and threw him against the wall. Matt hit with a resounding thud and then launched himself at his brother. Scared, I started across the room only to find Finn standing in my way, shaking her head.

"Don't. This is their way of working things out," she said. Then she slid an arm around my waist and led me to the kitchen where she poured me a glass of wine.

"All right. That gives us some time to talk." Suddenly Jim's method of *discussing* the situation looked pretty damned good. Maybe it wasn't such a bad thing that my folks had already left. I had a feeling they wouldn't approve of what I planned to do. "I'll start by pointing out that I am not nor have I ever been an omega."

"Maggie, the last thing in the world you are is an omega." Finn laughed gaily. Then she draped an arm across my shoulders and gave me a hug.

As if to prove I wasn't an omega, one of our kind who soothed and healed, my fist balled at my side. If Finn didn't start explaining pretty damned quick, I'd take a page out of Jim's book and see if I could beat some answers out of her. Frankly, if I wasn't sure she could – and would – wipe the floor with me and barely break a sweat, I'd already have tried to deck her. But I'd learned that lesson as a kid. She had always been stronger and faster than me.

And, judging by her smug look, she remembered it as well.

"Finn," I growled. "Damn it, I'm tired of being blindsided and I'm tired of being told by my Alphas that I'm something I'm not."

"Maggie, why do you keep insisting I'm trying to say you're something that you're not?"

"Why?" I'd have tossed my hands into the air if I hadn't been holding the wineglass. Instead, I lifted it to my lips and drained it. "First Declan names me as a tracker and sends me and the others out without proper training. When I find that bastard Volk, he's got a feral with him and it damned near killed me. As if that wasn't enough to throw me for a curve, I realize I've found my mate, something I'd never really believed in until I met Jim. Now you and Matt have named me Omega to Jim's Alpha. I'm not an omega and never will be and I won't play that sort of game. It's not fair to the pride or the clan or, most of all, to Jim."

"Maggie, I never said you were an omega. I'd never insult you that way."

"What?" Okay, that was the last thing I'd expected. "Then why did you say it?"

"I didn't say it. Alton did." That damned smile was back. If she didn't explain and quickly, I really would try to wipe it off her face. It would be worth a few cuts and bruises just to get a little satisfaction.

"You didn't dispute it."

"Maggie." She smiled and shook her head. "Why in the world would I insult another Alpha, especially one almost as strong as I am, by calling her an Omega? If you think back, I asked if you were ready to stand at your mate's side and support him as Alpha of the Denton pride."

"Same damned thing as saying I'm an Omega."

"Not at all." She leaned against the counter and sipped her wine, watching as I tried to figure out what she was saying. "I very carefully asked if you were ready to support Jim as an alpha."

She was playing word games. The way she'd phrased it could mean was I ready to support Jim in his role as alpha. It could also mean was I, as an alpha, ready to support him.

Oh my God.

For a moment, all I could do was stare at Finn in disbelief. She'd lost her mind. There was no other explanation. I was no more an alpha than I was an omega.

"Before you start arguing with me, Maggie, just think." When I opened my mouth to interrupt, Finn shook her head. Then she motioned for me to take a seat at the table and waited until I complied. "I suspected it at that first clan meeting. There you were, injured and anything but sure about your role. Hell, Maggs, you were still reeling from realizing you and Jim were mates. Yet you not only stood up to Brittney, you wiped the floor with her without breaking a sweat.

"Then there's Volk. I know you feel Jim is why you managed to hold out against the drugs that bastard gave you. I'll even admit he's part of the reason why you were able to. But the main reason is you. Your strength and your commitment to do whatever it took to beat him and keep Jim's safe.

"But the final confirmation came when the other clan leaders were here. You treated Matt and me with the same respect and deference you always do when others are present. You honored me by the respect you showed my grandmother. But the other clan leaders, well, you treated them as equals. Your tiger recognized the fact you're an alpha, their equal, even if you didn't realize it."

"Finn's right," Matt said from the doorway.

His shirt was torn and his right eye was swelling. He'd have a black eye before long. Jim didn't look much better. But there was no mistaking the fact that they had worked out their problems. Too bad Finn and I hadn't – yet.

"You're both out of your minds," I said softly.

"Sweetheart, I think we're going to have to let them have their way." Jim pulled a chair up next to mine and was seated. Then he reached for my hand. "I've never wanted to be an alpha. But Matt's shown me that he needs me to step up now. The pride needs a leader, one who knows those in the clan and who will look out for them.

"This business with Volk also proved that we each have to accept our roles, whether we want to or not. I can't help feeling that the day is coming when our existence will be revealed to the normals. Before that happens, we have to be prepared. You and I can help with that."

"Maggie, I know how you feel," Finn said. The humor was gone. In its place was a seriousness that told me I needed to listen. "That day in the parking garage when Jennings' trackers almost captured me was the day my life turned upside down. In a matter of days, I went from being on the run to being Matt's mate and female alpha for the clan. I resisted and, I'll admit, I was scared to death. But this is right. I know it now, just as you will when you've had time to think about it." She reached out and patted my hand. Then she stood. "Remember what you've done and what you've gained since coming here. When you do, you'll see that this is right."

"What I want to do is find a nice beach to lie on with my mate," I growled.

"Which we will do and soon," Jim promised.

"We'll take our leave now, you two. Why don't we have dinner tomorrow at our place?" Matt suggested. "Irene and Adam will be there and we'd love it if your parents and sister would come as well, Maggie."

I nodded, not sure I trusted my voice.

"Are you all right?" Jim asked softly as he shut the front door behind them a short time later.

"Hell if I know." I shook my head, a slight smile playing at my lips. "An Alpha?"

"Damn, baby, if we aren't a pair." He laughed and pulled me close. "Tell you what, if I'm an Alpha, so are you. How's that sound?"

"All right I guess." Not really, but I'd be able to wrap my mind around it come morning – I hoped. "I'll tell you what sounds better."

"What?"

I pulled his head down and whispered in his ear. I swear, I could hear his eyes rolling back in his head. Then he laughed and lifted me in a rib-creaking hug. "I do like the way your mind works, Maggie Thrasher."

Grinning, I had to agree, especially when he swung me up in his arms and moved quickly in the direction of the bedroom. Now that was one thing I was more than happy to wrap my mind around. Everything else could wait until morning.

REQUEST FROM THE AUTHOR

It has long been said that the best form of advertising is word of mouth. That is especially true when it comes to books. Friends and family members trust reviews and suggestions for books that come from people they know.

That word of mouth goes even further in this digital age. If you enjoyed this book, do me a favor. Spread the word. Tell people on your various social media accounts. Leave a review on Amazon. If you're a blogger, write a post about it. All that does help. Besides, it is the one way we, as authors, know you really enjoyed our work.

Thanks!

AUTHOR'S NOTE

I've had so much fun putting this expanded and updated edition of *Tracked* together. The characters have been favorites of mine from the very beginning. Getting to come back to revisit—and expand—their stories has been a joy.

This expanded edition is the second of the re-releases for the series. *Hunted* is now available for download and *Prey* (previously released as *Hunter's Home*) will be released next month. As with *Tracked*, both books have been re-edited and, in some instances, parts have been re-written.

All this is in preparation to relaunching the series with a new book, *Snared*, which will be released next summer (of not sooner).

I hope you enjoy returning to the world of Finn, Maggie & Company as much as I have. Please check out my Facebook Page for further information about upcoming books.

ALSO BY THE AUTHOR

Written as Sam Schall

TAKING FLIGHT

BATTLE BOUND

BATTLE WOUNDS

VENGEANCE FROM ASHES

DUTY FROM ASHES

HONOR FROM ASHES

FIRE FROM ASHES

Written as Amanda S. Green

NOCTURNAL ORIGINS

NOCTURNAL SERENADE

NOCTURNAL INTERLUDE

NOCTURNAL HAUNTS

NOCTURNAL CHALLENGE

NOCTURNAL REBELLION

SWORD OF ARELION

DAGGER OF ELANNA

Written as Ellie Ferguson

SKELETONS IN THE CLOSET

www.ingramcontent.com/pod-product-compliance
Lightning Source LLC
Chambersburg PA
CBHW031957190626
46808CB00018B/1627